WHITE LION

Walter Williams

AuthorHouse™
1663 Liberty Drive
Bloomington, IN 47403
www.authorhouse.com
Phone: 1-800-839-8640

© 2011 Walter Williams. All rights reserved.
No part of this book may be reproduced, stored in a retrieval system, or transmitted by any means without the written permission of the author.
First published by AuthorHouse   05/27/2011

ISBN: 978-1-4567-5121-0 (sc)
ISBN: 978-1-4567-5123-4 (hc)
ISBN: 978-1-4567-5122-7 (e)

Library of Congress Control Number: 2011905194

Printed in the United States of America
Any people depicted in stock imagery provided by Thinkstock are models, and such images are being used for illustrative purposes only.
Certain stock imagery © Thinkstock.
This book is printed on acid-free paper.
Because of the dynamic nature of the Internet, any web addresses or links contained in this book may have changed since publication and may no longer be valid. The views expressed in this work are solely those of the author and do not necessarily reflect the views of the publisher, and the publisher hereby disclaims any responsibility for them.

This book dedicated to:
CPL Richard L. Musser
Killed in Action 3-7-69

A special thank you to:
My good friend Zora Richards
For teaching me grammar
My wife Judy
For her support and encouragement

I don't know why, but the smells of the jungle always drew my attention. There was the sweet smell of fresh vegetation, flowers, moist soil. The musky, yet pleasing smell of rotting vegetation and the smells of fresh bananas and other fruits belied the terror and fear that lurked in the thick, almost impenetrable hell. There were other smells as well: gun powder, sulphur from the bombs, burned vegetation, rotting human corpses, the smell of death. Death was a smell we all feared; but I figured as long as I could smell it, I was ok. I'd watched some of my friends die; I learned not to make too many friends, because it was easier to let people go if I didn't know much about them. I learned how to kill quickly and efficiently and not feel anything about doing it. I didn't know my personality could change so quickly from an isolated country boy to a man whose main job was to kill the enemy. After six months in the place they call Viet Nam, the Republic of, I figured I was about as far from my life back home as I could ever get.

Contents

CHAPTER 1	The Carefree Years	1
CHAPTER 2	Welcome to Manhood	5
CHAPTER 3	In the Army Now	9
CHAPTER 4	The real Training	13
CHAPTER 5	The end of training	19
CHAPTER 6	Welcome to the Nam	23
CHAPTER 7	Deep Into Indian Country	41
CHAPTER 8	The Snake Hunt	45
CHAPTER 9	Becoming a Real Soldier	53
CHAPTER 10	Time off for bad Behavior	63
CHAPTER 11	Into No Man's Land	69
CHAPTER 12	A Mission That Never Happened	83
CHAPTER 13	Stalking the VC	93
CHAPTER 14	Heading Home	99
CHAPTER 15	A Free Man?	103
CHAPTER 16	Heading West	107
CHAPTER 17	Back To the Woods	119
CHAPTER 18	Return to Hell	127
CHAPTER 19	Back to the World, Again	145
CHAPTER 20	The Ministry Grows	159
CHAPTER 21	My True Mission	163
CHAPTER 20	A Love Renewed	167
CHAPTER 22	A New Life	181

CHAPTER 1

The Carefree Years

I grew up in a small town in rural Pennsylvania. It was a good life. I had parents who loved me and three older sisters who loved me sometimes. I had lots of aunts, uncles and cousins and a group of friends around my own age that hung out together and did things kids normally do. My friends and I would spend our summers playing baseball, mowing grass, making hay or anything else we could find to make a few dollars. As teenagers growing up in the early 1960's, our lives were very ordinary. Most every summer day we would wind up swimming in the local creek, swinging from a rope tied to "the tree". Even though there were lots of trees in the area, that one was special because it had several heavy limbs that hung out over the water. We would roast hotdogs, corn, potatoes and sometimes bull frogs over an open fire. We smoked cigarettes we stole from our parents. When one of us was able to get it, we would drink beer, wine or liquor that was confiscated from our parents. The trick to not getting caught stealing cigarettes was to just take two or three out of an already opened pack - nobody would ever notice. The same technique would work for booze as well. I remember one day taking a little bit from four or five different bottles of whiskey and pouring it all in a mason jar. That day we hit the mother load as one of my friends did the same thing. I think there were five or six of us and we all got drunk just before we all got sick. Just ordinary kids doing what kids do.

Because of where we grew up we knew very little about crime. Most of our parents never locked their doors at night and hardly anyone locked their car doors. Everybody knew everybody else and there was a sense of trust in the community. (Except for the occasional cigarette or booze thieves.) We knew nothing about street crime or gangs or rape or murder, except for what we might see on TV. At that age we didn't know if people were kidding or not when they said "don't touch black people, the black might rub off on your hands." We didn't have any black people in our community to touch. I always wondered, but never really asked anyone, if black people told their children not to touch white people because it might rub off.

In our lives at that time the most important things in life were sports, girls, what kind of car we would have when we got our driver's license, girls, who was the strongest among us, girls, who would be the first among us to actually have sex and what it was really like, and, of course, GIRLS.

As a group, our all time favorite thing to do was sleeping outside or camping. Sometimes it was as simple as throwing a sleeping bag on the back porch of somebody's house or the back porch of the local elementary school, where nobody could see us. Our main source of entertainment was looking at Playboy magazines somebody swiped from somewhere, or lighting farts. If you have never done this, it is really funny to see a blue flame shooting out of somebody's butt. It takes passing gas to a whole new level. Warning: it could be dangerous to your health. Teenage boys generally have hair on their butts that can and will catch fire. Also explaining to your mother how you got a burn mark on the back of your underwear can be problem. Another reason for sleeping out was generally there was a slumber party somewhere in the area. At these slumber parties were - you guessed it - girls. Need I say more?

We also loved to hike in the mountains near our homes and sleep out under the stars with a big campfire. This was one of the few things we did where no girls were allowed. I don't know why, but it was an unwritten rule. Our hikes would often last a few days. We would build lean-tos into the side of a bank, or build a roof over a depression in the ground. We would line the floors with hemlock limbs and pine needles and it was quite comfortable. We had one favorite spot where the creek split and there was a small island in the middle. Unfortunately every spring it would get washed away when the high waters came. We hiked, camped, played war games or army as we called it, and generally just loved being out in the woods. When we younger, we were allowed to carry BB guns. When we were in the woods, no bird or chipmunk was safe. As we got older, 14 or so, our parents allowed us to carry .22 rifles. This was our way of life. From a young age, we were "Never point a gun at another person, whether it's loaded or not." Even with the BB guns this was a rule we adhered to. We were taught to respect guns, not fear them. For us it was an embarrassment and inexcusable to point a gun at anyone else.

We did lots of shooting. In the '60's, you could buy a box of fifty .22 rounds for 40 or 50 cents. We naturally become very good shots. We could shoot acorns off tall oak trees; we could shoot bottle caps at 50 yards. One of my friends could consistently shoot bumble bees flying through the air.

We learned what plants were edible; we learned to lay hot rocks from a campfire on the ground beneath us in our lean-to to keep us warm at night. We learned to survive on what we had and loved it all. Little did we know, for some of us these skills would be put to the test someday.

One of the pleasures of summertime we had was the town reservoir that was located on the mountain near where we camped. At night we would climb the chain link fence that surrounded the reservoir and skinny dip in the water that everybody in town was drinking. We joked about peeing in the water and hoping a certain teacher we didn't like was drinking that water. We were so stupid it took us a while to realize that some of us were drinking the same water at home. We all heard about the war in Viet Nam, but we really didn't know much about it. Mostly what we knew about war was the stories we heard from our parents and other relatives about WWII or Korea. We were all pretty naive and just assumed we would all be around and be friends for the rest of our lives.

CHAPTER 2

Welcome to Manhood

Fast forward a few years to 1968. Things had changed. We were now old enough to go to war, but not to vote. Some of my friends were in college; some were already fighting the Vietnam War. The rest of us received our draft notices. The days of innocence were over. In January of 1968, I received word one of my childhood friends, Carl, had been shot, but would survive. A few weeks later, I visited Carl at his parents' home. He was badly wounded in his right leg and faced a long recovery. He would never fully recover from the wound and would always walk with a limp. He told me that being shot at and shot sucks. He said he hoped I never had the experience. I saw the pain in his eyes and I heard it in the way he talked. It wasn't the pain in his leg that I saw, it was deeper than that. His speech was deliberate and filled with pauses, he seemed distant. He wasn't the same joking, impulsive guy I grew up with. It was the look in his eyes that stuck with me - a distant, hollow look. Carl had changed; I guessed that's what war does to you.

I wished him well, as I knew he would be going to rehab for quite a while. I told him it was great to see him again, and chatted with his parents a bit. As I was leaving, Carl grabbed my hand and whispered in my ear "if you go over there man be careful, it ain't no picnic."

My visit with Carl caused me to think. I was twice his size and a bigger target. I couldn't help but think about the guy that shot Carl; his dad apparently didn't teach him to never point a gun at anybody. For me personally, that was the first time the Vietnam War was real. Carl was a guy I really cared about.

In two weeks I'd be taking my physical for the draft. Would I get shot? Would I be like Carl and come home crippled? Would I come home at all?

Two weeks went fast, and I reported for the physical. It was like a huge locker room with guys standing in lines in their underwear. Doctors were checking for I don't know what. Some guy told me to drop my drawers, bend over and spread 'em. Why the hell did he stick his finger up my butt? They were poking in my mouth, my ears, grabbing my nuts and telling me to cough and shining a light in my eyes. They gave me a bunch of papers and told me to get dressed. Some Army guy out front told me he would see me later. What the hell does that mean? Did I pass or fail?

The following week I got a notice that I passed the physical. I had to decide if I wanted to enlist or wait to be drafted.

The week after the notice came; I got a call from a friend that one of our mutual friends, Don, had been killed in action. His body would be flown home next week for burial. Holy shit, he's the first person from our little town to be killed over there.

The next week, my friends and I met outside the funeral home for Don's funeral. We decided to all go in together. Out of the six of us, two had received their orders to report, two of us were awaiting orders and two had college deferments. Now a friend of ours was dead. There was an air of somberness among us, not the joking or grab-assing we would normally have. Don was only 19 years old, a year older than me, and now he was gone. When I looked at my friends I saw fear, indecision, and a lot of tears. That day had changed us all. As we said goodbye, I think we were all secretly asking ourselves who would be next. I had lost family members and friends before, but this was different. This wasn't an accident or natural causes. Don was shot to death, fighting in a war in a place most of us didn't even know existed a couple of years ago, in some province I couldn't even pronounce.

One by one we were all called up to active duty. Rob was first, then Stu, then Tom. We were now being called men. Just last year, as high school seniors, we were boys. What made the difference? Did being eligible to be shot make you a man? I remember as a child someone would call me a little man or young man. Usually when my dad called me a young man, I knew I screwed up somehow. As teenagers we wanted to be looked upon as men, but we didn't have a clue what that meant. Was this what it took to be a man? To be scared out of your mind, to risk your life for your country, leave your family not knowing if you would ever see them again? Hell, I didn't know.

The next big question was, do I enlist or wait to be drafted? Everybody had an opinion on this. If you enlist in the Air Force or Navy, the chances of going to Vietnam were less, but it was a four year commitment. If you enlist in the Army or Marines it was a four year commitment as well, but according to the recruiters you got to choose the job you wanted, if it was available. Yeah right. If you waited to be drafted, it was a two year commitment, but you would probably wind up in the Nam. How the hell does an eighteen year old make the right decision about that? Somehow enlisting in the Air Force or Navy didn't seem right to me. I had never flown on an airplane and I got seasick, even on small boats. So I narrowed it down to the Army or Marines. Enlist or be drafted? My decision was made for me two weeks later; I got my notice to report for induction into the U. S. Army in thirty days. I was drafted.

Four days later I received another phone call. My good friend Dick had been killed in action in Vietnam. Dick grew up four houses away from Don on the same street. I'd known him most of my life. We went to the same school and church, played ball, roamed the woods, fished and swam together. He was tall and thin and was a pretty good baseball pitcher. We called him Dick the Stick. The next day I stopped to see his parents. His dad was always a rough speaking, sort of intimidating man; that day his words were barely audible. I'd never seen a man cry so much before. It was a helpless feeling for me, not knowing what to say or do to comfort him. He thanked me for coming and asked if I would mind being a pall bearer at the funeral. I said I would be honored to do so. He hugged me and it was one of those moments when nothing was said, but the pain we each felt was understood by the other as we both cried.

My friends and I got together that evening in the woods. None of us were old enough to drink, but we were drinking beer anyhow. A few of us looked old enough, and it was never a problem to get some beer. Somehow it just didn't seem to make sense again: we were not old enough to drink, but now, two of us were dead. There were only four of us tonight, and although none of us wanted to admit it, we were all scared. We reminisced about Dick: what a good curve ball he had, how he could eat like a pig and never gain weight, and how shy he was around girls. We couldn't remember of him ever going on a date. We built a fire and slept around it all night. Even though we drank beer all night none of us really got drunk. I think we all felt this might be the last time we would have the chance to do this together for a while or maybe ever. Over the years, we had our share of fights, arguments and pissing matches with each other, but there was a bond among us that we didn't even share with our own family members.

There were a lot of people at Dick's funeral and I knew most of them. I could see Don's grave not far away, fresh enough that new grass had not started to grow over it yet. As pall bearers, we were all very nervous. I know when the honor guard gave their gun salute, we all jumped. When Taps was played, we all cried. The one thing that stuck with me that day and will until the day I die, was Dick's father shaking the hands of the pall bearers and saying to all of us "thanks a million boys, Dick loved all of you." All I could say was "you're welcome." I wanted to say you don't have to thank me, I'm honored to do it, but I didn't. It just didn't seem real, but it was all too real. Part of me wanted to seek revenge for the death of my friends, part of me was scared to death, and yet another part of me wanted to go back to being an irresponsible teenager. The reality of it all hung like a dark thunderstorm cloud over all of us that day.

CHAPTER 3

In the Army Now

Welcome to Fort Dix, NJ. We got off a bus and some guy was barking orders to us that we didn't understand. He talked so fast that we were all confused. We moved like a herd of sheep, following one another. If the first guy went to the wrong place, we were all going to the wrong place. We reported to a building where there are barbers shaving guys' heads. The smart asses asked us how we wanted our hair cut and then shaved everyone down to the roots. Next they issued us clothing called fatigues. There was no modesty; we were all naked and putting on military issued underwear and fatigues. Some of the guys were bitching their clothes didn't fit; mine were ok. We marched to a building they called a barracks. Two rows of bunk beds, a big bathroom with a row of sinks and one big shower. The building to me looked like a cattle barn. I grabbed a lower bunk and a black guy grabbed the bunk above me. I introduced myself, we shook hands and he said his name was James Robinson. He's from a town near Richmond, VA. A little while later I realized that was only the second time I had ever touched a black man. Talk about being a country hick! The first time was my junior year in high school, during a wrestling match. The guys on my team were riding me pretty hard about wrestling a black guy. I was unsure about it myself. Once the match started, it was obviously no different than wrestling a white guy. After the match was over, we shook hands and talked about wrestling a bit and he seemed like a nice guy. Afterwards I thought about how weird it must have been for him; he was the only black kid in the whole gym.

That wasn't a problem for James Robinson; it looked like almost half of the guys in the barracks were black. As I was making my bed, I glanced at my right hand and noticed the black from James' hand didn't come off onto my hand. I'm sure my face turned beet red as I realized what a stupid thing that was to think. I sure didn't want James to think I was so dumb. I never really got the courage to ask him if he worried about the white coming off my hand. There were a few guys arguing over bunks, but that was short lived. Shortly the drill instructor was in the barracks barking orders. According to him, we were the dumbest people on earth and the only things we needed to know, he would teach us. That was a little hard for me to swallow, but the guy was pretty intimidating. He ran us through some formations outside and, after observing us for half an hour, maybe we were the dumbest people on earth. The next morning we were up before the sun, doing calisthenics and running and running and running. I was 5' 10" and 190 pounds. My body was made for running over things, not around them all day. I didn't really mind the calisthenics, but all that damn running sucked.

There were men from a lot of different areas and it was funny how we all had ideas of each other and certain geographic areas. I told people I was from Pennsylvania and right away they thought of Philadelphia or Pittsburgh and that's just a small part of PA. I always ended up explaining I was a country boy and where I was from it's mostly farm land and mountains. I'm of German descent and many from my area speak Dutch. I normally talked very slowly and do have a Dutch accent. I took a lot of kidding from some of the guys because of the way I talked. James Robinson talked almost in a foreign language to me; I really had to listen closely to understand him. Robinson called me country and that's ok with me - I'm proud of my heritage. I made a new friend from Arkansas, Jake Morgan. He was a country boy like me and even though he talked funny, we hit it off really well. Jake and I shared an interest in the outdoors, hunting and fishing, and just spending time in the woods.

The day finally came when we got to shoot guns. Jake and I hung together on the range and had a friendly competition between us. After learning the M-16 rifle inside and out, we enjoyed shooting the weapons. Some of the rest of the guys didn't seem to be enjoying it very much. Obviously they had little or no experience in handling firearms. I was kind of shocked at how many people did not know anything about guns and that they were afraid of them. I had to realize these guys grew up in a different culture than I did. Even though I was able to keep up with the calisthenics, I took some ribbing about my running ability. Now it was my turn to shine. Jake and I were far ahead of a lot of the other men in our platoon when it came to shooting. Being 18 years old, it was my turn to throw some digs at the guys who were on me about running. We were feeling pretty good about ourselves until Robinson pointed out that this was the Army and probably the best shots with a rifle were going to go to the front lines in the war. In our gloating, Jake and I hadn't really thought about that. I don't know if our drill instructor had our barracks bugged or not, but he always seemed to know what was going on or what the topic of conversation was at the time. The following day after exercising, running and some other drills, the instructor took Jake and me to the rifle range. He informed us that he noticed we both could shoot well. He said he hoped that after discussing the advantages and disadvantages of being a good shot with our fellow recruits that we didn't entertain the idea of blowing our next opportunity on the range. Of course Jake and I responded "No, Sir." How the hell did he know just last night Jake and I discussed doing that very same thing?

He introduced us to the range master, who brought out two really nice looking bolt action .308 caliber rifles equipped with 6-24 x 50mm scopes. He explained to us that we were going to do our best and the guns were both zeroed in at 200 yards. We would first shoot at 100 yards, then 200 yards, 300 yards, and then 400 yards. We would each have three shots at each distance. If, in his opinion, and his was the only one that counted, we did not perform to the best of our ability, Jake and I would be subject to drilling and workouts that would turn our sorry assholes inside out. Whoever shot the best would be given a special reward. I thought cool, maybe he would give one of us a weekend pass or something like that.

At 100 yards we each had one inch groups, at 200 yards the same. These guns really shot well! At 300 yards my group was two inches, Jake's was 1.5 inches; at 400 yards, my group was 2 ½ inches and Jake's was 3 inches. We were virtually tied. When the drill instructor counted the bull's eyes, Jake had one more than me. Jake got the special reward – a lousy can of Pepsi, the cheap bastard. Nothing was said about our shooting ability and we were sent back to the rest of recruits. As basic training was winding down, it was kind of amazing to see this group of men developing into a unit working as one. It took a while to sink in, but I guess that's what this was all about in the first place. As we were patting each other on the back for getting through this training we all realized we might never see each other again. Jake and I shared a special bond and enjoyed each other's company. We found out to no one's surprise we were both going to Advanced Individual Training, or in this case, advanced infantry training at Fort Benning, GA.

CHAPTER 4

The real Training

When we arrived at Fort Benning, we found out they were looking for volunteers to take sniper training. We looked at each other and it was like we were both thinking what the hell, let's do it. We signed up and were assigned bunks with six other guys who had already signed up the day before. That evening, it was explained the eight of us would be part of a unit to be trained as scouts and snipers. We would spend two weeks in the A.I.T. program with the rest of the troops. Along with that, we would receive specialized training in bullet trajectories, ballistics, judging yardage and wind direction, map reading and orienteering, and the latest technology in optics. After that we would spend six more weeks of intense training in survival, hand to hand combat, stealth techniques, and camouflage. We would be shooting dozens of rounds a day from a variety of weapons at ranges from 100 – 1000 yards. We would need to score a minimum of 90% at 800 yards to graduate. We were told we would be kept to high standards and if we couldn't cut it we would be washed out of the program and sent back to our regular unit, not home. We would work in two man teams and as such, each team needed to be compatible and have complete confidence in each other's abilities. Jake and I were naturals together and we teamed up. We would find out later we were actually recommended for the program by our old drill instructor and if we would not have "volunteered" for the program, we would have been chosen to serve. So much for having a choice. That night, the eight of us sat around discussing what we might have gotten ourselves into. It seemed most of us were suited for this kind of duty and what the hell we were at least going to get some good equipment to use. Somehow two guys sneaking around in the jungle by themselves didn't seem like a really cool thing to do.

Those two weeks went really fast. We went through the regular A.I.T. and spent our off hours studying charts and graphs, reading books, and receiving a constant grilling about what we learned. We studied until our eyes bled; we slept 2 -4 hours a day and caught little cat naps of 15 -20 minutes whenever we could. We were beat and didn't realize this lack of sleep was actually part of our training. We were given 2 days off before the start of our next training; we went drinking the first day and slept the next one. We knew if we got through the next six weeks of training we would be heading to Nam to do our jobs.

The sniper training started with a workout and, of course, running. I was actually starting to like running. We would spend four hours in the classroom studying firearm care and maintenance. Then off to the shooting range for at least four more hours of shooting instruction. Our training included self defense, survival, orienteering, hand to hand combat, first aid, concealment techniques and stealth maneuvers. I normally shoot right handed but I learned to shoot left handed also. It was not that hard for me because I am naturally left handed. I throw a ball and bat a ball left handed and can write and eat with either hand. When I was a young boy my dad forced me to learn to shoot right handed because he was left handed and he always had trouble finding left handed guns. I was amazed at how my shooting improved. I never really thought much about proper breathing techniques, relaxing into the gun, proper body posture and how all of that can improve accuracy. I'd never used a range finder before – it was almost like cheating. But we were not preparing for a game!

Each day we grew stronger and more confident in our abilities. I was running six miles a day and I wasn't complaining. I was in the best shape of my life. We were running with full packs of 50 – 60 pounds, as well as carrying our weapons and ammo. We had everything in our packs to survive a week or more if necessary. For a guy who thought he knew everything he needed to know about surviving in the wild, I sure had learned a lot in the past few weeks.

After two full weeks of training, Jake and I were measured and fitted for custom stocks for our sniper weapons. Somebody must have figured we were going to make it through our training or they would not have bothered to fit us up with custom stocks. I had no idea the Army had its own gunsmiths. I was finding out there was a lot I did not know!

The equipment we were using was some of the best I had ever seen and it certainly made us look good. As a unit most of us are shooting 4-5 inch groups at 1000 yards. Back home I never shot farther than 300 yards. During our training we had shot enough pumpkins and cabbage heads to keep my hometown in pumpkin pies and cold slaw for an entire year. Our instructors told us a head of cabbage is the same relative density as the human head. We were using stuff I never heard of before: scopes with illuminated crosshairs, turrets mounted on top of scopes for windage and yardage adjustments, bipods with telescoping legs, a little gadget between the trigger guard and the trigger that forces you to squeeze the trigger, and bolts polished so finely they slide open with barely a sound. I was feeling like the"country bumpkin" who just came to the big city for the first time. In a lot of ways, I was.

The final week of our training our custom guns were finished and we could not wait to try them out. Mine were both on a model 70 Winchester frame with match grade barrels, one in a .30-06 caliber short to medium range and the other chambered in .300 Winchester Magnum for long range shooting. The .30-06 was equipped with a Leopold 3 – 9 x 40mm custom scope and the .300 Mag. was equipped with a Leopold 6 – 24 x 40mm custom scope. We were told that these guns are valued at over $4000 each, so take good care of them and they would take good care of us. Mine fit me like an old shoe. Jake and I headed to the range to play with our new toys. We both could cut bullet holes out to 500 yards, so the wagering began $5.00 per target. We both had 15 rounds of ammo, 3 at each of the remaining targets, closest to the bull's eye wins. I won at 600 and 700 yards and Jake won at 800 and 900 yards, leaving the final target at 1000 yards. For us, this was the seventh game of the World Series or the final round of the Masters Golf tournament. My first and second shots were 3 inches and 2.5 inches from the bull's eye, my third was 1.5 inches. Jakes first shot was 2 inches high, the second 2.5 inches, and the third 3 inches. I won by ½ inch. Jake blamed it on the wind gusting at the time he was shooting, but I didn't care – I won. We joked around about it and started wrestling around on the ground for a while. I think we both realized that for the first time in a month and a half, we had both just taken time to be 18 year old boys instead of men.

We both agreed on one thing: this was the most physically and mentally demanding training we had ever been through. We had six more days left in our training. The next morning started like all the rest: exercising and running. Afterwards we were told to put on our full gear and grab our weapons and ammo and then we hiked to a ridge top overlooking a mock village in the valley below. We were given a photo and description of our target. Our target would appear but we were not told when. We flipped a coin to see who would shoot first, and Jake won. We would each be given one shot and I spotted for Jake. We waited and waited and waited – there were pigs, chickens, and dogs wandering around the village. The "people" were pop up targets that randomly appeared and they all had different faces and clothing on them. We were 455 yards from the center of the village and there were several people who popped up, but through the spotting scope I saw they were not our target.

It was 4:00pm and we had been sitting for 6 hours. This sucked! All the push ups and sit ups and running we had done were to prepare us for sitting on our butts for hours on end? I was looking through the spotting scope and Jake was manning the gun. I farted and Jake rolled up his nose. It was pretty bad. My eyes hurt from looking through the spotting scope so long and Jake flipped a stone at me and hit me in the ear - now my ear hurt that asshole. We could not move very much as we could not give away our position. There were instructors positioned somewhere with laser lights and if they hit us with a laser light, we were dead. We did not know where they were and hopefully they did not know where we were. We could urinate from the position but had to wait until after dark to do anything else.

The previous week, we had attached a length of ¼" plastic tubing to our water bottles and then attached the tubing to our shirt collars to minimize movement when we needed a drink. Our meals were c–rations and peanut butter crackers - better than nothing. It was 6:00pm and getting dark fast and it looked like we would be spending the night here. We took turns sleeping and watching during the night. Around 3:30am, I could hear something moving below us and I woke Jake. We were watching and listening, with our weapons ready, when a skunk popped out about 10 feet in front of us. We both froze in place and the little bastard sniffed around us and wandered off up over the hill behind us. Pheeew! Thankfully he did not leave us with his calling card!

At 7:10am, I saw the target through the spotting scope and gave Jake a poke in the ribs to wake him up. He was on the gun and I called the shot at 330 yards, downhill and no wind. Jake made the shot. Within a few minutes, we were radioed to take a break for 15 minutes, and then it would be my turn to shoot. Again we sat and waited. At 2:35pm, Jake spotted the target and there were two other "people" with him, one on each side. The range was 368 yards downhill with a slight wind from the right. One shot and it was over. For the next three days, we went through the same exercises: climbing ridges, walking creek bottoms, and taking shots anywhere from point blank out to 1000 yards. Our final two days were spent going over the mental stresses we would face, briefings on protocol if we were captured, and basically what we could expect and how we should react.

CHAPTER 5

The end of training

We were given a two week leave. We were told we could not tell our families exactly what we would be doing or where we were going. That was not a problem because we did not know. Ah, the Army. We were not to wear our uniforms while on leave and we were not given a dress uniform. We were told it was for our own protection, as we would need to keep our identity hidden from the enemy. Our instructions were to tell our families we would probably be serving in transportation somewhere in Germany.

Leave was great. It was good to see my folks, but it was hard to not to be able to tell them what I would be doing. I visited with some of my old friends, including my high school sweetheart, Trudy. While away at training, I realized the strong feelings I had for her. The image of her beautiful eyes stuck with me and now she looked better than ever to me. We talked about marriage but decided it would be best to wait until I got out of the service. I didn't really like not being honest with everyone but I thought it might be best for them so they didn't worry too much about me.

It was kind of weird, but I did miss Jake. We had spent almost everyday together for the last three months. We had some disagreements, and at times we both needed our space, but he had become my best friend. I couldn't think of anyone else I would want covering my butt, except for my dad. My dad and I had a special bond. He was my best friend until Jake came along. We shared a love of the outdoors and sports and he was always my biggest fan when

I played sports. Hunting was what we loved the most. My dad taught me a lot from the time I was able to tag along rabbit hunting at age 7 or 8 until that day. He never told me I could not go, just that I had to keep up with him and his hunting buddies. He taught me how to spot a rabbit's eye while the rabbit hid in a pile of brush, how to bark like a squirrel and get them to move in a tree top. The most important thing my dad taught me was how to move slowly and quietly in the woods. If I had to make noise, I should move like a deer or squirrel, not a man. One of his favorite sayings was "move like there is a piece of game behind every tree." If there was one thing that he and I could do better than most hunters, it was move quietly. We would almost always make a game of trying to sneak up on each other whether we were hunting or not. He taught me to take pride in getting as close to game as possible before taking a shot, as that always increased the odds of making a clean killing shot. He instilled in me the sheer joy of stalking, which is something I enjoy today, almost 60 years later. Although we enjoyed eating what we killed, the thrill was in the stalking. Taking a shot was almost anti-climactic after stalking close to a deer or turkey or even a rabbit, so close you could reach out and touch them. Or sitting stone cold still and letting a bird or animal step on you, or still enough that a chipmunk would climb up on your shoe and relax and chew on an acorn. That's hunting whether you kill something or not.

I would not be able to hunt with my dad that year for the first time since I was 12 years old, and I knew I would miss the hunt and him. My mother kept trying to fatten me up the whole time I was home, and I told her I would have to run an extra two miles a day to burn off the extra weight I gained since I was home. I had five pounds of cookies to take with me that she baked, and maybe I would share them with Jake. I told them all about him and they hoped they would get to meet him someday. The two weeks went really fast, and it was time to go back. My parents and sisters and Trudy saw me off with a whole bunch of hugs, kisses and tears. I promised to write when I could, and told mom to keep the cookies coming.

I had been trained to do a different type of hunting in a place I had never been, against a body of people I had never seen. I was ready. For the last three months, my mind was shaped, my body tuned to do something in my heart I knew was wrong - kill people. To this point in my life, I never even pointed a gun at another human being, and I knew that would soon change. We had been taught by our superiors that killing was not a game, we should take no pleasure in it nor should we gloat about it. Our mission as soldiers was to kill the enemy before they had a chance to kill one of us. Each life we took would save the life or lives of our fellow soldiers. I understood this and accepted it, and for a while this would be my job. I was committed to do the best I could and had confidence in my abilities and the skills taught to me by my father and my instructors. I also had some doubts – could I kill another person? How would I feel when I did it? Would I remember that person's face after time passed? How would I feel about myself afterwards?

All these questions and more were answered by instructors and psychologists as part of our training. We were taught not to take it personally. We were given a job to do, just do it. I knew the right answers, but could I apply them to myself.

I would soon find out.

CHAPTER 6

Welcome to the Nam

The air transport touched down on what looked like the remainder of a mountain top. It was October 17, 1968. I looked out around the place and I saw troops moving. Some were lying around apparently resting from some just completed patrols. When we were leaving the plane, the pilot said "welcome to the Nam, boys." Once on the ground, we heard cat-calls and whistles from the other troops and comments like "fresh meat" and "check out the ass on that one." We were escorted with two other men to half plywood, half canvas quarters where we met a Captain Myron Wilkins. Captain Wilkins would be our commanding officer. Wilkins was a tall man, about 6' 4", thin, and looked hard as nails. He introduced us to the other two "newbies": PFC Daryl Hayes and PFC Tom Sachs, who were a sniper team as well. We were informed that we would hook up with two other sniper teams that would arrive later that day. We could leave our gear outside his quarters. When the other two teams arrived, we would all be transported by helicopter to a firebase where we would based for at least the next two weeks. We were assigned to Sergeant Miles Cooper, who was a stocky built, muscular man and looked like he was a sumo wrestler back in the world. He wore ragged looking six pocket pants, no shirt and a beat up flack jacket, had curly red hair and thick, dark rimmed glasses. His teeth looked like they hadn't been brushed for a week. He informed us that we would be spending two weeks with him, learning the ropes of this country and hopefully teaching us how to cover our asses and not get them blown off. At that point we were dismissed and allowed to go to the mess tent and get something to eat and check out the base. We were reminded to keep our M-16's with us "because we were in Indian country now". We were also told not to go beyond the wire that encircled the camp. The wire was concertina and German wire to help keep the enemy out.

We could hear mortars going off in the distance, but the soldiers in the compound didn't seem to mind them. They were playing cards, washing up, taking naps and checking us out. I'm sure we stuck out like sore thumbs, our fatigues were spotless and it was obvious only "newbies" were spotless. It was the smell of this place that I noticed the most – a combination of aviation fuel, diesel fuel and something burning. I found out later that the something burning was a detail that we would probably get a turn at – burning the waste from the latrines.

We were flagged down by a guy who called himself Shorty, who was at least 6'5" tall and he had obviously been drinking. He asked us where we were from and what our MOS (Military Occupational Specialty) was. When we told him we were scout –snipers his response was "woo – you guys must be bad dudes. How many Gooks have you killed?" He apparently was the only one who hadn't noticed our shiny new clothes. When Shorty announced to some of the other guys hanging out nearby that we were snipers, we could hear comments from a few, like f------ murderers and blood thirsty bastards. We didn't know why they would say that, but we didn't like it. Jake and I figured we should make our way back to the captain's quarters before we said or did something we might regret. We both wanted to go back and kick some ass, but this time we would let it go. We were warned by our instructors some people would not understand why we did what we did.

Jake and I decided to sit on our duffels outside the captain's tent and behave ourselves. It was so damn hot and humid my clothes were soaked from sweat just walking a few hundred yards. I was sure it was 50% heat and 50% anxiety that caused the sweat. Sergeant Cooper sat down with us and welcomed us to the Nam as well. He said he read our profiles and could vaguely remember when he looked fresh like us. Hayes and Sachs wandered in and they were pissed. After saluting the Sergeant, they asked for "permission to go kick some ass, sir." Cooper's response was "permission denied."

It seems they had gotten similar comments to what we had heard from some of the troops. The Sergeant explained that most of these men didn't understand the value of our operations. He assured us that if we came back through here when our tour was up and these same assholes were still here, we could kick as much ass as we wanted.

As I looked around that place, I couldn't help but wonder if any of my friends from back home had come through here. My friend Dick's casket was closed at his funeral, and I was told it was because they only found pieces of him, not his entire body. I wondered how many guys came back that way. I made up my mind that I wasn't going to focus on dying; I was going to focus on staying alive. I was young and "full of piss and vinegar" as my dad liked to say, and ready for what ever Charlie could throw at me.

Enough daydreaming, the other four members of our unit arrived. PFCs Mitchell, Heller, Smith and Anderson met with the Captain and Sergeant Cooper and received their orders. With a sharp click of their heels and a "yes sir" in unison, they joined us along with Sergeant Cooper. We were all loaded onto a helicopter and whisked off to firebase Whiskey. After a 30 minute flight, we arrived at our destination. The base was half the size of the one at Pleiku, the one we had just come from. The same basic layout: bunkers, plywood and canvas quarters lined with sandbags, artillery and mortar placements, jeeps, half tracks and a small landing area, and the entire compound surrounded with a wire. I could see a road winding into this hilly location which I assumed was a supply road for the base. There was a small village about a half mile from the camp, a couple of dozen huts with some rice paddies next to them. We were taken to the quarters where the eight of us would bunk together. Sergeant Cooper would be the guide for Jake, me, Hayes and Sachs. The other four were assigned to a Sergeant Miller, a small man who didn't mince words. He was very direct in what he expected from us - attention to detail, no cowboying or hot-dogging, and just maybe, we would leave this place in one piece some day. In his words "the fun and games are over and we were now in Indian country." The NVA were quite happy to kill us any opportunity they got. We were told not to trust anyone, as any man, woman or child could kill us. To illustrate his point, he showed us an ugly looking 8" scar on his leg that he got from a 12 year old boy who led him into an ambush on the premise of helping his mother. For the next two weeks, we were taken out to different hides in hopes of killing the enemy. We also provided support for our patrols and learned how to work with them and gain respect for each other. There were strategic travel routes the enemy used through the thick, almost impenetrable country. We needed to be aware we were not the only snipers in the woods. The enemy was very adept at hit and run tactics. We would be most successful if we employed one shot – one kill tactics, remain mobile, and never use the same hide twice. Our job was to provide support for patrols, to limit enemy movement, and to make him think we were everywhere.

We settled into our quarters, tore down our weapons and cleaned them in preparation for the next day. The apprehension of what was coming was almost overwhelming and I doubt if any of us slept very much during the night. We were up at 0600 and had some breakfast. Then we were off to the rifle range to make sure our rifles were still zeroed in after all the travel. There were two patrols leaving that morning, and we could overhear the banter among them as we headed for the range. Some of them were ready to give Charlie hell, but most were complaining about sore feet, the f----- bugs, the heat, and who didn't want to go to this place or that place. At the rifle range all eight of us checked the zero on our rifles and, after a few minor adjustments; we were all ready to go. One thing was certain, everybody could shoot. Sergeants Miller and Cooper comments were "OK, you guys can shoot paper. Now let's see how you do humping it into the bush and how well you do when somebody shoots back at you." We were all really damn nervous at this point; it was "shit or git time." Hayes, Sachs, Jake and I went with Cooper, who was a highly decorated sniper himself, and we were told a great shot. We coordinated our hand signals, as once we were outside the wire there would be very little talking. We moved as slowly and quietly as possible. Five men made a lot of movement and too much noise for me, but I wasn't in charge.

It made me uncomfortable to be moving with this many men, as I could get shot for somebody else's mistake. I knew I was a loner and only felt comfortable with Jake. Cooper was good; he walked on his toes, never brushed against vegetation, never stopped in the open, and used the terrain for concealment. After two hours we reached our destination. It was a steep hill overlooking a trail that the enemy was known to use. Jake and I made ourselves comfortable behind a deadfall tree where we could rest our rifles. Hayes and Sachs sat up about 200 yards to our right to watch a trail that intersected the one we were watching. Cooper got us settled in and said he would be back in a few minutes after he got Hayes and Sachs settled in. Jake looked at me and said "let's saddle up man, this is the real rodeo." I had a lump in my throat that no amount of water would get rid of. We were positioned off the crest of the hill and it was 550 yards to the trail. Jake was manning the spotting scope and I had my Winchester Model 70, .300 Win Mag. with 176 grain Sierra boattail bullets. It was zeroed in for 500 yards and it would be a piece of cake shot. We sat for 1 ½ hours and saw nothing except a bunch of birds. The edge was coming off of both of us, the waiting calmed us down and we were actually getting bored. It was hot, the morning sun was up high and beating down on us, and the bugs were having a picnic on our fresh meat. My camo face paint was washing off from the sweat, so I reached down and got some moist, wet soil and rubbed it on my face and hands. It seemed to repel the bugs a little bit and kept my face cool until it dried and I'd have to put some more on. There were a lot of sounds: lots of birds I had never heard before, monkeys screaming, mortar and small arms fire, and what sounded like 50 or 60mm machine gun fire off in the distance. I could hear the whomp-whomp-whomping of helicopters and jets sailing off in the distance dropping their payloads of bombs which seemed to vibrate the very ground we were sitting on, even though they were falling more than a mile away.

All of a sudden, there it was, a single rifle shot close by. It made both of us jump. It came from Hayes and Sachs position. Then another shot and another, all evenly spaced, in the time it took to work the bolt on a rifle. There was return fire coming from the valley below and then it was quiet. My heart was in my throat and going 100 miles an hour. Jake was up on the spotting scope and clicked his fingers. I was taking some deep breaths trying to calm down. Through my scope I could make out movement coming down the trail. Jake whispered "you got him?" I nodded yes. Black pajamas carrying an AK-47, this was it, this was the enemy, an NVA soldier. He was sneaking along slowly and looking back the way he came. I centered the crosshairs on his chest and took a breath and eased it out while gently squeezing the trigger. I never felt the recoil from the rifle, but through the scope I could see the man's chest explode and he flew backwards off his feet. His legs kicked a few times and he was still. I could see movement behind him, but it disappeared as quickly as it appeared. A few seconds later I heard another shot from the other team's location. Again silence, nothing was moving, no birds and no monkeys. After about fifteen minutes, Cooper came on the radio and said they were coming over to our location. I felt surprisingly calm, but was still looking through my scope for any more movement. A twig snapped to our right and Jake poked me in the ribs. He had his M-16 ready just in case. Cooper gave the approach signal and we relaxed. Without a word said, Cooper indicated we were moving out. When we finally reached the safety of the wire outside camp, Cooper nodded and said "good job." Back at our quarters we discussed what happened. Hayes spotted four NVA's moving down the trail and he took out two of them, the other two got by them. I got the third one when he came our way and apparently in confusion the fourth man doubled back and Hayes took him out as well. The whole encounter may have lasted five minutes, but it seemed a lot longer. We were out about seven hours and I was exhausted, my legs were rubbery and my head was spinning. Hayes looked at me and asked "are you as shaky as I am?" I just nodded my head yes, as I was finding it hard to talk. Cooper came out of the command office and into our tent. After we stood and saluted he said "at ease boys – you guys want a beer?" He told us to get a beer and something to eat and we would debrief as soon as the other group got in.

We had some beer and chow and at that point I didn't know if I was going to throw up or not, my stomach was all knotted up. Jake asked me if I was all right, and I said I think so. Hayes and Sachs were pretty proud of themselves and that was ok. I felt like I needed some time to process all of what happened that night. That was the first person I ever killed. What was his name? How old was he? Did he have a family? I could still see the expression on his face as the bullet struck him, the shock, the fear and then a blank stare as he died with me watching him through my scope. I had to get past taking this personally – but it was personal. It was my job right now and this guy would have killed me if he had the chance, I knew that.

My thoughts were interrupted by the return of the other four members of our unit. They had not encountered any enemy today and they were bitching about the bugs, heat and the boredom of the day. When they heard we had four confirmed kills they wanted all the details. Hayes was the hero of the day and he did a good job. The guys congratulated us and they all wondered what it was like. Sergeants Cooper and Miller came through the tent flaps and we scrambled to get to our feet to salute and come to attention. We were told to get some rest as tomorrow we would be leaving at 0500 in two man teams. We would hook up with two guides in the morning. We needed to make sure our packs were full and we had plenty of ammo as we may be out for more than a day. Jake and I would be going with Cooper and he told us to grab our long range weapons and an M-16. For us that meant using our .300 Winchester Magnums for the longer ranges. We also carried .45 caliber handguns for close combat. We were told we all did ok that day and the next day we would be hunting more Indians in a different territory.

Cooper asked to see me outside. We walked to an empty bunker in the middle of the compound and he asked me how I was feeling. He said he could see I was bothered by something and asked if it was killing someone. I said I was dealing with it but had mixed emotions about it. He asked me if I could do it again. He said tomorrow his life and Jake's life may depend on my ability to do so and he wasn't willing to take a chance on me if I hesitated to pull the trigger. He needed to know right now – yes or no – no indecision. My answer was yes sir; there is no doubt in my mind, sir. He said good, he hoped we would never have this conversation again. In passing he said a good soldier never takes pleasure in killing but neither is he ashamed of it. It is simply what we do and we need to do it to the best of our ability.

I went back to our barracks and cleaned my weapons. The old Winchester was my favorite but I had a M21 – M14 with a Redfield scope that shot very well as my backup and I took really good care of both of them. Jake and I talked a while and he asked me what I was feeling. I told him I didn't think it was remorse or regret; it was just something I needed to work through in my mind. The next day it would be his turn to shoot first and maybe he would better understand what was going on inside my head.

We were up at 0430, had some breakfast, and were outside the wire in an hour. It was raining and hot and humid. Cooper was going slow, pointing out good locations for an ambush and spots we didn't want to get into. We not only needed to find a good spot to shoot from, the location needed to have at least one good escape route as well. I really liked moving at this slow pace, it was like the way my dad taught me to stalk deer back home. It was my favorite way to hunt, move eight or ten steps, stop and look over the area thoroughly, watch for movement - the flicker of an ear, sunlight shining off an antler - hunt like there was a deer behind every tree. In this case, hunt like Charlie was behind every tree. There was a great deal of personal satisfaction in going one on one with a deer, whether I got a shot or not. The hunt was in the stalk, not the kill. I was thinking I could get pretty good at this type of hunting.

We climbed to a hill overlooking a village and some kind of trail system winding away from the village. Cooper told us the trails led to what was suspected to be an entrance to one of the many tunnel systems throughout the area. Our mission that day was to observe for any enemy movement along the trails and to try to figure out if any of the villagers were enemy sympathizers. We ranged the center of the village at 820 yards and we could see the trails for another 100 yards into the thick jungle only in bits and pieces. I didn't bother to put on my raingear because it just made me sweat even more. I was soaked to the skin from rain and sweat and my boots were full of water. I didn't know if I'd ever get used to the heat and humidity. We constructed a hide by digging into the steep bank just off the crest of the hill making a flat spot to sit on. We rigged up some broad leaves above us to keep some of the rain off of us. I was soaked on the outside, but dry inside from climbing the steep hill, so I took a drink of water from my canteen. I thought to myself that was kind of stupid, all I would have to do was look up and open my mouth and I could have gotten a drink that way. We had to use our bipods because we didn't have anything to rest our weapons or spotting scope on. That day I was manning the spotting scope and Jake was doing the shooting. We observed the villagers moving about and doing their chores, small children running around and playing, it seemed like such a peaceful place. It appeared to be a very simple life; they grew or gathered whatever they needed. Their whole life was this isolated village in the middle of nowhere.

The peacefulness was broken by distant explosions of bombs, mortars, and gunfire. I was told the NVA would often take the rice and other food these people had, often leaving them near starvation. At this point we did not know which side these villagers were on. I could only imagine they would be on the side of whoever was in their village at a given time. We were also told the NVA would give someone in the village a rifle and 15-20 rounds of ammunition each day. Everyday the NVA would collect the spent casings and leave fresh rounds. If the villager did not fire off the rounds from the previous day they would be beaten or killed. It was a way for the NVA to know if we were in the area by our patrols returning fire at the villager doing the shooting. If we would happen to kill the villager, the NVA would pick someone else to do the shooting the next day.

It was nearing midday and several of the villagers were moving back to their huts. I was watching an old man through the spotting scope. He went into his hut and sure enough he came out with an old beat up long rifle. I told Jake to get on him with his rifle and Cooper said to wait, don't shoot. The old man had a bag with some ammo in it and he walked over to a bench and sat down. He loaded the rifle and fired 18 shots at nothing we could see. The old man gathered up the spent casings and put them back in the bag and took the rifle and the bag and put them back in his hut. Cooper said don't shoot him; all that would do is let Charlie know we were here. Killing that old man would accomplish nothing and besides, without any return fire from the old man's volley, Charlie might let his guard down.

About 3:00pm, I spotted some movement on one of the trails above the village. It was a dog. The dog wandered into the village stopping to piss on everything some other dog had pissed on before, marking his territory. I thought to myself in a way we were here to mark our territory. In a few minutes I saw more movement coming down the trail; it was hard to see because of the thick vegetation. I could make out a man in black pajamas carrying a weapon, then another and another. They were moving towards the village where it was more open, let them come. I wondered if they used the dog as a decoy to draw gunfire. Naw, they couldn't be that clever. Cooper said stay on them but don't shoot until we see what they are up to. As they entered the village behind the old man's hut, we saw one of them leave more ammo and take the bag of empties. The third man was carrying a backpack full of something. The three of them walked to the edge of the village where another trail led off into the jungle. Cooper told me to load up as he was positioning his weapon. Depending on what they were going to do we would take them all out at the same time. They were pulling land mines out of the backpack.

They were going to booby-trap the trail in case one of our patrols would stumble onto it. Cooper said "Boys, this is what we get paid for." We each picked a different target and on Cooper's mark we fired simultaneously. The three men flipped backwards and never knew what hit them. Cooper kept firing, and bingo, he set off one hell of an explosion. There were body parts scattered everywhere after the mines exploded.

It was time to boogie on out of there. Without a word, we were up and over the top of the ridge and down into the valley below. One thing I noticed was that we did not go out exactly the same way we went in, and I would remember that. It was after dark when we reached the compound wire. We signaled the sentries we were coming in. I tripped on one of the wires and set off a bunch of cans with stones in them to an awful rattling. The tension of a long day was broken, and we all laughed and howled once we were inside the compound. Jake said to me "you dumb ass, we just humped for miles through the jungle and I didn't here you make a sound all day." We both asked Cooper how he knew he could blow those mines. He said he didn't know, but he had to try. Although it was bloody, it was shockingly funny when they blew. It was truly one of those "holy shit moments."

We had done a good thing that day. We most likely saved the lives of some of our soldiers by disabling those mines. It took me a while, but I finally got it. Although I'd heard it many times before, this verified for me what we did was necessary. I was glad for Jake; he did not appear to be struggling with the emotions I was struggling with the day before. That day I became a real sniper. I thanked Cooper for his guidance and not losing faith in me. His response was "just do your job soldier."

When Jake and I got to our quarters, Hayes and Sachs were already there. They spent the day providing cover for a patrol that left early in the morning as well. They saw some Indians but did not fire a shot all day. I asked Jake how he felt and he said he understood some of what I felt yesterday. It was his first kill and he said it felt pretty weird. He found himself thinking about the man he shot on the way back in to camp and wondered if that was what was bothering me the day before. We both agreed it was a sobering experience. After that day's encounter, we also agreed we were both doing what we were destined to do. I apologized for not sharing my feelings with him the day before; I just didn't know how to express them. He said he knew me well enough to know that when I didn't want to talk, to just leave me alone. He said I was always a moody bastard from the first time he met me. My comment to him was I was just waiting for some intelligent conversation! That day we became even closer; we shared yet another experience neither of us would ever forget.

I was becoming excited about going out hunting each day; it was what I loved to do. Our credo was go slow, cover your ass, don't use the same hide twice and try for one shot – one kill. We drank a few beers and were discussing what the legal drinking age was in the People's Republic of Vietnam when our intelligent conversation was interrupted by the return of our other bunk mates. Mitchell and Smith each got their first kills that day. There was apparently some problem with Anderson, but we didn't know what it was. Heller, his partner, wasn't talking about it. We found out the next morning Anderson was being scratched from the unit. We all knew he wasn't happy and he did have a bad attitude. He questioned everything that was done and always had a better idea. That was not the Army way and Heller would need a new partner or be scratched from the unit as well.

The next week was pretty uneventful. We spent a lot of time perfecting our movement or lack of movement, concealment and patience. Patience was the hardest part: we were always looking for some adventure and it wasn't too hard to find one in this place. We did pick off a few more of the enemy and it seemed we earned the respect of the patrols operating out of the camp. Much of our time was spent observing enemy movement, studying different villages for enemy activity, reading the land, and almost getting used to the damn bugs and heat. We also got a lot of practice bailing out of helicopters without breaking our necks. Jake and I acquired a taste for the local snake population. Back home I had eaten rattlesnake and liked it, these snakes tasted the same and yes, it does taste like chicken. I talked to some guys who had eaten rats while out on patrol but I wasn't ready for that. The rats here were twice the size of the ones back home but I hadn't been that hungry yet.

My senses were becoming tuned to the surroundings. I was learning the smells of the jungle, there were so many in this fertile soil. The trees, flowers, rotting vegetation, the smell of a rice paddy - I learned to seek out the smell of wood smoke – especially when there was no village nearby. This would be coming from the underground tunnels Charlie used to hide from us. On several occasions I smelled the pungent odor of cat urine, and when I saw the large tracks 5-6" across the foot pad, I knew there was a tiger nearby marking his territory. Although I never saw one, I'm sure they saw me. I could smell human odors – sweat, urine, and feces, reminding me I was not alone in these woods. All too often I could smell rotting flesh, gunpowder, and burned out vegetation. There were just as many sounds – the almost constant chatter of birds and monkeys, the occasional bark of dogs, the braying of water buffalo, the squeal of pigs, the drone of airplanes, the whomping of helicopters, the explosion of mortars (I learned to distinguish the size of each round by the explosion), ground shaking bombs, and gunfire. The scariest sound was silence: when the birds and animals were quiet, something or someone was moving. I really enjoyed the scouting and sneaking around gathering information and observing without being seen. Sometimes it would be a game between us, to see how close we could get without getting caught. It was a dangerous game and somewhat foolish, but it was an extreme adrenaline rush to have the enemy walk by within touching distance and not know we were there. Sometimes when we were on reconnaissance and not allowed to use our weapons, we would try to sneak into an enemy camp and take a piece of clothing or something to prove we got in and out of a camp without detection. Jake and I had a collection of NVA stuff stashed in our quarters, clothing, sandals, knives, documents and various other items. The coolest thing we had - Jake came away with an AK-47 rifle one night, I don't know how he got it and he wouldn't tell me.

Jake and I were on our way back to camp late one day, almost to the wire when we spotted a couple of wild pigs feeding in an opening. We decided it would be great to have a bar-b-que and we shot the biggest one. It wasn't the smartest thing we ever did, the pig probably weighed 200 pounds and we had to carry it up hill for a half mile to get to camp. Once we got it into the compound we had plenty of help skinning it and about twenty different recommendations on how to prepare it. We left it up to the cook and he did a great job, by nightfall the pig was all gone. We caught hell for bringing a dead pig into the compound from the C.O. but he enjoyed eating some of it as well and just walked away shaking his head. I looked at Jake and could see the wheels turning in his head. He said we need to figure out how to get a live pig into the compound and see if that was ok with the C.O.

Jake and I were told we needed to get some sleep because we had a special assignment the next morning early. The sniper teams would be working 12 hour shifts until somebody took out an enemy sniper who started firing on the base the day before. He shot two of our guys and one of them had just died. The sniper was firing from the hill north of the base and our guys were lobbing artillery rounds over there, but it was unknown if we got him or not. He needed to be eliminated before he shot anybody else. It was dark out and we were keeping lighting to a minimum and nobody was allowed outside without wearing a flack jacket and a helmet. I hated those damn helmets; I didn't like anything on my head. The helmets were hot and heavy and I was afraid it would rub the hair off my head. Normally I wore a boonie hat: it was soft and light weight and the one I was wearing had been with me since sniper school. Everybody had some kind of lucky charm with them; I guess mine was that old boonie hat. We hit the sack and were back up by 0400 hours.

Sometime during the night, someone saw a muzzle flash coming from a different location on the same hill and there were several rounds that struck harmlessly in the compound, the sniper was still out there. The plan was to position four dummies in fatigues to be seated outside a bunker with their backs to the sniper. Jake, Mitchell, Smith and I would be in separate sentry towers before daylight to watch the area and try to get a fix on this guy. We were banking on the guy to still be in the area, but we would just have to wait. I crawled into the tower and got as comfortable as I could. The sun was coming up over my back and it was a beautiful sunrise, for a moment I forgot where I was and just admired the view, beautiful shades of red and yellow creeping along the horizon. As the sun got higher, I developed a greater appreciation for the guys who normally manned these towers. The metal roof and small opening didn't allow for much ventilation and it was getting hot. Hopefully with the bright sun we might catch a flash of a reflection off his gun or something else on his person, if he was there. These guys were supposed to be very good and probably didn't make many mistakes. Three hours had passed and no sign of the sniper; I was getting tired of staring through binoculars. My eyes were tired and I was constantly fighting off headaches. The base was more quiet than usual.

There was some activity, a forklift unloading supplies, mechanics working on equipment, but everyone was keeping something between them and the hill to the north. It was very unlikely a shot would come from another direction because the firebase only had that one spot to the north which was higher. The other three directions were a sharp drop off and seeing into the compound was impossible from those directions.

All of a sudden there was a sharp crack of a rifle from the hill we were watching, a short pause and then another shot. One of the dummies fell over and the other three didn't move, which should indicate to the sniper something was wrong – he'd been had. I heard a shot from Mitchell's position and he came on the radio to say he saw the second muzzleflash or a reflection from the scope. He fired a shot into the area but had no idea if he had a hit or not. He said the shot came from a different location on the hill than the day before – so this guy wasn't stupid. If he wasn't dead he was probably moving out right now. Cooper radioed to come down to his post immediately. We were told to gather our gear and we were going after the guy right now. We would try to flank him on either side and one team would pick up his trail. Jake and I were told to pick up his trail and the other two teams would try their best to out flank him and intercept him. Jake and I were pretty good trackers but I suspected our slow movement was the reason we were given the tracking job. The other two teams had to move fast to get ahead of this guy. Cooper and Sergeant Miller would remain in one of the towers and try to spot for us if we needed help. We marked a couple of landmarks where the shots came from and we were off. If this guy was alive he probably knew somebody would be coming after him. We passed through the wire and dropped down into the valley below. There was a small stream at the bottom of the valley that everybody called a river – it was only 12-15' wide – but if the Army called it a river, it was a river. There were a lot of human tracks along the river - some were boot tracks, some were barefoot, some were sandals. We had approximately a 500 yard climb to get to the sniper's position. Jake and I split up by 20 yards or so until either of us found his trail.

I came across his hide from the previous day. The earth was kicked up and fairly dry and the broken vegetation was turning brown. I noticed an odd slice out of the sole of his right boot track. It would help us to identify his trail. I signaled for Jake to come over and we would take up his trail together. There were spots on this hill that our guys bombed the day before that were very open, but a good amount was still thick vegetation. We were still 150 yards from that day's shooting location and it was hands and knees time, move a few yards and glass. Our movement was slow – the guy could be wounded and lying in ambush. We had to move slightly to our right as we approached the site and I could feel the butterflies in my stomach having a party. We stopped about 30 yards out and glassed every square inch we could. We found what we thought was his trail out and over the top of the hill. From here we would drop our packs and belly crawl until we found his hide. We could see a dead fall ahead of us and some broken limbs behind it; that had to be the place. The question - was he in there? Jake would keep his scope trained on the spot and I would crawl in above and take a look. Almost to the hide, I found a trip line attached to a punji stick. A punji was one to five sharpened sticks which when tripped would come up, drive through a boot or leg or crotch, and inflict a lot of pain. The most common method was to line the bottom of a hole in the ground with the sharpened sticks and when someone fell into the hole, a lot of damage would be done or even death. I disabled the punji and eased forward to check out the hide. It was empty. There were fresh boot tracks and the right boot had the same slice I found before. I signaled Jake to come on up. I found some blood, bright red in color and no air bubbles or anything in it, probably an arm or leg wound. If it was a chest hit the blood would be frothy, and if it was a lower abdomen hit there would be some type of waste matter in it. Mitchell's shot was just a little bit off. His trail led up and out over the top of the ridge and I had to keep telling myself to go slow and watch ahead. I went first and Jake would watch ahead, I would stop and glass and Jake would move up to me. Like my dad taught me, hunt like there's a deer behind every tree. I was not seeing in his tracks that he was dragging one of his feet, so he was probably hit in an arm or a slight head wound. The trail led us to the top of the ridge which was fairly open.

We radioed Cooper with what we found and the other two teams reported they had not crossed his trail coming out. The other teams could see us where we were at this point. It appeared the guy went down into the next valley and was somewhere between Jake and I and the other two teams. Cooper told us to "Go get him and be careful, you rednecks ain't huntin' deer now, this S.O.B. will shoot back." The other two teams were going to stay ahead of us and above us on each side of the valley and maybe pick him off if we pushed him out. Jake and I skirted around the burned out area, sticking to cover and started down into the valley. We reached the bottom of the valley and we found where he entered the river and crossed to other side. We each took a different side of the river; he was zig–zaging back and forth in the river to try to disguise his trail. After about 100 yards of this, his trail took off to the ridge to our left. I motioned for Jake to stop because now the sniper was above us and I did not like that. I eased down the river bank to talk to Jake. I was sliding down the bank when whomp – a bullet came whistling over my head and struck the mud bank above me. I had no idea where the bullet came from and made two leaps to get to the cover of the opposite river bank. I heard another shot and just froze under some tree roots on the bank. Jake was already hidden on the bank after the first shot. We were peeking out trying to get a fix on this guy and we were pretty sure he didn't have a shot at us from this position. It was thick and we couldn't see very far. If he wanted us he would have to come and get us. After about thirty minutes, Smitty came on the radio and said they got him. They saw him moving along the hillside and watched him set up and watch his back trail. Smitty said he couldn't pick him out until he fired. He said he hoped he wasn't too late and was glad we were ok. We could hear Smitty talking to Cooper but we couldn't hear Cooper because we were down in the valley. Smitty relayed the message to head on back to camp and to be careful, the shooting may have attracted some company. Jake said "let's follow the river back to camp" and along the way we bumped into some kids from the local village playing in the river. They were all young - probably under age 10, and reminded me of the gang I used to hang out with. They were looking for candy or anything else we could give them. I had some hard candy in my pocket and gave it to them. I remember being told not to trust anybody including woman and kids. It was hard to imagine these little kids could do us harm, but it was possible. This was a hard land and a culture different from any that I knew about.

It wasn't fun being shot at, and my ears were still ringing from that bullet going over my head. The guys out on patrol told me as long as I can hear them I'd be ok, the one that gets you is the one you don't hear. When we got back to camp we reported to Sergeant Cooper who was in the command office with Captain Wilkins. We briefed them on what occurred and while we were there Smitty and Mitchell reported in. They had a few souvenirs: a Russian made long gun and handgun, some maps, and other documents. Hayes and Sachs soon reported in, and we were truly glad to see one another. That day, we all worked together as a team and even though we were friends before, we formed a bond that would be difficult to break. I made a mistake that day and let myself out in the open too long and it could have cost me my life. I would not make that mistake again.

Mitchell said Charlie sniper man had a wound on his right forearm which was where he must have hit him initially. Maybe that's why he missed me. I thanked the guys for covering my butt and they laughed and said it wasn't easy because my butt was pretty big. We were all dismissed and in unison we all clicked our heels and saluted and then left the office. We got some chow and went back to our barracks to strip down and wash the mud and sweat off our bodies. Jake and I picked a few leeches off each other from wading around in the river. When we came back out, there was a group of men waiting outside our barracks. We didn't know what was going on and I was thinking I really didn't want to get in a fight with only a towel wrapped around my ass. These guys wanted to party – they had a couple of cases of beer, a boom-box and speakers and said we were going to have a dance! It was their way of saying thanks for taking care of the sniper. I never danced with a guy before, but what the hell. After a few beers nobody really cared. It was fun to act like a kid again and for a little while forget about the pressures of the day. We rocked to the Rolling Stones, The Beatles and Led Zeppelin until we were ordered to hit the sack. I knew I was going to have a big head in the morning. Some of the guys were passing around some joints but I didn't try any, maybe another time. Throughout the party, nobody could answer the question of what the legal drinking age was in Vietnam.

We had two days left to our training and none of us had any idea where we were going when it was over. Heller was shipped out to another sniper unit and Anderson was reassigned to a regular infantry unit. Jake and I were 20 years old, Mitchell was 22, and Smitty, Hayes, and Sachs were 21. All the training we had received was about to be put to the test. As a unit at this base, we had 19 confirmed kills in the past 12 days. A couple of us had been shot at, but fortunately no one was injured.

The next day was spent reviewing our mission and Captain Wilkins brought us two new rifles to try out. They were called a M24 – a revised M21 on a Remington 700 frame with a match grade barrel and fiberglass stock. They both had Leupold 3-9x40mm scopes and were chambered in 7.62x51 (.308). They were prototypes and they worked and shot very well. We could not keep them and we tried, but the brass was just trying them out. We were told that maybe next year we might see them again. He also had a XM-21/M14 with a silencer on it and a starlight scope attached to it which was supposed to gather light under low light conditions. That gun was only good out to 300 yards but it was supposed to be super quiet. It was a very heavy gun and I did not like that. We waited until near dark to shoot the gun and the scope worked really well but there seemed to be some accuracy issues. Captain Wilkins told us we could keep it and play with it to see if we could get it shooting better. The six of us spent the evening comparing opinions on the various rifles had and never really came to any consensus. We all agreed, knowing the Army we would probably never see the M24 again.

CHAPTER 7

Deep Into Indian Country

The next morning, I wrote a letter to my folks and to Trudy, and reread some of the ones I already received. After breakfast, we were told to get our gear together, as we would all be shipping out the next day. We had an hour to do so and then we would report to the command post. The Captain told Jake and me, we would be assigned to a part of the 9th Infantry Division at Dong Ha which was close to the demilitarized zone and not too far from the border of Laos, a region known as the Quang Tri Province. Mitchell and Smitty were going with us and they would move on to another base later. We were each given maps and told to study them. Hayes and Sachs would be staying and be part of a unit that was going to operate out of the base. The rest of the day was spent saying good byes, having a few beers, and studying the maps we were given of our new home base and the area around it. Jake and I were working on making our tiger stripe camo a bit more effective. We heard about and saw some Ghille suits, but we didn't have any. We collected some leaves from some of the local plants and made paper patterns of them. We then gathered some old tent material and old tee shirts, all olive drab green in color, and cut out leaves and sewed them on our shirts, pants and hats, which would help to break up our outlines. We took quite a bit of kidding from the other guys about cutting out paper dolls, but we didn't care. If it helped save our butts, we did not care what we looked like. Mitchell gave us a flower print shirt he had and told us to cut out the flowers and sew them on and we could be "flower children."

Maybe later it was time to get to sleep, but I doubted there would be much sleep that night.

Morning finally came and we grabbed some chow and by 0630, we were diving onto a chopper to head out to our new location. We flew over the village of Dong Ha, which was larger than the village close to our last base. I could see trails leading into the village from all directions and a decent dirt road leading from the village to the base. Welcome to firebase Billy. It looked like the other bases - red mud, plywood and tin shacks, bunkers and sandbags everywhere. There was, of course, a landing zone and plenty of artillery stations. There were guys milling around doing whatever they were supposed to do. We were told to report to the command office after we bailed out of the chopper. We all saluted and clicked our heels to a Captain Reynolds, he in turn introduced us to Sergeant Olson. Captain Reynolds was a short, stocky man who wore wire rimmed glasses and spoke with words I had not heard in a while. He was obviously a well educated man and at least for the moment was not cursing every other word. He thought before he spoke and I liked that. He informed us that as snipers here we would be used to destroy material targets, support patrols, provide multiple over-watch positions, provide intelligence about the enemy, and anything else he thought we could do. He stated that we were one mile from the Laotian border and he knew we were aware the U.S. Army had no presence in Laos. However a lot of material and enemy troops were coming out of Laos and a great deal of our effort would be to slow down or stop that movement.

We were given the rest of the day off to settle in and get acquainted with the base and the personnel. The next morning we would report to Sergeant Olson for our assignment. Mike Olson was a rough talking, very abrupt person, just the opposite of Captain Reynolds. My dad would say "he didn't have any couth" or was uncouth. It would take time to decide if I liked him or not. I did not have to like him, but I did have to respect him.

Mitchell and Smitty were moving on shortly and we said our good byes and good luck. I was going to miss them both, Mitchell was the first black man I could truly call my friend. That was the way it was, you met someone and get to enjoy their company and then one or both you move on. Jake and I were lucky - we had been together from the beginning and I put my complete trust in him and I think him in me as well.

We would be replacing two men who rotated out the day before; they were heading back to the world. We would be bunking with four other men who were also snipers - PFC Bill West and his partner Sergeant Mike Williams and PFC Tom Moore and his partner Corporal Harry Hood. When we entered our new barracks, West and Williams were catching up on some sleep, and even though we tried to be quiet, we woke them moving our gear into place. We apologized for waking them and went outside so they could get more sleep. I was sure we made a lousy first impression on those two guys. We learned that Moore and Hood were out with a patrol and might not be back for another day. Sergeant Olson showed us around the camp and we got the usual "fresh meat" and "newbie" comments from all the guys who had been here a while. Sergeant Olson told us he read our records and he knew both Captain Wilkins and Sergeant Cooper and served with both of them. He told us they recommended us for this post and they recommended we stay together as a team. Olson said he would decide that after he saw us in action. Normally newbies coming in were assigned to a partner who had been here awhile. He said that tomorrow he would take our asses out and see if we were any damn good. We would be going out to try to destroy some equipment that was supposed to be coming across the border. He told us that after lunch we would go check our weapons at the range. For now we were free to go jack off or whatever the hell we wanted to do but be at the range by 1300 hours.

Jake and I were kinda shocked, we had no idea they might split us up. Hell, we put in all this training together, we knew what the other was thinking without saying anything, we were a team. We vowed we would show that asshole Olson he would be stupid to split us up. We talked to a few of the troops and looked things over and then headed to the mess hall for something to eat. We spied West and Williams in there and they motioned for us to come over and sit with them. They said they were sorry if they seemed rude but they had been out most of the night. We agreed it was no big deal, we had been there ourselves.

West said he had been here for six months and Williams for eight months. They told us Olson wasn't a bad guy once you got to know him. Most important was he was a good teacher and good in the woods. We asked them about splitting us up and said how we thought it was a dumb thing to do. They told us to look at it from the Army's standpoint as it was safer to put a newbie with a veteran until they learned the lay of the land. At some point we would become the veterans and it would our turn to teach the new guys coming in. I guess they were right, we had not really thought about it that way. We still did not want to be split up. Williams told us the men we were replacing were very good and we would have some big shoes to fill. I asked to just give us a fair shake and if we screwed up to tell us. Jake said we were just a couple of dumb old country boys who liked to hunt and play in the woods. They laughed and said we would get plenty of chances to do that. Here we were again; we would have to earn everybody's respect all over again.

We met Olson at the rifle range, on time. We checked the zero on our rifles and everything was ok. We went back to our barracks and unpacked our gear. West asked what the hell we did with our camo. He looked it over and thought it was a good idea. I told him I would show him what we did but he would have to do his own sewing because I still had blisters on my fingers from all the sewing I did. We spent some time going over maps and hearing about some of the missions these guys were on. They also told us who was friendly in the area and who was not and most importantly do not trust anybody.

I had a question about being so close to Laos. Were we going in there? I knew what the Captain said but why were we so close to the border if we were not going in? The response was we would have to talk to the Captain about that. I had a feeling that we would be talking to somebody about that sooner or later.

Moore and Hood were not back yet and it was getting dark. Williams was telling us that this base would get hit about once a week with mortar rounds and some NVA trying to breech the wire but so far nobody got in. One of our jobs would be to try keeping enemy artillery from getting within range of the base. Most of the time they would wait until the patrols were out and most of the attacks would occur at night. According to the maps, there were only two decent ways to get in here: one was the supply road and the other was a hill to the west. That hill was pretty well defoliated and there were not a lot of places left to hide. Obviously we needed to keep the supply road open to keep our supplies coming in and Charlie was going to try to shut it down to keep our supplies out.

CHAPTER 8

The Snake Hunt

Olson had Jake and I up at 0530 hours and briefed us where we were headed that day. We each took a .50 caliber rifle and Olson had one as well. Intelligence had information of a shipment of supplies coming across the border and our job was to stop them. We slipped out through the wire and headed west towards the border. Our objective was a road about two miles northwest. We crossed one hill and down into the next valley and across to the other side and climbed to the top of the next hill. We could see into the next valley and the road we were looking for. We found a place to set up and settled in. Our job was to take out any vehicles carrying equipment and then destroy the equipment. After about an hour we could see four men moving down the road. Olson said not to shoot them because they were probably decoys sent out to draw any fire before the convoy came through. In fifteen minutes we could hear trucks coming down the road. There was a bit of an opening we were going to let them get into before we fired. First up was a personnel carrier with four men and a bunch of boxes on the back. Following were two trucks, one loaded with two generators and other supplies and the second appeared to have ammo and vehicle parts on the back. It looked like two men in each truck. We were 820 yards out.

We allowed the personnel carrier (PC) to get to the far right of the opening and I put a .50 caliber round in the engine block, Olson and Jake took out the four men riding in the back of the PC. I turned my gun on the driver of the carrier and these guys never knew what hit them. I then hit the first truck and took out the passenger; the driver tried to ram the PC off the road but did not succeed. The driver bailed out of the truck and ran around to the front of the truck and looked in our direction - it was the last thing he ever saw. Olson and Jake had taken out the two men in the second truck and then we all fired into the supplies and generators on the trucks. One of the guys in the second truck got off a few bursts of fire before he was killed, but he didn't have a clue where we were. I was watching for the four guys we let pass earlier to come back and check things out but did not see any sign of them. It was time to move out, so Olson radioed the patrol behind us to move in and blow up the trucks. That should plug up the road for a while. We moved in the direction of the four NVA soldiers that passed by just in case they might come back and give the patrol some trouble. We sat up and settled in to provide cover for the patrol coming in. We fired a lot of ammo into those trucks and could very well have given our previous position away. In about thirty minutes Olson said he could see the patrol moving in through his spotting scope. Their job was to rig some explosive charges and blow up the trucks and in a few minutes there was a huge explosion and fireball and parts and pieces were flying everywhere.

We were going to move to another location up the road where Olson said there was a trail intersecting the road where there may be some more of Charlie moving in to see what was going on. He put Jake and me on the guns and he was using the spotting scope. The patrol was going to do a sweep into this area and we would once again provide support for them. A few things were the same here as other places I had been "in country" – the bugs, the heat, and the sweating. Olson looked at our water bottles and said he liked the way we had them rigged up and said we could do the same for him. Or because he out ranked us, he could just take one of ours. Neither one of us said anything but I was thinking – not gonna happen. I didn't think I'd like this bastard. I had to take a leak and rolled over on my side to relieve myself. When I did a green tree snake slithered out from under my leg. I reached down and grabbed the snake behind its head and snapped its head from its spine to kill it. The snake was squirming and twitching and I threw it over at Jake. Jake put his foot on the snake until it was done squirming and I finished the task I started out to do. These snakes were not poisonous but were pretty aggressive.

I looked back at Olson and he was as white as a bed sheet. I thought to myself, he's afraid of snakes. I looked at Jake and winked and nodded for him to look at Olson, Jake looked back at me and smiled. Olson had one eye on the snake and one eye on the spotting scope. Jake looked at me and asked "you hungry?" I said yes, I hadn't eaten anything since breakfast. He cut the skin behind its head and peeled it down over the back and cut a piece of flesh off and ate it. He then cut a piece off and handed it to me and I swallowed it whole. Now, I had never eaten raw snake before and I was pretty sure Jake never did either. But if we could gross out Olson and show him we deserved to be together, it would be worth it. It worked, Olson whispered "you f------ hogs, I can't believe you just ate a f------ snake, let alone raw!" Jake said "the next piece is yours, sir." Olson said get that damn thing out of here. Jake cut two more pieces off and tossed the rest of the snake into the bushes. We each ate one more piece and as my grandpa used to say "we were grinning like a possum eatin' shit!"

We were at this location for another hour when we heard some gun fire out in front of us. Olson said he could see our patrol moving through the area where the shots came from and we were to watch that nobody could flank them. Jake picked up some movement along the edge of the trail and Olson identified it as an NVA. Jake had him in his scope and one Charlie was done sneaking. A few minutes later the platoon leader radioed they were on the trail we were watching and that they killed three NVA back in the bush and they thought one of them got away. Olson told the platoon leader the NVA did not get away. We could hear the Sergeant tell Olson one of his men got hit, not bad, and they were going to make their way back to the base. Olson told him we would do the same.

Olson looked at both of us and said "ok snake boys, lead the way back to camp." It was almost dark when we got to the wire and Jake and I were snickering about the snake. When we reached our barracks all four of our bunkmates were there. Olson said to the four of them "these f------ guys are crazy, you don't want to go huntin' with them" and then he left. Obviously we had to explain the whole thing to them. They howled and laughed and I think at that point we were accepted. Moore and Hood introduced themselves and then Hoody handed us a beer and a "welcome to the unit." It was really funny, we thought it would take a couple of weeks to earn some respect and that silly little green snake helped us earn at least some of it in a day. They all said Olson was a tough SOB, but when it came to snakes he was a big wuss. We all headed for the mess tent to get something to eat and inside was Olson eating by himself. I couldn't resist asking the cook if he had any fried snake meat on the menu. Olson flipped me the bird and motioned for us to come and sit with him. It was time to let the snake thing die, if we pushed Olson too hard he could make life pretty miserable for us.

The next week or so Jake and I did share duty with some of the other guys and we learned a lot about this part of Indian country and the other guys in the unit. The tenth day there, we were sitting around shooting the bull after dark. We had just come back from a scouting mission when all hell broke loose. There were 60mm and 120mm mortars falling into the compound and gun fire coming from somewhere. We could see a couple of guys get hit by shrapnel, and Jake and I went out and dragged them into a bunker outside of our barracks. One of them was Olson and he was torn up pretty bad. He was hit in the back and his right arm was badly broken, he was covered in blood and dirt. The other guy I did not know and he had a least a broken leg and a lot of cuts on his chest and legs. A medic showed up and attended to both men. Jake and I were in our underwear and our combat boots but it didn't matter, we grabbed our rifles and belly crawled to a bunker lower on the hill just inside the wire. There were night flares illuminating the area where the mortars were coming from and our guys were lobbing mortars back at them. We could make out some movement from where the enemy mortars were located but it was hard to pick out a target. We lined up on what we thought were men and waited for the next flare to light them up. I picked out an outline and fired and I could see legs kicking after I shot. Jake and the other guys were spread out in other bunkers and were firing on the enemy positions as well. We started to get some return fire from across the hill - both automatic and machine gun. I could here somebody on the hill above me calling for more flares. We were picking off a few but there was a lot of fire power coming off that hill. Our guys finally got three artillery guns up and running and we started to push them back. We were able to pick off a number of NVAs trying to move across the bombed out more open areas of the hill. The night flares were a big help. A lot of our shots were taken at muzzle flashes coming out of the darkness and they were not a very high percentage shot. The problem was the enemy could see our muzzle blasts as well. We had bullets smacking around us and over our heads. We were shooting through port holes in the sandbags and were reasonably well protected. We did have a mortar round throw a bunch of dirt over us and the concussion rocked us a bit. This siege lasted about six hours and we held our positions until daylight just in case Charlie had not had enough. Every now and then we would pick off a straggler. Position was everything and we had superior position as well as superior fire power, at least in this battle. This type of fighting was not what snipers were best at - we were more of a hit and run unit, but we did the best we could.

We moved back to our barracks and found the front of it had been hit by a mortar round. There were two evac choppers loading up wounded and we went over to help. There were also five body bags on the ground. We were looking for Olson but didn't find him. We checked the body bags and none of them had him in them. We saw Moore lying on the ground on a stretcher waiting to be loaded on a chopper. He said he was hit in the leg but was ok and he'd be back. Hoody came over and was really worried about his partner; we all helped load Moore onto the chopper and wished him luck. Hoody told us Olson was dead and his body went out on a chopper earlier. We were all taken back by Olson's death. He was our leader and just that quick he was gone. Just that quick our unit was down to five men.

We found out later there were seven killed and fifteen wounded that night. We stowed our rifles and started cleaning up the mess. We had some plywood and sheet metal to put back up and a lot of red mud to clean up. We filled sandbags with dirt and rebuilt the bunkers. Captain Reynolds stopped by and thanked us for pulling the two men to safety and even though Olson didn't make it, the other soldier, Tom Hill, would survive his wounds and we should stop over to the infirmary to see him. He told Sergeant Mike Williams he would be the new unit leader and he should report to his office at 1400 hours. For Jake and me, it was the first time somebody we soldiered with was killed. It was a somber time and even though I didn't really like Olson that much, he was a good soldier and took good care of us. Williams told us to gather up Olson's things and put them in order. While packing Olson's things, West found a log that he kept. In it he had nicknames assigned to all of us that we didn't know about. Jake was of course Jake the Snake or Snake, I was Dirt Hog, West was Cowboy, Williams was Hank, Hoody was Hoody, and Moore was Les. We all chuckled that maybe the guy did have a sense of humor. We decided that these would all become our new call names, as a way to honor the man. I guess I was Dirt Hog because I was always rubbing dirt on myself for more camo and to help keep the bugs off me.

The word came out that there would be a bombing run on the hill opposite us to clear it and open up the jungle remaining there so Charlie wouldn't feel comfortable crawling around over there. That run would be at 1530 hours.

We cleaned up our area and went around helping out where ever we could. There were sandbags to fill, buildings to repair, holes to fill, everybody was busy. There was a helicopter with some damage to the rear propeller and some guys were tearing it apart to get it back up and running. These helicopters were the backbone of every base and the guys that flew them had brass balls.

We could hear the jets coming and right on time. They hammered the hill with bombs and the ground shook under our feet even though they were hitting ¼ mile away. They included a defoliant called Agent Orange that completely destroyed the vegetation. Anything left on that hill was gone and it would make this base a lot safer. I looked down into the village below us and there was no one moving around. I was sure these people were all hiding after the previous night's fire fight and now the bombing. I tried to imagine how their lives had been turned upside down by this war. They were mostly simple farmers and I'm sure the terror they felt almost daily was a real hardship. It had to be one hell of a way to live.

We all met with Captain Reynolds that evening and he told us the base would be ramping up its operations in the coming weeks. There would be two more platoons coming in and our unit would be doubled in size to ten men. We had five new snipers coming in and we had one week to get them broken in. He informed West, Jake and I that we were in line for promotions to Corporal and he would push it through. We would all be responsible to train the new men coming in as this area was going to get hotter because Charlie wanted it as much as we did.

I wasn't too crazy about training somebody but I didn't make the rules. I just wanted to do what I did best on my own or with Jake. Williams said "you guys know the game; we are all going to have to suck it up". It was up to us to create a good team here.

Most of the guys on base left us alone. I didn't know if they thought we were weird or nuts or what. We did do things in a different way but as a unit we were effective. Between the seven of us we probably accounted for over 100 dead enemies in the last two weeks. I didn't know how many confirmed kills I had; I knew Olson kept a scorecard, but I never saw it. I knew Williams had it now and maybe someday I would look at it. I didn't particularly care for this whole body count thing but it was the way the Army wanted it done.

It was fairly quiet in the compound that night, no dances; we were all beat physically and emotionally. I crawled into my bunk and found some clumps of dirt in it. I was so tired I just pushed them aside; I would clean them up later. We had not slept for over a day and the emotions of the day had me worn out.

The next day Jake and I were told to take a jeep down into the village and deliver some food and clothing to the people of the village. Each week we gave them some supplies to maintain some good will with them. I wasn't sure what day of the week it was. But I knew it was always done on a different day and time just in case Charlie was trying to pattern us. We parked the jeep and handed out the supplies and some candy to the kids. We had strict orders to accept nothing from the villagers, as it could be booby-trapped. These were such humble and grateful people; it was hard to believe they could kill us. We did have a few women who came on base to do laundry and cleaning. I recognized one of them in the crowd as Mai Lin who did some laundry for us. I guessed she was 30-35 years old and some what attractive but too skinny for me. We gave her a ride back to the base but had to drop her off at the gate so she could be searched before entering. In her broken English she said thank you. It was hard to tell what these people thought of us. I'm sure they were grateful for the supplies. I'm also sure they wished we would get the hell out of their country and let them live their own lives. I tried to envision if the roles were reversed what I would feel. If Viet Nam came in and bombed and shot up the land that I loved my beloved mountains and killed some of my family, what would I feel?

I realized a little bit of what these people felt. They would take what we gave them, because we had taken so much from them. But I also understood that they would also kill us given the opportunity, because that was what I would do if the roles were reversed. From that point on I would never trust any of them. It was the only way to survive in this hellish place. Another part of what we were trained became a reality today – never trust anyone, man, woman or child. Respect them as human beings, but always cover your ass.

CHAPTER 9

Becoming a Real Soldier

I bumped into the medic who tried to save Olson when we got back from the village. I needed to know if there was anything more I could have done to save him. He told me there was nothing anybody could have done. He was bleeding internally and lost so much blood that it was only minutes after he tried to treat him that he was gone. He shook my hand and said it was a brave thing I did dragging Sergeant Olson out of danger's way. I didn't think I was brave; it was something I would do for any fellow soldier. I hoped they would do the same for me, if necessary. I looked down at my boots and they were covered with Olson's dried blood and for the first time since he died, I cried. I did not get to know Olson well but he taught me things that would serve me well in the future and I would not forget him. That day I became a complete soldier. The experiences of the last two days hardened me, toughened me to become the man I had to be to survive. It was really the first time I thought of myself as a man. Before I felt like a boy in a man's world and I didn't feel equal to the men around me. I guess all the training I had over the last few months were to prepare me for this moment.

I never thought much about destiny and I never thought much about God. Its ironic how being in a place like that forces you to think about such things. I heard that God predestined our lives in Sunday school as a kid, but it never really sank in. I only went to church because my parents made me go, and that was not very often. I began thinking - I was born at the right time, I grew up in the right environment, and I was taught a set of values that seemed to fit perfectly for me to be in this place at this time.

The training my dad gave me in woodsmanship, the games my friends and I played as kids, the independence and self-sufficiency we learned as kids roaming around the mountains, my decision to volunteer to be a sniper, could that really be true? Could God have known before I was born that I would be here now? If that was true then what was my purpose for being here? Was it to kill as many enemy soldiers as possible? Was I here for some other reason? Was I supposed to save somebody's life or would I die here?

This was getting to be some pretty heavy thinking and I thought when you became a man you knew all the answers! I had just asked more questions of myself than I could possibly answer. Maybe I shouldn't ask so many questions and just do what I'm told. That was the Army way, but it was not my way. I knew at some point in the future the Army way and my way would clash. I understood that most everything the Army taught me had been beneficial and had gotten me this far with all my body parts intact. Although at certain times I questioned why they did things a certain way, I found time after time they were right. My instructors moved me through my training at the right pace. They taught me as much as they thought I could handle and then we moved on. I guess what was really bugging me was now they were asking me at 20 years old to train someone else. The Army must think I was ready, therefore I must think I was ready. I'm here to do a job and I would to do it to the best of my ability. That was the way I was brought up and I did not know any other way.

Jake grabbed me by the shoulder and asked "man are you all right?" I looked at him and asked "yeah, why?" He said "you've been staring at the wall for the past 20 minutes". I responded "I guess I was just trying to figure out how I got here and what the hell I'm gonna do while I'm here." He asked "figured it out?" I said "yeah, we're going out in the woods and do some hunting".

The next morning I awoke to something scratching on the wall next to my bunk. Instinctively I reached for my rifle, which now was always within arms reach and hanging on the wall next to my bunk. Looking down the sight on my M-16, I saw the biggest rat I ever saw in my life. It was as big as a cottontail rabbit. Everybody else was still sleeping so I didn't shoot. I had a new mission – kill that rat. I eased out of my bunk and the rat ran out the back of the barracks through a hole in the wall. I sneaked out the front door (we didn't have a back door). I grabbed a couple of cookies my mom sent me and went stalking for mega rat. I didn't see him so I laid half of a cookie on the ground as bait and I ate the other half. After a few minutes, he stuck his head out from under the plywood wall. Somebody inside got out of bed and scared him back under the building. It was just breaking daylight and I was getting cold sitting in my underwear on the ground. Finally the rat came out - no creature could resist my mom's cookies! I let him clear the building and whacked him with one shot. One shot – one kill that was our motto. That one shot caused quite a stir, my other bunk mates were up and out the door with their weapons before I could pick up the rat. They came around the corner of the building and saw me sitting there and wondered what the hell I was doing. I announced that I had just killed a world record rat! If looks could kill, I'd have been dead. They were not impressed to say the least. Williams suggested a place I could put the rat and West volunteered to put it in there. Jake, my only friend at the moment, picked it up and said "nice rat." I decided I was going to skin this rat and tan the hide and put it on our barracks wall along with a few of the snake skins we accumulated. The guys all said they were going to get some breakfast before our new recruits got here. I decided I should probably eat before skinning the rat also. A couple of other guys in the mess hall asked "what that shot was this morning". My buddies all pointed at me. I told them the cook was running low on meat so I shot a rat and gave it to him to mix with the SOS they were eating. The Captain overheard our conversation and just shook his head. I quickly ate breakfast and got to skinning the rat outside the back of our barracks.

    I heard a chopper coming in and thought I better hurry because it was probably our new guys coming in.

    In a few minutes, I heard talking at the front of our barracks including some strange voices. The new recruits were here and I wasn't done skinning the rat. Williams came around the building leading the five new men and introduced me as the camp cook, preparing a survival meal for them for lunch today. The look on their faces was priceless! They didn't want to act grossed out but they were.

    I finished my task of skinning – stole some salt from the kitchen to dry the skin and I was done. Hank (Williams) told me to get dressed (I forgot I was still in my underwear) and he would assign me to a new trainee. I did so and he introduced me to PFC Eduardo Sanchez. The other four newbies were PFC Carter, PFC Edmonds, PFC Walker and PFC Trimble. They all had a tendency to salute but were reminded when we were outside or in the bush, no saluting. If Charlie was watching he would always pick off the officer first as we were trained. Besides I was not a superior to them – I was still a PFC myself.

Sanchez asked "so you're not the camp cook?" I told him I was just the cook's assistant. I was not ready to let them off the hook just yet. We all left for the rifle range after they stowed their gear. Our barracks was pretty full now; we only had room for two more guys. They all shot well at the range and we only had to make a few adjustments. I was interested in the way these men moved. Sanchez was short and stocky like me and moved slow and deliberate, I liked that. Carter and Edmonds were both tall and thin with long legs and moved fast, we would have work on that. Walker and Trimble were average in their pace and would be all right with a little more training.

We started the boys off with some map reading and studying of the terrain and native plants, what you could eat and what you did not want to eat. A man could never starve in this country as there were a number of fruits and tubers that were edible (as well as snakes and rats). It was time for lunch and as we entered the mess tent the "chef" hollered our special was ready. The newbies were trying to be cool eating rat stew but I could see in their faces this was an "oh shit" moment for them. They each took small sips and looked at each other in surprise. Sanchez said "this ain't bad". The rest of us laughed and said "welcome to the unit". We never told them it was not rat meat in the stew. We were all glad they had the balls to try it and follow orders; they had passed their first test. A little humor in this place really helped.

The plan was to move out in groups of two and show these new guys some Indian country. We mostly wanted to see how they moved and how attentive they were to details. I took Sanchez and once outside the wire I told him to follow in my footsteps as best as he could. This was to teach him a slow pace and to make sure he did not snap any twigs or make any noise. He did well and seemed eager to learn. He talked a little too much but then, compared to me, everybody talked too much. I pointed out some trails and likely ambush sites and places that were too open to move through. None of us encountered Charlie that day and I thought that was a good thing. It took the edge off for the new guys and we got to know each other better. Sanchez asked how I got the name Dirt Hog and I showed him and told him where it came from. I assured him at some point he would be given a nickname as well. For me it was a little scary having a guy I did not know very well following me with a loaded weapon but we made it back to camp without an incident. We had a lot to show these guys in a week and I hoped for their sakes they were paying attention. With ten of us now in this unit, the odds were pretty high somebody was not going to make it home alive. After dark the new guys all had questions about combat and any encounters we had in the past and of course, how many kills we each had. I really did not like talking about number of kills and making it some kind of competition as some people did. I tried to emphasize it was not the number of kills that was important, but whether you came back each night. Williams told them it was ok to be scared, this was a scary place, all of us have been scared and as long as we could keep our emotions in check, we would have a better chance of survival.

That night it was unusually quiet in that sector; there were some bombs in the distance but nothing close. Edmonds snored like a wild man during the night and we would have to do something about that. He kept me and the rest of the guys awake most of the night. While he was eating breakfast the next morning, Jake and I moved his bunk outside. When Edmonds saw the bunk outside, he knew it was his. Apparently he had the same problem where ever he went. He told us if he slept on his belly – he didn't snore. We gave him one more chance and moved his bunk back inside and he was as good as his word. Every now and then we would have to throw something at him to get him to roll over on his belly and then he would be quiet. I was a bit worried about him snoring out in the bush - it could be deadly.

The Captain called me and Jake into his office and said our promotions came through and he would have a brief ceremony at 0830 that morning. After a little saluting and hand shakes in his office, we were both Corporals in the U.S. Army. Then it was back to work.

Jake and I were to take our new guys and go with a patrol to check out the road we plugged up with junk a few days ago. Charlie was probably trying to clean it up and get the road open. The Captain was thinking the enemy might try to keep us busy here at the base so we couldn't stop them from their clean up job. He noticed last night was quiet also and figured Charlie was up to something. We were to check out any activity in that area and communicate to the patrol what was going on. We would provide support for the patrol as needed. He had intelligence that reported some movement in that area. He would have some artillery ready for backup if we needed it.

I was really glad to get out with Jake again, and Sanchez and Carter would have to watch and learn. The other teams were going to set up a perimeter around the base and be prepared for any attack on the base. Snake and I were headed for a spot we called the mud hole. It was a spot where Charlie had built a bridge across the river. The bridge was blown up long ago but they made a dam of sorts and drove across the lower side of the dam where the water was lower. It was a funnel where two roads came together, and a lot of locals used the crossing as well. The crossing was narrow and only wide enough for a jeep sized vehicle to come through. Charlie liked to try to blend in with the locals and move through this area undetected.

It was raining that day and a little cooler, the bugs were not too bad or maybe I was just getting used to them. I showed Sanchez and Carter my little trick with the mud to keep the bugs off of them and they tried it. It was good to get back in the bush, I felt comfortable there, and that was my environment. Sanchez and Carter were both itching for some action. Snake just said "be careful what you wish for." We sat up in a hide we made a week ago for observation. The previous week when we left we put a thin piece of thread around the area and it was still intact so no one had been here and discovered our hide away. We showed the boys how to lay out some sticks and dead leaves on the ground in a perimeter around our hide to alert us of any intruders. We also made what we called a fence, which were just simply some logs or other debris to block anyone from slipping in on us. Carter asked "you guys want me to put out this bag of rice?" I asked "what do mean?" He said he was told Charlie would put some rice behind his hides to attract birds. If something came in from behind – the birds would flush and let him know there was something or somebody moving in from behind. Snake and I looked at each other and asked "why didn't we think of that?" We both agreed it was a great idea and told Carter to spread the rice 100 yards behind us. We were now ready to watch and wait. It was about 500-520 yards to the dam and we had a clear view of the crossing from where we were.

There were a number of locals moving up and down the roads and it was hard to tell if they were enemy or not. We had to watch for people acting spooky or spot a weapon or someone acting rough with the locals. Our goal was mostly recon, but we would remind Charlie that we were everywhere if we had the chance. We reminded Carter and Sanchez – one shot - one kill. Snake was on the spotting scope and I was trying to help him out with my rifle scope. We spotted a few questionable folks but were not sure. The last thing we wanted to do was kill some innocent farmer. Carter and Sanchez were having a hard time with the bugs and I told them to smear some mud on their ears and faces and handed each of them a piece of garlic. I learned a long time ago that garlic in your system helped repel flies and mosquitoes, why I don't know, but it worked. Jake looked over and whispered "oh great, now we are going to have a little troop of dirt hogs stinking like garlic. I can't imagine what our barracks is going to smell like." I just flipped him the bird.

It was past noon and we could hear a vehicle coming down the road. An old compact truck came into view and we thought we might be in business. On the truck were six NVA soldiers each of them holding a small child. They were using the children as shields. Even the driver was holding a child. The only shots we had were head shots and it was too risky - we might hit one of the children. I decided to shoot out a front tire, somebody was going to have to change it and he couldn't change it holding a child. I waited until the truck was in the middle of the river and shot the tire. The truck stopped on the edge of the bank on the opposite side of the river, it would not climb out of the river with the flat tire. The men bailed out of the truck still holding the children, but they didn't know where the shot came from. Apparently the sound of the running water muffled the sound of the gun shot. Four of them dove on the opposite side of the truck from us and two of them dove under the same side of the truck that we were on. The two children the men closest to us had escaped the men's grips and ran into the bush. I told Carter and Sanchez to take the two men out now and they did.

One of the men on the other side of the truck stepped out with a handgun pointed at the child's head that he was still holding. It was obvious he was threatening to kill the child if we didn't show ourselves. He was hollering in Vietnamese and I had no clue what he was saying but understood his intentions. I put my crosshairs on his head and it was a tense few minutes. Then he did it - he shot the child he was holding. Just as quickly I shot him in the head, the rotten bastard! It made me sick, literally, to see that child's life blown away, she could have only been four or five years old. The other three men came out from behind the truck with their hands up. My first thought was to kill them; they deserved to die after what they did to that innocent little girl. My crosshairs were centered on the chest of one of the men and my safety was off. I looked at Jake and he said waste them all. "We don't want to deal with prisoners, hell we don't even know what to do with prisoners, and they deserve to die." I agreed but we had two men here we were trying to teach the right thing to do. I told Carter and Sanchez to stay put and Jake and I would go get them. If they tried anything, anything at all, shoot them. We hollered for them to lie down on the ground and they understood. We carefully worked our way down to them and Jake and I argued the whole way down whether to kill them or not. When we got to them, we made them strip down to their underwear to make sure they were not booby-trapped. We pocketed their handguns (Russian made) and tied their hands behind their backs. Then we tied the same rope around each of their waists and I took the lead back up the hill with Jake bringing up the rear. As we were walking away from the truck, some locals came out of the bush and gathered up the little girl who was shot and carried her off. They were waving to us and bowing to us I think was a gesture of thanking us. Our prisoners were jabbering to us in Vietnamese and it just made me angrier.

I stopped and put a gag in each of their mouths. I had no compassion for these men, if they suffocated from lack of oxygen that was their problem. Maybe Snake was right, we should just shoot them, and it was going to be a pain in the ass to get these guys back to the base. When we got back to Carter and Sanchez, we took a little break. Snake took a drink of water and one of the prisoners gestured he wanted a drink, we didn't give him any. We all four argued over killing them and letting them here or dragging them back to camp. I did not want to be responsible for Carter and Sanchez having to live with murdering these three men for the rest of their lives, we decided to them back. I told Sanchez to plot a new course back to camp as we not going to take the same route we came out. Hell, now we had seven damn people to try to sneak through the woods, we were almost a damn platoon. There was not a word said among us the whole way back to camp. The prisoners really smelled bad from body odor and it just made them that much more disgusting to be around. I told Sanchez to go ahead of us and to alert the sentry we were coming in with prisoners. It was close to dark and I could smell fuel and burned garbage as we got close to camp.

Hank came down to greet us and asked "what the hell you got there?" I said to Hank "I heard you guys were hiring and I brought some new recruits." Hank said to drag their asses up to the Intel office and they would have to deal with them. We delivered them as ordered and gave the intelligence officer the papers and maps we had found in their shirt pockets.

We went back to our barracks and dumped our gear. Snake asked Carter and Sanchez how they were doing. He told them "the first one's the hardest, they both needed to realize that they did a good thing today, saving the lives of several children, sometimes the call to kill someone is not that easy to make." We both told them to sort out their feelings and if they needed, to talk to us. Snake looked at me and said "it didn't take long for your promotion to go to your head; you were bossing us around out there today like you have been doing it for ever. Now since I'm the same rank as you I'm giving you an order – fill out the report for today, you made the call." I was taken back by Jake's remark, I knew he was pissed at me for not killing the three enemies but I didn't think he took it personally. I wanted to lash out at him but I thought I'd just let it go for now and let him cool off.

I did fill out the report and gave to Hank. He read it and asked me why we just didn't waste these three guys instead of dragging them back here? I told him "they surrendered, they dropped their weapons and released the children they were holding and even though I wanted to kill them, I could not shoot unarmed men. I'm not a damn assassin, sir. What the hell would you have done Hank?" He said "probably the same thing but you put yourself in danger by going down there. If you would have shot them nobody would have known the difference". I said "I'm sorry, sir, you're wrong; I would have known the difference and there are three other men who would know the difference as well. It is a call I had to make and I can live with it, sir." Hank looked me in the eyes and didn't speak right away and then simply said "duly noted." I thought to myself – this was a no win situation.

I didn't sleep very well that night and the mood in the barracks was thick enough to cut it with a knife. The next morning Snake called me outside and said "look man, you're my best friend; I didn't sleep for shit last night and I should have told you this then but I was pissed. You were right and I didn't want to admit it at the time, I should not have second guessed you. If we would have killed those gooks yesterday we would all have to live with that the rest of our lives." We shook hands and got ready for another day in the woods. That meant a lot to me - I didn't really care what other people thought of me but it was important to me what Snake thought.

The rest of the week was pretty routine. Our new guys were learning well and they fit in nicely. We showed the boys the ropes including how to skin, clean and cook a snake. Our unit racked up some more kills but Charlie was laying low for some reason. We all sensed it wasn't going to last for long. A lot of our time was being spent scouting out new areas and gathering information. At times it was boring, sitting for hours looking through binoculars or spotting scopes but it was necessary.

Sanchez came to me with a problem. He was struggling with troops from outside our unit calling us cold hearted killers, assassins or blood thirsty. I told him what my old C.O. told me – if those guys who are giving you trouble are still here when your tour is up, you have my permission to punch them in the mouth. I also told him to remember those kids we saved, it might very well be the best thing he would do while he was in country. He said well sir; it's a little late to tell me that, last night I punched out a guy who was bad mouthing our unit. He said he didn't know it at the time but the guy he punched was a Sergeant. Another oh shit moment. It wasn't long before Hank and Sanchez were called into the Captain's office. Sanchez came back and said he just got busted back to a Buck Private. He also got a good ass chewing from the Captain and he had latrine duty for three day. Such is life in the U.S. Army.

CHAPTER 10

Time off for bad Behavior

Our week as trainers was over. Snake told Sergeant. Williams he hoped he and the Dirt Hog could finally get cut loose to do their own thing as a team. Once again, be careful what you wish for! Capt. Reynolds called us in and told us we each had a three day pass to Saigon tomorrow if we could catch a ride to get there. Also, when we came back, we were going to be flown north on a scouting trip. We were to make no contact with the enemy, only observe. Intel had a report of a new road coming out of Laos that Charlie was using and moving a lot of material across the border. Our mission was to find out where they were coming from and to take photographs and notes. There was a suspected training camp and troop buildup somewhere in the area. The Captain dismissed us and ordered us to be back here ready to ride at 0600 hours in three days. As we were leaving he said to me "Dirt, please do not bring any prisoners back from Saigon." I simply replied "Yes, Sir." Jake looked at me and said "hell Dirt, I think the Captain just cracked a joke." The Captain was not known for his sense of humor.

Three days in Saigon, all right! Neither one of us had been to the big city yet and we could sure use a break. We were supposed to get a break after our last training but they rushed us through to get here. Now we had to find a ride to get there. We checked with three different chopper pilots and finally found one who would drop us off on his way to get some personnel coming back here. He was leaving in one hour. The pilot told us if were not on the chopper in one hour he would leave without us. We had not had a day off in eight weeks - we would be on the chopper on time. A few of the guys in our unit told us we needed to go here or there or see this or that. Hell, we only had three days and half of one of them would be spent flying. I think the best advice we got was to make sure our Johnsons wore a raincoat. In thirty minutes, we were on the chopper waiting for the pilot. We helped to load two men who were being taken to the hospital there and we were off.

We caught a ride from the airbase with some MPs into the city and got a lengthy lecture on what we should and should not do, plus some good advice on where and what to eat. If we encountered any trouble there was a restaurant that was owned by an American who we could trust and the owner knew how to get in touch with them. The MPs told us to not eat at that restaurant, the owner could be trusted but the food was lousy. When we got to town the first thing we did was find a hotel that offered private baths. This was a service that was highly recommended by everyone. It was the best bath I ever had. There were two female attendants to wash each person and I almost fell in love right then and there. After showering with a bunch of stinky men for months, this was wonderful. After the bath, we went looking for something to eat. We ate so many shrimp and mussels it's a wonder we didn't get sick. That night we slept in real beds with real sheets, another luxury I previously took for granted.

We slept until noon the next day and I was seriously considering another personal bath when I got up. Jake wanted to shop for some gifts for his family and I agreed I should pick up some things for my folks and Trudy as well. I ended up buying a radio and a nice pocket knife for myself as well as some nice things to be sent back home. We hit a few bars and bullshit with some of the other troops, trying to forget the war for a little while. There was a presence of war here but nothing like where we came from. There were military personnel here from all the different branches and some other countries. We spent some time with some fellows from Australia and had a great time with them. It seemed like everybody wanted to get in our wallets, street hustlers selling whatever you could think of from watches to booze, women selling themselves, and drug dealers peddling their stuff.

We went into a bar that evening to get something to eat and had a few beers while we were waiting. There were some Marines at the bar having a good time. One of them came over to our table and said he noticed our patches that signified we were with the 9th Infantry. He asked if we might know his cousin who was with the 9th but we did not. He asked what our

MOS was we told him we were part of a scout –sniper unit. He rolled his eyes and hollered to his buddies that "we have a pair of genuine U.S. Army snipers sitting here having a beer." He asked us if we were aware the Marine Corps had the best snipers in the world and there just happened to be two of them sitting at the bar right now. I could count six Marines at the bar, so chances are we were in for some trouble. These guys obviously had been drinking for quite a while and were feeling no pain. The two snipers came over and introduced themselves as James and Schmidt. We invited them to sit down and offered to buy them a beer. They sat down and we talked about how long we were each here and where we were stationed, what kind of weapons we used and of course how many kills each had. These guys had been in country for five and six months respectively and had seen more action than we had.

They sort of apologized for their buddies' big mouth and they went back to the bar. We ate our meals and had a few more beers and thought we would leave before one of us said something we might regret later. Too late - Mr. Bigmouth came over and tried to get us to challenge the Marines to a shooting match. We were in downtown Saigon, our weapons were back at the base, and a shooting match was not going to happen. This clown was getting to be a pain in the ass. I had about enough to drink and my temper was getting short. Then the guy said "ok chicken shit, how about an arm wrestling match? How about it – Army verses Marines, right here right now?"

I looked at the guy and said "ok, dick head, you and me right now. If I beat you, you go over to the bar and sit down and shut your big mouth." He was stumbling drunk and I was not, I beat him.

His buddies came over and dragged him back to the bar while he was mumbling two out of three. Schmidt came over and said ok now this is an honor thing and I can't let you beat up on my friend, so he challenged me to take him on. I'd always had pretty good upper body strength and had done a lot of arm wrestling over the years and Schmidt was right this had become an honor thing; I was tired of these Marines pissing on us. Snake was rubbing my shoulders and egging me on, as if I needed any encouragement. I stood up and took my long sleeve shirt off, stripping down to my tee shirt. Snake said let's make this interesting and laid $5.00 on the table and all five of the Marines took him up on it. Schmidt was strong but not strong enough and Snake made $25.00. James said it was his turn. He was a bit bigger than me but I had the adrenalin flowing and a lot of courage from the beer and my cheer leader Snake, who was already laying $5.00 bucks on the table again. The Snake made another $25.00 bucks and I was doing all the work. The bastard better split it with me! I thought we were done and started to put my shirt back on when James said "wait a minute – I got one more for you Army. I saw a big black man hanging out with these guys and James motioned for him to come over and I thought oh shit. Snake poured another beer in me and one on me because I was sweating pretty badly. The black guy shook my hand and said his name was Harley, I don't know if it was his first name or last name but he was a big man. His hands were huge. James asked Snake "how about double or nothing?" Snake didn't even ask me, he just said "oh yeah, we'll take that action." If I was going to beat this guy I would have to get a jump on him. A little trick I learned was to shift my body weight quickly and put my whole body into it. It worked, I got Harley off center right away and he was never able to recover as big as he was. He was very strong but had poor technique. We made $100 and quieted down the Marines for a while at least, except for Mr. Bigmouth who was still cocking off about a rematch.

We bought the marines a round of beers and decided it was time to move on before they wanted to challenge us to something else. We stopped at another bar around the corner and bumped into our friends from Australia and they had already heard about our encounter with the Marines. They wanted to buy us a beer but did not want to arm wrestle. I was glad because I was tired and I think I pulled something in my back after that last tussle with Harley. We went into this bar figuring to blow the $100 we won, but the Aussies wouldn't let us buy a thing. It turned out they had a bit of a run in with the same group of Marines before we got there and they left before things got out of hand. A few of the Aussies wanted us to go with them and go back to kick some ass but I said no way, I fought the only battle I was fighting tonight. We wished the Aussies well and left the bar. I told Snake I wanted my $50 and I was going to blow it on another one of those baths in the morning and we headed back to our room. We had one more night to sleep in a decent bed.

The next morning we both spent our $50 on a deluxe bath and it was worth ever penny of it, those ladies sure knew how to make you relax. I'd never had someone shave me before and that hot bath sure felt good on my sore back.

We had to be back at the airbase by 0900 hours and we found the M.P. station and caught a ride back to the airbase with them. On the way back they asked what we did and in the course of the conversation we told them about our arm wrestling match with the Marines. The driver stopped the jeep and turned around and looked at us and asked "that was you guys?" Snake said yes it was and I'll put my buddy Dirt here up against anybody in the military. I poked him in the ribs and told him to shut up! The driver said they helped some other MPs last night break up a fight in a bar between some Marines and some Australian soldiers and a number of them were headed for the brig that day.

That was funny; those damn Aussies did go back and pick a fight. I asked who won the fight and the other MP said nobody they were all too drunk to do much damage to anybody. I thought to myself, I finally made a good decision and did not get involved in that fight. The MPs dropped us off at the airbase and wished us well and we waited for a chopper to come in that could take us back to the firebase.

We caught our ride back to the base with a chopper taking three replacements out to the base. These guys were new and were full of questions just like we were when we first got here. I was thinking on the way back - where in the hell are we going to end up now.

CHAPTER 11

Into No Man's Land

When we got back to the base, we stowed our gear and reported in to the Captain. He gave us each a map and some coordinates Intel had provided and told us to pack heavy - we may be out there for a while. We would fly out at 0600 hours tomorrow. He reminded us to not engage the enemy unless our butts were on the line and to try our best to not use our weapons. He gave us each a 35mm camera with 200mm lenses and a lot of film. We would only use the radio to call in a chopper when our mission was complete and we returned to the landing zone (LZ). We would have no backup patrols or artillery, when we left the chopper we would be on our own. He asked if we had any questions. Snake asked how long the Captain thought we would be out there. He said if we were not back in ten days he was going to be worried. We saluted, he wished us luck, and we went back to our barracks.

We looked over the map and it appeared we had eighteen to twenty miles to hump it after we got off the chopper. There were two roads that were on the map and they both led to the same general area to the West. Our LZ was due North of where we were now. We were going into the heart of Indian country, definitely into Laos but we were not allowed to talk about it, because the U.S. Army did not have a military presence in Laos. In a little more than two weeks it would be Christmas and it appeared we were going to have some Christmas vacation.

We asked Hank if he had ever been in there. He hesitated but said yes, he was in there about three months ago, doing some scouting. He said the brass would like to bomb the hell out of it, but the politicians would not let them. He said Charlie felt safe in there and let his guard down a little bit. The brass needed more Intel so they could convince the politicians to let us go in and blow up the place. It would be up to me and Snake to bring back the proof they needed, so what we were doing was very important. It was also important we didn't get our asses shot off before we got the information back here. The word was there was a big push coming from the North and we wanted to be ready. He told us we were the best team he had in the woods and felt we could handle this mission. Besides, he heard we kicked some Marines' butts last night and figured we were all pumped up and ready to go after our vacation.

Snake and I looked at each other in disbelief, how the hell he knew about last night. We didn't have time to tell anybody about that since we got back. We had to know – did he send a babysitter to look out for us? Hank told us his brother was an MP in Saigon - he was one of the guys that brought us back to the airbase. He talked to his brother on the phone that morning and his brother told him two guys from his unit dusted off some Marines in a bar downtown last night. Hell, this place was like my hometown, nothing was a secret.

I told Hank the story and clarified who dusted off the Marines while his buddy collected the money. Snake just smiled. Hank told us he would buy us a beer when we got back and he gave us some tips on what he remembered from being in this area before.

I put everything in my pack I could: rope, rain gear, extra socks, foot powder, moleskin, elastic bandages, extra batteries, fire starter, fishing line, hooks, sutures, first aid kit, flares, mesh kit, food, and more. I would also take my .45 caliber handgun and my M16 rifle and a couple of knives. There was no need to take a long range rifle if we could not shoot anybody. I was as ready for this mission as I was going to be.

In a way I was excited about this mission - it was what I really liked to do: explore new country, be alone with my best friend, and try to outsmart the enemy. I had to remind myself this was no camping trip with the boys. Speaking of boys, I'd been so busy and so focused on the task at hand I just realized in another day I'd be 21 years old. Isn't that a hell of a thing – to forget your own birthday. Maybe Snake and I would have a party.

We climbed aboard the chopper the next morning and the smart ass pilot asked for our tickets. We showed him our M16s and he said that would do. After about forty minutes of flying, the pilot told us we would have to get off quick, he would not be able to land because this area was pretty hot. He was right; we got some machine gun fire going in. The side gunner was giving it back and we bailed out the opposite side from the gunner still four feet off the ground. We hustled it to the tree line and it didn't seem like we were drawing any fire. We worked our way up onto a ridge away from the gun fire. We plotted our course and we were off. It was 0700 hours and I was soaked with sweat. We figured it would take us a good two days of steady travel to get to our destination and that was based on not encountering any trouble along the way. There were some pretty steep mountains ahead of us and we would have to climb at least two of them. From the top of the first mountain we could some trails in the valley below that were not on the map we had. It looked like Charlie was using these trails to move men and light supplies. We decided to watch that trail from above and ate a little bit while we watched. We saw 62 NVA move along that trail in an hour.

It was nasty going - there were thick brush and vines grabbing at our feet and bodies every step we took. It would have been easier to follow the trails, but not very safe. I thought below us was the border of Laos. There were no signs saying welcome to Laos, but there was not as much sign of a war going on. No burned out vegetation, no bomb craters, and very little sound of gun fire. Most of the gun fire was behind us. Below us was a beautiful valley, rice paddies galore, a river winding through it, grass huts scattered about, a few natives out working in the paddies, pigs and chickens running around, and one man working a paddy with a water buffalo dragging a plow.

I was using my binoculars and Snake was looking through the spotting scope. I asked him what he thought we should do and he said he thought we should have one of those chickens for supper. For now we needed to get closer to the valley floor and check it out. Something shiny caught his eye, but he could not make it out. It was in a tree line behind some of the huts.

We eased down the mountain and it was slow going because this side was just as steep as the other. We were both scratched up from the thorns and brush, and the mosquitoes and flies loved us. We stopped about 400 yards from two of the huts and we were still a little bit above them so we could see well. Snake put the spotting scope where he saw something shiny earlier and said "holy shit; there are two trucks and a whole bunch of NVA laying around in the shade." We were just above the river and there were rice paddies on the other side of the river about 200 yards wide.

We talked it over and decided to wait to see what was going on here.

The sun was starting to go down behind the mountain and the valley was in the shade. The NVA pulled the trucks out of the cover and started loading baskets of rice from out of the farmers' storage huts. The bastards were stealing food from the farmers. There was obviously a road in this valley that was not on our maps. We watched as the six NVA stopped at each storage hut and loaded rice that these people had stored for themselves and their families. Along the way they shot some pigs and chickens and took them as well. The two trucks then disappeared driving on up the valley and out of our sight. The way it looked, the road they were on intersected with a road that was on our map.

We decided to spend the night there and we didn't have the heart to kill one of their chickens, these people had to eat also. That night the menu was good old pork and beans. We couldn't make a fire because we were too close to the village. We decided we would sleep awhile and took turns doing so. We loaded up our gear and headed out before daylight so nobody would see us crossing the valley.

We got across the valley without incident and now we had another steep mountain to climb. Again it was thick, our packs were constantly getting caught on limbs and brush and it made for tough going. We reached the top of the mountain and came across a well used trail. I was sure many of these trails could not be seen from the air because of the thick vegetation overhead. This was a foot trail Charlie was using a lot. The trail was indented into the soft soil and it was not wide enough for anything other then a bicycle. We were seeing a pattern - Charlie appeared to be running these mountain tops off the main road to our North. We decided to move on as we lost some time yesterday and we still had a long way to go to be able to check out everything on our mission.

The other side of the mountain was a little more open and made for a bit easier travel. Again, below us was another fertile looking valley and village. This village was larger and more spread out than the last one. It was also on our map and a notation as being NVA sympathetic. Halfway down the mountain, we noticed a trail switch backing its way up just below us. We never crossed the trail higher up the mountain and that seemed weird that it would just end. We dropped our packs and belly crawled closer to the trail. It was a narrow foot trail that seemed to go nowhere. We watched and waited for almost an hour about 60 yards from where the trail seemed to end. Then the ground lifted up and an NVA soldier crawled out of it, then another and another and they just kept coming out like ants coming out of an ant hill. One by one they came out, 40 in all, and worked their way down towards the valley below.

We heard some noise behind us and slowly turned to see another group of soldiers emerging form the ground about 75 yards form us. There were about the same number of men in this group. I hoped to hell we were not laying on top of another trap door. Here we were with 80 enemy soldiers on either side of us. Fortunately, they were all headed down the hill away from us. We waited until they were all down in the valley, in the open and then we slithered on our bellies back to where we dropped our packs.

Like one of my old friends used to say, we were in a situation. We could see more troops moving around in the village and another group of 40-50 moving towards the village from the North. There must be 150-200 NVA in and around this village. We could see what looked like an obstacle course to the south and targets on the opposite side of the village just inside the tree line. With standard air surveillance, this would look like an ordinary village. We apparently just found one of their training camps. If we had come through a few hours earlier we would have been in deep shit, trapped between the village and the troops coming out of the tunnels. We got our cameras out and started photographing everything we saw. While we were taking pictures, another group came in from the West - now we had 250 enemy soldiers in front of us.

We got the pictures we needed and wrote down everything we could about the area and decided we would have to swing to the south to get around this place without being seen. Jake said he was disappointed – he thought we might get a room and a hot bath in the village tonight.

We moved real slowly - I kept thinking we were going to see another trap door open. We slipped around the lower end of the obstacle course along a drainage ditch and there was a big sigh of relief when we reached the river bottom. We only had to cross the river and we had a short distance to be in the cover of the trees again. We got across the river safely and started up the steep muddy river bank when we heard men talking above us. There was a cut back on the bank with a log hanging out over it 20 feet to our right. We eased over to and under the log and listened. We could hear them talking and laughing but we couldn't see them. I was sure they didn't see us or they wouldn't be laughing and joking around, so we just waited. I could hear three, maybe four voices, but I did not know what they were saying. It sounded like they were drinking. It was getting dark fast and we were both trying hard to get comfortable hanging onto this muddy bank. We both kept digging our heels in to keep from sliding down the bank and we rubbed mud on ourselves and scooted our butts deeper into the mud to blend in better. It must have worked. All I could see of Snake was the whites of his eyes.

I could hear somebody walking closer to us. The log over top of us bounced and a guy sat down on the log with his feet hanging two feet from my head. I don't know if that slimy feeling in my pants was mud or something else. This just was not good; we were really trying not to breathe hard. We had been trained for situations like this to focus on something pleasurable to keep our breathing under control. I kept my eyes closed and waited for this guy to move. Finally I heard someone else say "Di Di Mau" which I think meant let's go or move it and I felt the log move again. When the log quit bouncing, I squinted my eyes open and his feet were gone. We could hear them talking and they sounded like they were moving away. It was totally dark now and the tension was really thick - we were not sure if we could safely move or not. We waited about fifteen minutes and did not hear anybody. One of us had to take a look. I whispered to Snake that my legs were asleep. He said "so are mine." I said "ok, I'll try to take a look." With all the mud and being soaking wet it felt like my body weight doubled as I struggled to get to the top of the river bank. I couldn't see or hear anyone, they were gone. I motioned for Snake to come on up. Neither one of us could walk, our legs were asleep. We crawled to the tree line about 20 yards away. We were slapping our legs and stomping our feet to get the circulation going and finally were able to stand.

We had to get out of there because we left one hell of a trail behind us on that river bank. Hopefully the next day who ever found it would think it was made by one of their own men screwing around in the river. We made a mistake that night by trying to save some time and not swinging wide enough around the camp to better conceal ourselves. There would be no sleep that night - we had to get as much distance between us and that camp as possible.

Day three began with us on top of the next mountain after climbing all night long. We were looking at a foot path along the top of the mountain just like the other paths we had seen. We dropped down the other side of the mountain about 200 yards and found a depression in the ground to settle in and rest a little bit. Snake looked at me and said "you really are a dirt hog now." We were both covered with dry mud and I'm sure we looked like hell.

We got lucky, it started to rain and that would probably wash out the trail we left down by the river. We were a slimy mess with the rain but we were still alive. Snake checked the map and, according to it, we should have one more ridge to cross before we reached our destination. We decided to move further South to try to stay away from the NVA troops we encountered the previous day. It seemed all the movement was from here north.

We ate a bit, and worked our way down into the next river valley. It was a very narrow valley - only 100 yards wide - and we could not see any sign of human habitation anywhere. We followed the river south and saw very little sign of anyone. We decided to take some time to wash out the clothes we were wearing in the river. We each took a turn washing and standing watch. I had one change of fatigues in a plastic bag but decided to put the wet clothes back on because it was still raining. I felt ten pounds lighter with all the mud washed off and it felt good to at least be clean. My feet were wet and sore and my boots were wet inside. There wasn't much I could do about it until the rain stopped. We continued moving up the ridge in front of us, hoping this would be the last one we had to climb. I would have liked to stay in that little valley for a while; it was very quiet and peaceful.

We eased our way to the top of this ridge and, sure enough, there was a trail across it just like all the other ridges we had crossed. This trail was being used a lot. We could not see the valley below but we could hear machinery running. We moved down the ridge to a rock outcropping where we could see down into the valley. This must be the place - there were numerous buildings all with camo netting over them. We could see equipment like trucks, jeeps, APCs, a helicopter, and two tanks. There were also artillery guns and boxes of ammo. We couldn't see in the buildings but one of them appeared to be a repair shop because we could see welding flashes coming from inside. Snake said "it could be some kind of electric shock torture chamber." I guessed it could be. We got the cameras out and started taking pictures.

There were a lot of NVA moving around doing whatever their job was. There were trucks being loaded and unloaded and moving up and down a road headed to the north. The question for us was - do we want to try to get closer and see what was in those buildings? For now we would stay put and observe as much as we could. It was late afternoon and we worked at camouflaging our location a little better. It finally quit raining and now maybe we could dry out our clothes. We took turns making a little nest for ourselves to rest in. This always turned into some kind of competition between us to see whose was the most comfortable. We then spread out some rice behind us and to each side so the birds in the area would act as a warning signal in case somebody tried to sneak in on us. We also put out some trip wires and stacks of dead limbs to serve as a warning if somebody got too close.

We took turns glassing and sleeping. I told Snake since I was older I would take the first nap (he would be 21 in January). Even though I was soaking wet it only took a few minutes to fall asleep. We worked in two hour shifts and my two hours went fast. Snake shook me and said Dirt, it's your turn. It was a clear night and the moon was full and we had to be careful our gear did not throw any reflection with the bright moon. I took my shirt and pants off and laid them on some brush to dry out. There was a lot of activity down there even at night - Charlie must be planning something. I spent part of the night tying strips of camo material around our cameras and the rest of the night just watching and taking notes.

Day four dawned bright and sunny which meant it was going to be hot. We decided against trying to get any closer, there were just too many ways to get into trouble. There were sentries in towers, a wire to cross, probably a mine field we didn't know about, and troops moving all around the place. We had all the pictures we needed but we needed to find out where all this stuff was going. That meant we had to head north. We thought it would be safer to go back to the other side of the ridge where there were no trails and hopefully no troops and follow the ridge north. We had to come to the main road eventually.

Twice we had to squat down as patrols were working the top of the ridge - if we got caught here, we were in deep shit. We humped it three, maybe four miles and we could hear vehicles moving ahead of us. We eased to the edge of a steep drop off and the road was below us. I was ready for a break, we had been walking along the side of that ridge for a few hours and the weight of my pack wanted to pull me down the hill and it made for nasty walking. It was time to eat something, so we parked our butts to watch what was going on.

A truck came in from the west and stopped below us and then backed into the steep bank underneath us and disappeared. We looked at each other and each said what the hell. We couldn't see where the truck went; it just disappeared into the bank. We had to be sitting on top of some kind of tunnel. After about 45 minutes the truck came back out – empty. We had to check this out. We waited until after dark and crawled down off the ridge to take a look. There were two doors opening into the side of the mountain and they were not locked. I told Snake I was going in to take a look and he said he would stand watch outside. I cracked one door open and it was pitch black inside so I sneaked in. I didn't know if there was anybody inside or not so I just listened for a few a minutes. I could hear or see nothing. I turned my flashlight on and it was another of those holy shit moments. There were generators, ammo boxes, boxes of grenades, artillery rounds, and boxes of food. Food, I had to check that out – I grabbed some rice cakes, canned pineapples and some salted pork and stuffed my pockets full. Thank God for BDU pants - I had all six pockets full. I got out of there and Snake and I beat it back into the bush to our lookout above the road. He looked at me and asked "what the hell you grinnin' about?" I said "tonight my friend we are going to have a feast." I unloaded my pockets with the grub and his eyes bugged out. I said "tonight Charlie is buying dinner." After three days of cold c-rations this was good. We ate our fill and decided to cross the valley and head back east to the next mountain top while paralleling the road. We needed to find out if there were any more of these caches along the road. It made sense now, the trails along the tops of the mountains led to these caches of supplies.

We made it to the top of the next mountain by daylight and saw a trail leading off the mountain to the road. We shied away from the trail but wanted to see if there was another cache dug into the side of this mountain. Snake said he would crawl down and take a look and I would watch the road and the trail. While Snake was down at the road a truck came by where he was and I hoped he heard it coming.

I saw the truck go past the location he was in and hoped he was ok. In about a half hour he came back and said that truck just came around a corner as he stepped onto the road and they damn near saw him. He said he dove back into the brush and they kept on going. He then took a quick look and there was a set of double doors just like the one we saw yesterday built into the side of the mountain. We needed to take a look inside this one but not until nighttime. We made ourselves a hide and settled in for the day. It was almost like a day off - we took turns watching and sleeping throughout the day. There were trucks moving equipment up and down the road all day long and two patrols came by on the trail but never noticed us. Every hour a jeep with four guys came by - they must be patrolling the road. Late in the evening another patrol came down the trail and disappeared into the cache in the dirt bank. After about twenty minutes they came back out and stood around on the road talking - there were six of them. In a while, an empty truck came down the road, they flagged it down and all hopped in and took off. They were probably supposed to walk back to their camp and finish their patrol, but what the hell, it was hot.

After dark we were well rested and ready to go. We made up our minds that we would travel mostly at night as it was much safer. We had three more mountain ranges to cross to get back to our pick up point.

We both slipped down to the road and Snake went inside the cache to take a look. He came out and said it was basically the same as the last one and it was filled out to the doors. He grabbed some more food for us and that night we were going eat on the run. We had not seen much traffic on this road lately, so we decided to stay on it and make better time. If somebody was driving on it, we only had to drop over the edge to hide.

The top of the next mountain had a cache built into it as well and it was even bigger than the last two. These Vietnamese really liked to dig in the dirt. We had to be more careful because the next valley was where the training camp was located. As we got closer we could see sentries at the entrance to the camp. We would have to drop off the opposite edge of the road to get by them. It was slow going because it was very steep and difficult walking. It was past daybreak when we got past the camp entrance and made our way back up to the road. When it was clear, we crossed the road and beat it up into the bush away from the road. Our plan was to get to near the top of the mountain and take a break and maybe see what was going on down in the training camp. We found a decent place to set up and dropped our packs. It really felt good to rest. We both had sore feet from side hilling during the night. We both decided we were putting in for new boots when we got back. There was a lot of activity around the camp - guys were drilling and shooting, other guys were running the obstacle course. It seemed like there were more troops now than a few days ago. I was looking through the spotting scope and could see officers barking out orders and it would be an easy shot but not today. Snake said he'd give a month's pay for one of them hot baths and tiny little girls to wash his back right now. So would I my friend. We both really smelled bad and we hadn't shaved in almost a week. God must have heard us complaining because it started to rain again. I laid out a piece of plastic to catch some rain water to fill my canteen and took my shirt off to try to wash some of the stink off of me. I don't know how much weight I lost but it was a bunch, I just had to put another hole in my belt for the third time since we got here. We both took off our boots while they were dry inside and washed our feet and powdered them. Now I knew how an old beagle felt after chasing rabbits all day long.

We got into a discussion of what would happen to us if we got caught here. I figured they would probably shoot us after they tortured us for a while. Snake asked "what would you tell them?" I guessed I would tell them we got lost and were trying to get back to our unit. Snake said "hell they ain't supposed to be here either, maybe we could tell em' we came to arrest them for trespassing!" I said "it works for me." He asked "what do think the brass is going to do with all this information we're going to give them." I said "I don't know but I hope they come in and bomb the hell out of this place."

We were going to wait until dark to move over the top of the mountain and again we took turns resting and watching until it got dark. I was resting and it was nearly dark when I heard birds fly up and make a racket behind us. I could also hear crunching of dead limbs off to the side. I sat up and turned to see Snake stand up and lunge at a man coming at him. Just that quick I felt someone grab me from behind and a sharp burning in the back of my shoulder. I reached over the top of my head with both hands and flipped the NVA soldier over my head and onto his back. I was able to grab his chin in my left hand and the back of his head by my right hand and snap his neck before he recovered. I turned to see Snake stabbing the man he jumped as I was pulling my handgun from its holster. I could not see or hear anyone else. The only thing I could hear was the gurgling sound from the man Snake stabbed as he died. Snake and I sat back to back for a few minutes and no one else showed up. Snake asked me if I was ok and I said I think so, just stabbed in the back. Snake asked what the hell I was talking about. He thought I was referring to him not covering my butt while I was sleeping. I said no, that SOB laying there stabbed me in the back! He looked at my back and said "holy hell Dirt, you are bleeding, you were stabbed in the back." He ripped my shirt and applied some pressure to try to stop the bleeding. Once the bleeding stopped he put some antiseptic on it and applied a bandage. Apparently there were only two NVA soldiers and now we had to hide the bodies. If these bodies were found there would be patrols out looking for us, we were not supposed to be here. We found a depression in the ground and dumped the bodies into it and covered them with some brush. We then peed as much as we could around the bodies to keep the wild pigs from digging them up for a day or so.

My shoulder was really getting sore and was throbbing quite a bit. Snake took a look at it and said I probably needed stitches. I told him there were some sutures in my bag and get them out and do it, we needed to get the hell out of here. I bit down on a stick as he sewed me up and Snake asked me if it hurt. I said yes, it feels like somebody's poking a needle in my skin and it made the tears run so I bit down harder on the stick. He helped me get my shirt and pack back on and we moved out. We crossed the top of the mountain and down into the next valley and then worked our way up to the road again to see if there was another cache at the last mountain crossing before we got back to our pick up point. My shoulder hurt like hell but it was tempered a little bit by some rice wine we took off one of the NVA. We had a shit load of intel and photos to get back to Capt. Reynolds and we still had 5-6 miles to go over some pretty rough terrain.

We found another cache on this mountain as well, basically the same as the rest of them. It was breaking daylight and we had to get out of there. Snake grabbed some food and we took off into the jungle again. We only had to cross the next valley and up the other side and we would be back where we started. We stayed north of the little village we first encountered on our way in and I had to keep the Snake from trying to catch a chicken for supper once again. We had to cross the valley on our hands and knees so the farmers wouldn't see us. Once we got to the river and across to the other side we were safely in the cover of trees again. I was having a lot of pain in my shoulder and Snake kept pushing me to get to the top of the mountain; we finally made it. When we peeked over the edge to the little opening where we landed seven days ago, there was an NVA patrol camped on the opposite edge of it. Now what? Both of us were pumped up with adrenalin knowing we would soon be out of here. We couldn't call a chopper back in here and we couldn't kill them because it would make too much noise. The Captain gave us an alternative pick up point but that was five clicks to the south. That adrenalin rush left quickly, we would have to hump it to the secondary LZ.

After getting our bearings we snuck out of there, leaving Charlie to his picnic. We climbed down off the mountain and into the river valley we had just come from, only this time south of the village. It was 1800 hours until we got to the next LZ and I radioed to the base our location and told them we were waiting on a bus. I got a call back that said "Roger that Dirt Hog sit tight till tomorrow morning and we'll send in a taxi first thing." We didn't see any sign of Charlie in this area but we needed to be careful anyway. I told Snake I was going to take a bath in the river and he could be next. I was saving some baking soda for this moment, the water was cold but it felt great. Snake took his turn and for the first time in a week, we were clean. Snake redressed my wound and he said it looked pretty good; maybe he would go to med. school when we got back to the world.

After pulling a few leeches off of each other we then pulled out our clean clothes and settled in for the night. These rivers were full of leeches and we thought about eating them but we were never that hungry.

We dug out the food we stole from Charlie: rice cakes, canned fruit, and some jerky that we thought was made from water buffalo. The night went fast after alternating sleeping and standing watch. Right after daylight we heard the whoomp, whoomp of a helicopter coming up the river valley - it was a good sound. We put out the flares and our ride was there. We climbed on and I thought how much I loved these choppers.

Back at the base, we reported in to Capt. Reynolds and he was waiting for us. He said "you guys look like hell, any problems." Snake told him about my stab wound and the Capt. told me to report to the infirmary right away. He asked "what do you guys have for me?" We gave him everything we had and he dismissed us. After being checked at the infirmary, they told me I would live and have a scar about as ugly as me - these guys were always so compassionate. We both went to our barracks and collapsed in our bunks.

CHAPTER 12

A Mission That Never Happened

The next day we were allowed to rest and ordered to shave. The Capt. seemed pleased with the recon we'd done. He reminded us that we were not in Laos and we both just said yes, sir. It seemed that Charlie was protecting those supplies pretty well and he told us we were going back in there to cause some trouble and keep him occupied for a little while. Carter and Sanchez would go with us and our mission was to take out as many officers as possible and cause as much confusion as possible. We would need to be mobile and under no circumstances were we to be within 500 yards of that supply road at any time. He said there would be two platoons coming in after us to mop things up after the bombing runs were over. The Capt. said in three or four days all hell was going to break loose, he would keep in radio contact with us through out the raid. He asked if I was sure I was fit to go back in there and I said "yes, sir."

Two days later we were all dropped off at the LZ where Snake and I were picked earlier. Sanchez went with me and Carter went with Snake. We knew there was a patrol working the ridge top ahead of us, and that was our first objective. I remembered there were six of them, we would try to get them in a cross fire and we had to take them all out. We were on the left of the trail and the other team was on the right. After waiting a couple of hours, there they came. They were getting comfortable and sloppy working this trail: they were talking, not paying attention, and they were all dead in a minute. I reminded Sanchez that this is what happens when you don't pay attention. We dragged the bodies off the trail and hid them, and then disabled their weapons. Sanchez kept a souvenir handgun.

We moved out across the ridge to the north. We got to where we could see the supply road below us. Knowing the bombing would not start for a couple of more days, we decided to move to the opposite side of the road where we had a good vantage point to the road and still be safe from the bombing. Sanchez picked a spot about 850 yards from the road with a good view from above. Sanchez and I would stay there; Snake and Carter were going further east to a bend in the road we couldn't see from there. We picked a spot in between as a meeting place for later that night. We had a long ridge to work from and a deep ravine below us that nobody would likely climb up to get at us. The road was cut into the side of the mountain in front of us.

After an hour or so, I heard two shots from Snake's position. It wasn't long before we had three guys sneaking down the road to us – Sanchez took out the first and the last one and I took out the one in the middle. Now we had bait on the road - anyone coming by would stop and check them out. A little while later, a vehicle came up the road with four guys in it, one of them an officer. They slowed to check out the dead men and I shot the officer. The other three returned fire but they didn't know where we were. Sanchez took out two of them and I shot the third one as he was trying to crawl under the vehicle. Now we had to move to another location so no one would get a fix on us. Our next set up was about 100 yards west and a little bit higher to another good vantage point. I knew we were moving closer to the training camp entrance and there were 200-250 troops in there and we were not interested in taking all of them on. Sooner or later they would be coming after us and I knew they had artillery as well; we had to keep on our toes and keep moving around.

We had trucks moving up and down the road all day; we would shoot at them just to let them know we were here and to make them nervous. It wasn't long before a patrol came sneaking up the road and they had some artillery coming on behind them. I could pick out two NVA carrying handguns and they had some type of insignia on their shoulders. I told Sanchez to take the first one and I took the second one. We fired and both men dropped. The rest of the patrol fired back, some in our direction, some in the opposite direction. They did not know where we were and we were able to kill a few more before they scattered into the bush. I could see the artillery gun being set up and aiming in our direction so we gathered up our gear and moved out as quickly as we could. We moved higher up the mountain and further west before the artillery started coming. They were hitting the area where we used to be but nothing close to our new location. We ceased fire and sat tight. Charlie eventually quit firing and we could see them turn the big gun around and start firing on the opposite side of the road from us. They were just guessing where we were. They eventually quit firing and we could see bits and pieces of them sneaking back the way they came but nothing we could shoot at except the artillery unit, so we hammered it pretty hard and did some serious damage to it I believe. We needed to make every shot count, no wild shooting at movement. We moved again to keep them guessing.

We played this cat and mouse game until almost dark, when we started to move back to our rendezvous point with Snake and Carter. We met up with them after dark and compared notes on what happened that day. Snake and Carter had taken out thirteen NVA, including at least three officers, and Sanchez and I had shot seventeen including four officers and crippled the artillery unit as well. A pretty good day's work. We needed to move off this ridge because Charlie was probably going to move some more artillery tomorrow and blow the hell out of this area.

The question was where the hell we were going to go. Charlie was pissed at us and was going to come after us the next day; if we went back across the road, our own guys were going to bomb the hell out of it in two days. That day was like a pigeon shoot; it would get tougher tomorrow, and they knew we were there. Snake said "let's move east along the road, we haven't been there yet and Charlie is probably expecting us to hit the training camp tomorrow. Maybe we won't get our asses blown off down there." Good old Snake, always looking out for my ass. We all agreed that plan made sense.

I radioed the Captain and reported in on that day's mission, and he seemed impressed with our body count for that day. I told him we were moving about three clicks to the east because we stirred up quite a hornets' nest. I gave him what our coordinates would be and he told us to stay out of the west end until the party was over. They would commence at 0700 hours the day after tomorrow. He would make sure we were outside the party area.

We started moving east that night and Carter asked when we were going to sleep. Snake said probably not until Saturday - it was Thursday, I think. We moved to the next location without incident. It was still dark so we had to wait until daylight to find a good place to set up for the day. Snake told Carter and Sanchez they had two hours to get sleep and they didn't argue. Snake and I were checking out the map and found a spot nearby where we could sit and screw with Charlie.

We were each going to take a position on opposite sides of the road. We flipped a coin to see who had to crawl off this mountain and climb the other one and I lost. I woke Sanchez and he and I worked our way down to the road and back up the other side. We moved a little further down the road than Snake and found a good overlook of the road. I told Sanchez I was going to catch a couple of Zs. Traffic was slower that day probably because we put Charlie on alert the day before. We noticed there were more locals on the road that day - Charlie was sending them out as bait and we had to watch for him mixed in with the locals. We could hear artillery going off where we were the day before; it was good we moved because they were really hammering the hill where we were.

I heard a shot from Snake's location and just that quick Sanchez's rifle barked and I almost fell off the stump I was sitting on. He picked off a lone NVA running up the road. I was focused on some movement down in the bush and not on the road. I didn't know what I saw, but I needed to find out. I told Sanchez to sit tight; we might have somebody trying to move in from below. We were looking, looking, looking, when finally I spotted him. It was a wild pig working his way up to us! All I could see was pork chops on the hoof. But we wouldn't be able to cook because we could not make a fire there. I let Mr. Pig walk on by.

Awhile later, a group of locals with a water buffalo pulling a cart came into view. There was a tarp over the back of the cart. Sanchez was on the spotting scope and said he could see a shoe and a leg sticking out the back. I said I was going to shoot the leg and when I did an NVA came rolling out the back of the cart along with seven of his friends. I shot one other NVA and missed a second one and they all scattered into the bush. They were returning fire in our direction and Snake and Carter got in the game. They took out two enemies and we still had five more to take care of. We were taking fire from below and they were getting closer. I told Sanchez to follow me and we belly crawled up to a depression in the ground behind us to a point directly above the NVA. We got two more and Snake and Carter shot one trying to sneak out the back. There were still two more to go and they were below the road in the bush. They set off a mortar round that landed about 50 yards in front of us and then a second that hit 20 yards in front. That was getting too close; we had to move again. We moved to our left as quick as we could and a third mortar landed damn near where we just left. I told Sanchez to keep moving to the left and try to cover me; I was going to go down and try to take these guys out. I slid down the steep bank until I thought I had a good angle on them. They must have thought they got us because they turned around and were ready to lob another mortar in Snake's direction. I saw one guy getting ready to put a mortar down the pipe and I nailed him in the chest. The second guy spread eagled out on the ground and all I could see was his head. That was enough, these clowns had been neutralized. I radioed to Snake that I was down low and to watch for my signal and please don't shoot me. I signaled him with my mirror and he came back and said "Roger that Dirt, I saw the whole show, thanks for the help." I told him I was going back up and we would move another click to the east and set up again. He responded they would do the same.

When I got back to Sanchez, he said he had been hit in the back of his leg and he was bleeding. I had him drop his pants and it looked like he'd been hit by a piece of rock or shrapnel. I put some antiseptic on it and bandaged it and told him we'd better get out of here, I would take a look at it later. He said he could walk but it really burned. We found a new location and signaled to Snake and he returned my signal. I radioed him that Sanchez had been hit and maybe they should come over to our location when it was safe. I looked at Sanchez's leg and there was a piece of shrapnel imbedded in his leg about an inch deep. I told him to bite on something; I was going to dig it out. I poured some antiseptic on my knife and I had to make the incision a little bigger to get the shrapnel out. After removing it, I cleaned the wound and let it bleed a little to help clean it out. I put in a few sutures and bandaged him up. He was a tough bastard - I thought he would pass out from the pain but he didn't. He did say if I ever performed surgery on him again, he wanted to bite down on my hand just to let me know how it felt. He told me to reach in his pack, there was a plastic case with some antibiotics in it and get them out. He said his brother-in-law was a doctor and he stocked him up before he left home.

The rest of the day we had no more incidents. Although Charlie was moving up and down the road, he wasn't giving us any shots. Snake and Carter found their way over to us after dark and we settled in for the night. We radioed in our location and were advised to keep our heads down as the party would begin at 0700 hours. I was told to radio in at 0800 hours for further instructions. We would offer support for our boys tomorrow. I told the Captain we had one wounded and I would like to get him out the next day. He responded "Roger that, we will find you in the morning." Sanchez said he was ok and wanted to stay. I told him "no way, I want somebody to check you out tomorrow, I'm not a doctor and I might need you next week."

Carter asked "you guys know in two days it will be Christmas." I hadn't even thought about it, Snake and I had been on the run for 12 of the last 14 days. It looked like we were going to have a great Christmas day; I wondered what my family was going to be doing. My mom was probably cooking up a storm; she made the best coconut cream pie I ever ate. I was hoping there would be some Christmas cookies back at the base that she sent over whenever we got back. I guess we all have our favorite memories of Christmas; the Christmas of 1968 would be my first away from home. Snake said we should sneak down and grab some food out of one of those bunkers. I said go ahead and see if you can get some steak and lobster while you're at it. After he thought about it, it was probably 3-4 miles down the road to the next cache and we were all beat for the day. It looked like a gourmet meal of canned meatloaf for that night. Snake did find a surprise in his pack – a can of pineapples he put in last week and forgot about; we split it four ways and enjoyed it.

While taking turns standing watch during the night, we could hear vehicles moving up and down the road but we left them alone. We did not want to give up our position and in the past two days we put a pretty good hurt on old Charles. Our little band had eliminated almost forty enemy, five of which we knew for sure were officers. It should help in adding some confusion once the big dogs came in.

Surprise, surprise it was raining in the morning. We were all pretty anxious about the bombing run that morning. The pilots were supposed to know our location and we were at least two miles from where the last drop was to be made but mistakes have been made before.

Sanchez said his leg was really sore and he would probably be walking like Chester on Gun Smoke for a few days. Bingo – Sanchez just got his new nickname – Chester. It was a couple of minutes before 0700 and we could hear the planes coming. They hit the supply camp and the training camp first and then the road and the caches along the road. The noise was overpowering and we felt the shock waves as far away as we were. The second wave of bombs was just the same. There were secondary explosions from ammo and fuel and fireballs rising up from each of them. We had dirt and leaves drifting our way even with the rain coming down. As quick as it started, it was over - the planes were gone.

I radioed the Captain and he said the extraction chopper was on its way and he gave us a pick up point behind us. He told me after we loaded up Sanchez, the three of us were to make our way west as quick as we could and provide him with some Intel on the damage and provide support for the patrols that would be coming in shortly. The patrols were on the ground and would be sweeping in from the south into the training area first. Hank and Cowboy were going to come in from the west and provide cover for the patrols sweeping the supply camp. The brass wanted this rat's nest cleaned up quickly and all of us out of this area as soon as possible. It wasn't long before we had old Chester loaded on a chopper and on his way back to the base. Carter, Snake and I headed for the mountain overlooking the training camp. It took us about four hours to get there. From the top of the mountain it looked like the bombs did their job - there was a lot of damage down in that valley. Snake and I marked the location of the tunnels on our maps when we were here before. One of us was going to have to drop some white phosphorus hand grenades down those tunnels to smoke Charlie out, if he was in there. We could see some movement down in the camp so we didn't get everybody. My guess was a lot of them headed into the tunnels when the bombing started. I radioed Lt. Andrews who was leading a patrol into this area. I gave him our location and our plan and asked if he could bring some of his men in below the tunnels - if Charlie was in there we would have them trapped in the middle.

We would try to keep them from coming over the top. Snake and I flipped a coin to see who was going down to throw the smoke grenades in the holes. I lost; I was going to have to check that damn coin he had, I don't think I ever won a coin toss with him. I loaded up five grenades we took off the chopper that took Chester. I belly crawled to where I thought the tunnels were - they were really hard to find. I was trying to find the one in the middle and I was using my fist to pound on the ground to hear a hollow spot. I finally found it and dumped all five grenades in the hole. I hustled back up the mountain as fast as I could. Before I got up to Snake and Carter, they were firing. I dove into my hide and grabbed my rifle. Some of them were trying to sneak up the mountain; the three of us were spread out about 100 yards apart to try to stop them.

Smoke was pouring out of the tunnel lids and so was Charlie. They were probably temporarily blinded by the smoke. Some were stumbling down the hill and were being cut down by our guys from the tree line below. A few were making it up to our location and we were taking them down as well. One young boy maybe 12-14 years old came running straight at me firing his weapon. I had to shoot him, damn it, I had to shoot him. I probably shot others his age but this kid was close enough that I could see the fear in his eyes. I saw his legs kick out from under him and the steam of hot air leave his chest. I hated this part of it - killing kids that Charlie forced to fight. It made me want to kill more of the people responsible for it. The shooting was getting more intense down near the camp and my focus turned down there. Our patrols were trying to move up the drainage ditches running along the training fields.

I could see Charlie trying to set up some mortars along the edge of the camp and zeroed in on them. My first shot hit low and must have hit the mortar base and spun it around. My next shot was on target and the other Gooks dove behind a bunker and forgot about the mortars. I wasn't seeing anybody moving up the hill towards us anymore and that was a good thing - I didn't want anybody behind me. I radioed Snake and he had no movement over his way either. We decided to stay put and keep Charlie pinned down while the patrols moved in. This battle lasted 6-8 hours with enemy losses very high, mostly from the bombing. The three of us held our position while the patrols moved in and mopped things up. I was just about out of ammo for my long gun; I had 12 rounds left. I had plenty for my M-16 but I was about 300 yards too far away to do any good with that.

I radioed Lt. Andrews and was told he was dead. I spoke to a Sergeant. Mills and asked him what he wanted us to do. He told us to come on down, they were in the process of mopping things up. Mills told me he had some choppers coming in to extract the wounded and the dead and if we wanted we could hop a ride back to Billy. He said he knew we had been here a while and we were responsible for this whole shooting match. I rounded up Carter and Snake and we moved out. Smoke was still coming out of the tunnels when we went by them. Carter wondered what they were like and asked if we had ever been in one of them. I said hell; I can't even fit in the damn trap door. Snake told him to go take a look, but be careful they might have it booby trapped. Carter said he was just gonna' stick his head in one and look around. He did – the dumb ass - and came up coughing and gagging and his eyes watering. Snake and I laughed and Snake asked "you ok, Smokey?" Carter just became Smokey. We had another 20 minutes to the fields and Smokey was coughing the whole way down. We finally met up with Sergeant. Mills and I said I was sorry to here about losing his Lt. He thanked us for our help and said we saved a lot of other men from getting shot today and he would tell our Captain to give us a few days off. We looked around the camp while waiting for a ride out and it was bad. There were women and children in the camp and they were among some of the dead. These damn Gooks always used them as shields. As much contempt as I had for the NVA, it was always sickening to see the lives of little children wasted. None of us signed up for this kind of duty. I didn't know it at the time, but sights like this would stay in my mind the rest of my life.

There were a few gun shots here and there but the battle was almost over. A medic came over and asked Smokey if he needed help and Snake said yes he does, he needs to see a shrink. Carter drank some water and relaxed and he was ok. The choppers arrived and we helped to load up the wounded and the dead. This was always a sobering experience. The reality of war always sank in at these moments. We hopped a ride on the last chopper out and although we were glad to get out of that place, it was a grim ride - there were four dead soldiers riding with us.

The rest of our unit was still out except for Chester - he was lying in bed resting. He said the doctor who treated him told him to tell me not to quit my day job. He wasn't too impressed with my suture work on his wound, although it worked. They put new stitches in and he would be fine in a week.

It turned out this was a very successful campaign. We destroyed the supply depot, the training camp, the supply bunkers and a good portion of the road as well. Enemy casualties were estimated at 300-350. Our losses were 14 dead and 54 wounded. Snake and I were each awarded a commendation for our part in this battle. It was nice to be recognized but we were just doing our jobs. Chester got a purple heart for his injury; Smokey did not. Snake and I got the reputation of being a couple of bad asses and kind of crazy. Most of the troops on the base left us alone or at least didn't mess with us and that was ok. Apparently the whole snake eating thing had grown quite a bit. The rumor was we never carried food with us, we just ate off the land, some were speculating we even ate Charlie out of spite. Some of these guys were smoking too much wacky-weed. Now we were training Chester and Smokey to be just like us, according to the rumor. We never really told anybody but Chester and Smokey about the food caches we found on the last mission, we kind of enjoyed the reputation we had received on the base.

CHAPTER 13

Stalking the VC

The war raged on: we would clean up one area and move out and in a few days Charlie would move back in. A lot of it didn't make any sense. After nine months of being in country, Snake, Chester, Smokey and I were still together. Snake and I mostly teamed up together although we each became comfortable working with Chester and Smokey. The other old timers: Hank, Cowboy, Hoody and Les, had all rotated out. Les was wounded a second time and was sent home early; the other three made it out in one piece. They had been replaced by four newbies and two transfers from another unit. We spent a little time training the new guys but left a lot of it to Chester and Smokey. Something happened to Snake and me as well, we had become hardened, emotionless and we didn't joke around as much as we used to. I didn't like to think so but we had become killers.

We perfected our craft of stalking and unlike earlier, we looked forward to killing. We were called spooky by other enlisted men on the base and we didn't mind. We were both drinking more and we tried smoking pot as well. I thought it smelled awful but it did make me forget for a while. The hangovers from smoking were bad for me so I mostly stuck to drinking. Chester and Smokey were both into smoking weed also. I didn't care as long as they were sharp when we went out on the job.

Snake and I would probably be Sergeants, if we hadn't been busted for fighting with some Marines in a bar.

I started the fight and six Marines kicked our asses. We were still Corporals and had to take orders from a Sergeant Allen who was an ok guy but didn't know shit about this country. He pretty much let us do our thing and we made him look good.

We were given the task of eliminating some VC. The Viet Cong were communist sympathizers living in the south. They could be anybody, anywhere - a village chief, a business owner, even a member of the ARVN troops, who were supposed to be on our side. Our first target was an ARVN Colonel who was selling information to the NVA. This guy was a traitor; we would have no problem taking him out. We found him where he was supposed to be, Snake took the shot and the traitor would not be passing any information any longer. Our next target was a man and woman who ran a fishing boat up and down the river, transporting enemy soldiers on the boat. We had to wait for two days until the boat came up the river to our location. We had clear shots at the two of them as they came by a very slow speed. Snake shot the man in the chest and my first shot on the woman was low in the thigh and it took a second shot in the chest to kill her. We had a grenade launcher with us and neither one us remembered how to use it. We lobbed four grenades before finally hitting the boat with the fifth one and it slowly sank in the river.

This was what we did for the next month. We would sneak in, take the shot, and sneak out. We were now assassins; we killed on command and we were damn good at it. I'd send letters to my family and friends telling them bits and pieces but never totally what I did. They knew I was in the Nam but I did not tell them about all the killing I had done. I was not ashamed of it but at this point I did not think they would completely understand.

The Captain called us in individually to try to get us to sign up for another four year tour of duty. He promised we would be promoted to Sergeant. as soon as we signed the papers. We would then be given jobs of training snipers for the remainder of our tour here. We both had two months left in this damn place. I told him I had to think about it and Snake said the same thing. I said to Snake "what the hell they gonna' do to us if we don't reenlist - send us to hell? We're already there." He said "Dirt, let's sleep on it, after we have a beer." Then he said "Sergeant. Dirt Hog. That sounds real nice don't it!" Yeah, like Sergeant. Snake sounds any better.

The next month dragged on with us doing some recon and support for patrols. We were short timers and still hadn't decided if we were going to reup or not. Our captain came into our quarters and said "boys, you each got thirty days left on your tour and I'm sorry, but you both are going to be extended another sixty days." Talk about a kick in the teeth, we were short timers. I asked "what's the deal, sir?" He said we were needed up north until replacements got in and they would not be here for at least another month. There was a small base north of us that had some heavy losses and Snake, Chester, Smokey and I were going up there tomorrow to provide some support and shake Charlie up a little. To say we were pissed was an understatement! I made up my mind right then and there; no way was I going to sign up for another tour. We would fly up there at 0700 hours the next morning - we had our orders and there wasn't a damn thing we could do about it.

We all climbed aboard the chopper the next morning, we were going deeper into the Quang Tri province – right into the heart of Indian country. As we were landing at our new base, it looked in rough shape; these guys had been hit pretty hard recently.

Welcome to firebase Cougar. The place was busy with reconstruction, repairs being done from previous artillery drops and dozers grading landing strips and landing pads. There were choppers moving in with new troops and trucks moving artillery and other equipment. It looked like we were moving to a real hornets' nest.

We reported to a Lt. Apple and he wanted us to go to work right away. Our first objective was to slow down Charlie moving into the area directly west of the base. He said he heard we were good and got the job done and this job needed done now. He needed us to cripple Charlie and make it really nasty for them to be here. We would have artillery support when ever we needed it and he would be sending in some patrols to sweep the area when ever we were ready.

After studying maps of the area and talking to troops who had been here a while, we were ready to go to work. There were signs of Charlie right outside the wire, which was too close. We needed to make this a place he didn't want to screw with. We found a drainage that the NVA were using to conceal themselves to get close to the base. We placed some explosives along the bottom of the drainage and booby trapped a few other spots along the way. Snake and I would take a spot above one side of the drainage and Chester and Smokey would take a spot on the opposite side. We were going to hit and run as much as we could; the first evening was slow. At daylight, we caught six NVA moving along the trail in the drainage and they stumbled into our first trap with a big bang. We finished off the survivors of the explosion and moved deeper into the jungle, paralleling the trail the enemy was using. Between our two teams we would intermittently move up the trail to see where it led. Throughout the day we would pick off some more of the enemy moving along the trail. Late in the day we found a camp with maybe 50-60 NVA in a little hidden valley. Apparently this was where a lot of the trouble at our base was originating from. We could see some mortars and grenade launchers and small artillery units on the ground. We debated what to do and decided to call in an air strike for this one and sit tight. The guys from the friendly skies did a good job and we were able to mop up what they did not get. It is very unnerving to see a bomb coming from behind you and sail over your head on its way to a target. After a while you sort of get used to it, and also to trust the pilots, but in the back of your mind you hope there is not one coming from behind that is a little too low.

We spent the next six weeks doing pretty much the same thing. Scout out an area, kill as many as we could, move on, call in artillery or an air strike and help out patrols sweeping through a given area. Smokey got hit in his left hand by some gunfire and was out of action for a few days but he was ok. We all kidded him about it being self inflicted so he could go home. All in all this camp was now more secure.

It had become really just a job to me and I enjoyed some of it. I no longer felt bad about pulling the trigger on another human being. Snake and I had been in country for over a year and luckily neither one of us had taken a direct hit, other than my being stabbed. We were careful and did not take too many chances. We'd both been hit by shrapnel and flying dirt and rocks and we had plenty of scars from the brush and thorns and a few fist fights. We both had bad feet from all the walking and being wet most of the time, most of the G.I. s called it jungle rot. The guys on this base treated us like every other place we'd been, I think they respected what we did but they looked at us like we were some kind of nut cases – hell, maybe they were right.

26 Nov. 1969, a day I will never forget. We came back to camp late at night after three days of scouting. I think we slept most of the next day. I awoke to the sound of artillery and mortar fire and there was a lot of hollering and commotion outside. We all bailed out of our bunks and grabbed our weapons and slipped outside to a bunker beside our barracks. There was a gunner running a 60mm to our left and he got hit. Chester crawled over to the 60 and started firing. I went back to the barracks and got my .50 caliber rifle. When I came out, I saw Snake helping to set up a 105mm howitzer and load it up with beehive rounds. I could see muzzle flashes coming from the hillside in front of us and started firing at those

flashes. I looked over at Smokey to tell him I was going to move to a bunker in front of us and he was dead. Damn. We were throwing night flares and I could pick out movement and fired at it. I moved to get a better angle and it's hard to explain, I was knocked off my feet, and felt an awful burning in my shoulder and then my leg. Everything was in slow motion – like the first time I smoked a joint. I could see blood running from my arm and my leg. I tried to crawl to some cover but my left arm and left leg wouldn't move. I guessed I was shot and there were shots falling around me. It didn't hurt like I thought it would. My arm was numb and it wouldn't move at all. My head was spinning and I was having trouble focusing, the rifle and artillery fire were becoming faint. I could hear footsteps behind me and somebody said my name and grabbed me under my arms and was dragging me backwards into a hole. I heard gun shots hit close by and blood splattered over me and the dragging stopped. I must have passed out and when I woke up I was in a bunker. Someone was lying behind me - it's Snake, and I think he's dead. I looked at the blank stare in his eyes and I know I've seen that look too many times before, damn it, not Snake; he's gone. My best friend was gone, he's dead, hell maybe I'm dead. Everything was very foggy.

I don't remember anything until the next morning. I was being treated by a medic and he said I'd been hit in the thigh through and through and in the shoulder where I'm going to need some surgery. I told the medic I didn't feel anything and he said that's because he pumped me full of morphine. I asked about Snake and he said he was sorry, he knew we were close, but he was gone. He told me that Snake probably saved my life by dragging me into a bunker and he was hit afterwards. Damn, it wasn't a dream; Snake was dead. He got shot saving me. We only had another 30 days to go; if the bastards hadn't extended our tours, Snake would still be alive. I asked to see Snake one final time and after some hesitation the medic agreed. The medic wheeled me over to Snake's body bag. I was hoping he would just get up and say to me "Got Ya!" But this was no joke, he was really dead. For thirteen months we covered each others butts, now he was gone. Every soldier that came here knew it could happen but this was hard to handle.

Chester came by and he and I both cried. Snake was dead, Smokey was dead. Chester said we held the base and it looked like I a got a ticket out of here. He wanted me to know that it was a pleasure serving with me and Snake and that he would never forget us. All I could say was thanks.

I knew Chester helped to load me on a chopper and I saw him salute me. I would probably never see him again.

The next thing I remember was being in a hospital unit and somebody said something about fixing my shoulder and she asked me if that is ok. I said yes that's ok, I don't know what's wrong with it. I woke up and my arm was in a sling, my shoulder was all wrapped up and my leg was wrapped with a bandage. There was a needle in my right arm and I couldn't move. I was alive but I had no idea what day it was or where I was. A nurse came in and asked me how I was doing. I said ok. She told me I had a broken shoulder blade and it was repaired yesterday, the surgery went fine and in a few months with some rehab it should be good as new. My leg wound was not as serious and it would heal faster because there was no bone damage. She told me it was Friday and I was shot on Tuesday. She told me I would stay here a few more days to make sure I did not have any infection and then I would be shipped stateside for some further medical treatment and rehab.

I felt very alone. For a guy who liked being alone, I guess that sounds really silly. I spent the last thirteen months living in a jungle, in the mud and filth, eating crap and never knowing if I would live or die each day. Now I was in this clean environment, people dressed in white - I wondered if anybody gave me a bath. I wasn't sure how to talk to these people - did they know what my job was and would it matter to them? I had this overpowering feeling of guilt because Snake and Smokey were dead. I felt like I let them down. Chester - who was going to know him well enough to cover his butt and take care of him? Was I going to be a cripple? I was really confused. It was hard to think about life without Snake, we'd been inseparable for so long, and it just felt like a dream.

CHAPTER 14

Heading Home

In three days I was on a plane headed for the USA. My leg was sore but I was able to walk with a cane. My shoulder was really sore and the long plane ride didn't help. I had a chance to talk to some other G.I.s at the hospital and sat with a few others on the plane ride and I felt more comfortable around them. We landed at the Baltimore Airport and the other guys helped me with my bag. While going through the terminal to catch our ride to the base hospital, a lot of people were staring at us. I heard a woman say – damn baby killers. As we were leaving the terminal, two long haired guys and a woman spit on us and told us we should be ashamed of ourselves. I wanted to punch them in the mouth but wasn't physically able. Two other guys with me made the threat. What the hell was wrong with these people, we just got our asses shot at and some good people lost their lives, so we could come back here to be spit on?

What a great welcome home. I knew about the war protestors and all that but I didn't expect this. I got dropped off at the base hospital and settled in. I called my parents and it was great to talk to them. They were going to come see me the next day and maybe spend a few days in the area and maybe I could go home with them for a few days. I met some other guys at the hospital and we shared some stories. A chaplain came by and said if there was anything I needed to talk about, he would be available. One of the guys on my floor had his leg blown off and came over and asked where I had been. I told him about the guilt I felt about losing Snake and Smokey and how I wasn't sure how to deal with it. He told me there were a lot of guys here feeling the same way and he would hook me up with some of them and maybe we could help each other. He told me to be careful who I talked to about the killing because the only people who understood were the ones that were there. I told him thanks and I would remember that. I'd already decided nobody would really know what I did in the Nam.

My folks stopped by the next day and it was a great reunion. It was the first time I ever saw my dad cry. My mom said I looked too thin and she would take care of that. I was carrying a lot inside me and I let some of it go when I saw them. Dad asked if I wanted to talk about losing my friends and I said not now, I just wanted to hear about home. We talked for a while and a nurse came in and explained to my parents and me what I was in for as far as rehab. They would be evaluating me that day and if things went ok, I could go home for a few days, maybe a week. The next day the nurse came back and said I could go home for a week as long as I had someone to change my bandages and make sure I didn't do something dumb with my shoulder. My mom volunteered, saying she spent 18 years trying to make sure I didn't do something dumb, she thought she could do it for another week.

When we got home Mom made me a big, juicy, rare steak and a pan full of fried potatoes; it was the best meal I had since Saigon nine months ago.

My sisters and some of their children stopped by to see me as well as some of our neighbors and I was exhausted that night. My old bed felt really good, I didn't think it would take long to get used to sleeping in a real bed again. The next week went really fast, I saw some of my old friends. Trudy and I spent some time together and I still had that old spark and hoped that she did as well. We made plans for her to come and visit me at the hospital the next week; it was a three hour drive from home. I was happy to be home but I still felt very confused and I had this feeling of not belonging anymore, like I didn't fit in. People talked about their lives and things that were going on in their lives and I didn't know much of what they were talking about. They all acted like I should just fit right in and I did not. I missed Snake a lot and I knew I was carrying a lot of guilt for his death; I was struggling over him dying to save me. Everybody seemed to want to avoid talking to me about it and acted like its ok, you're home now and everything will be ok. Well it was not ok, I was having trouble sleeping, I found myself sleeping in a corner sometimes and I was having some awful nightmares. Maybe the guys at the hospital could help me; they at least knew what I was feeling.

The next couple of weeks at the hospital were spent seeing doctors, filling out papers, meeting with the chaplain and other guys at the hospital. The following week the sling came off and I started rehab on the shoulder. My leg was pretty good, just a little pain every now and then. It took two weeks of rehab to get my shoulder back to 50% mobility. They told me I would need to work at it for six months and I should regain full use of it. I received my discharge from the hospital and the next day I received my discharge from the military as well. I guess they didn't want a one armed man trying to kill Charlie and that was fine with me, I'd had enough. I was a free man.

CHAPTER 15

A Free Man?

I spent a few days loafing around home and realized I needed to find a job at some point. Being back in the world was kind of scary. Now I was supposed to be this responsible citizen and I wasn't sure what that even meant. I realized just how wild we lived in the Nam; we didn't have many holds on us. We decided who lived and died, most of the time we decided where we went and what we did. Nobody told us how to do our jobs when we were on a mission; we knew how to do it better than most of our superiors. This was going to be different.

I got a job working in a cabinet factory and I knew a lot of the people who worked there. It was incredibly boring, standing at a machine doing the same thing hour after hour. I was pretty jumpy around loud noises because to me, a loud noise was something that could kill you. My second week on the job, a fork lift driver lost a load of pallets and they hit the floor with a loud boom. I instinctively dove under my machine to hide and when I realized what I did, I was really embarrassed. A friend came over and asked if I was ok. I said "yeah, but I feel like an idiot." He said "its ok man, I'm sure you went through hell over there." I looked around and could see some of the men with concern on their faces and others were laughing.

It was hard for me to talk to most of these guys: I wasn't up on current events, and I didn't know the local gossip, corn or wheat prices or who was sleeping with whom. Hunting or fishing was the only thing in common I had with them and I had not done that for two years. I mostly kept my mouth shut and listened. One young fellow said to me he heard I was some kind of hot shot sniper over there. I told him I had a job to do and I did it very well. He said "it must be pretty cool to go out everyday and just blow people away." He then asked like everyone else "how many people you kill?" I told him "there was nothing cool about seeing a man's head explode and be splattered over the ground. There was nothing cool about watching the steam come out of a man's chest while his arms and legs were kicking like a deer that had just been shot. As to how many did I shoot – too many." I walked away and went into the bathroom and secretly cried once again.

Later that same day, I was standing over my machine working, when I heard a loud crash. Again I dove under my machine to hide. I turned to look behind me and saw two guys laughing at me after they had dropped a pallet on the floor. I lost it. I dove across some metal rollers separating us and knocked the two of them on the floor. I beat one of them pretty bad and threw the other one across the metal rollers and started beating on him. A couple of other guys pulled me off him or I would have probably beaten him badly as well. I left the factory with everybody staring at me as I left. I stopped at a local bar and had a few beers to cool off. I was sure I just lost my job and probably worse. I should not have beaten on them so bad, but for now that was who I was. Maybe I should not even be here; I didn't seem to fit in anymore.

I decided to go home and face the music. I explained things to my mom and she was upset of course. While we were talking, the local sheriff pulled in the driveway and said we needed to talk. I told him my side of the story, he knew me, his two sons and I grew up together. He said the two guys I beat up wanted to press assault charges. One of them had a broken nose and possibly a broken jaw. He said as a vet he understood, but I might want to get a lawyer. He told me I had to go with him and he would take my formal statement. While walking into the Sheriff's office, the father of one of the guys I beat up approached us and called me an animal and said I didn't belong here among decent people. I really screwed up this time, I was home for two weeks and now I was in jail. My mother showed up with an attorney and he told me to say nothing.

Two days later I was taken before a judge for a bail hearing. The District Attorney presented me as a trained killer; he said my hands should have been registered as lethal weapons. My attorney said that was ridiculous, I was simply acting upon an assault on me. He indicated I was a decorated veteran with an outstanding military record, who only had 60% use of his left shoulder. These two men should be ashamed of themselves for their actions. Bail was set at $10,000 and posted that day.

I was fired from my job and I understood. My former boss told he also fired the two guys who pulled the stunt on me. I got another job working for a contractor friend doing masonry work. I liked it better anyway because I got to work outside. I had already made up my mind if I got past this assault charge, I was moving away from here; I felt like I embarrassed my family and friends. I kept to myself, mostly spending time in the woods, doing my job and drinking a lot of beer. I was wrestling with nightmares and flashbacks and I really missed the Snake. At times I felt like he was the lucky one, he didn't have to deal with this shit.

There were a lot of people who supported me and that kept me going. My dad was the only one I was able to open up to and I told him most everything I did in the Nam. He said he didn't care what I did, I was his son and he was proud of me. Besides he told me if I wouldn't have given those two knuckleheads a beating, he would have. Trudy and some other friends kept after me to go out with them and do things but I was afraid if somebody would say something stupid about me or the war, I wouldn't react very well.

I kept my nose clean for three months and the trial was going to begin. It began as me being painted as a killer, a trained assassin. According to the official Army record I was credited with 52 confirmed kills and many more that were not confirmed. I didn't even know how many confirmed I had, it was never important to me. My attorney's opening statement said I was a decorated soldier; I had received two commendations for valor, was a unit leader for six months and received two purple hearts in combat. He stated my military record was outstanding and I was a true American hero. It was a travesty to have this man on trial for defending himself. I thought he laid it on pretty thick.

The D.A. went through a number of witnesses who painted me as a man out of control and one who seemed to drink a lot. He even dragged up my being busted in rank for a fight while I was in Nam. My attorney did a pretty good job of shooting them down. Now it was his turn. Our first couple of witnesses were former co-workers who thought I was an ok guy and the two guys got what they deserved. The next witness was a shrink who examined me and said I was experiencing normal post combat adjustment problems and he did not feel I was out of control.

The next witness called was Corporal Eduardo Sanchez. Chester, I wasn't sure if he could come, but there he was. Man it was good to see him, as he walked by me he stopped and saluted me. I wasn't in uniform and it wasn't appropriate, but I appreciated it. I felt tears welling up in my eyes as he took the witness stand. Chester testified as to my character, how I trained him and taught him compassion and respect. He stated if wasn't for me, he would not have lasted a week in Vietnam. He said I was a role model for all new recruits coming into the sniper program. He concluded he was proud to serve under me and would be honored to do so again.

Next it was my turn. I told my story and when asked if I had any remorse for my actions, I said yes, as a trained soldier, I was embarrassed that I lost control of my emotions. For these two men to make a mockery of me and the soldiers I have served with was simply more than I could take. I was not only defending my honor but that of my men as well. I was sorry for what I did to these two men however they need to accept some of the responsibility for their actions as well.

The jury was out for two hours and came back with a verdict of not guilty of assault. I was ordered to pay their medical expenses not covered by insurance. All tolled, it cost me $600 plus $1200 in lawyer fees.

I had Chester meet my folks and he came home with us for dinner. He delighted in telling them all the Dirt Hog stories he could remember. We hugged and I thanked him for coming, he said he had to leave tonight and tried his best to talk me into coming back. I said I would seriously think about it and honestly I was. He had another year to serve and was thinking about going back to the Nam. We exchanged addresses and I wished him well then he hopped in his rental car and was gone.

CHAPTER 16

Heading West

I bought a '64 Chevy pickup truck and stocked it with a tent, sleeping bag, and other camping supplies and I decided I was going to do some traveling. I'd saved a few thousand dollars and it was time to see the country. My parents were not too happy about my leaving again but I think they understood I needed to find something and they wished me well. Trudy and I talked and we both decided it was best for both of us to take our time with our relationship. I told her not to wait for me, she deserved better. I really cared for her but I couldn't stay here anymore and right now I felt I had nothing to offer her. I sensed she was somewhat afraid of me since I came back but didn't want to admit it. I was different and I needed to find out why, if I could.

It was springtime and I decided to head west. I had no destination in mind, I just wanted to go. I decided to go southwest first to try to catch some good weather and then maybe head north after the snow melted. Texas was sort of my goal, I heard a lot about it and besides I had always wanted to be a cowboy since I was a little boy. I headed south into Virginia and then started west from southern Virginia. I stopped at campgrounds along the way and sometimes when the weather was nice just slept in the back of the truck. I avoided big cities any time I could, preferring back roads and small towns. I felt too confined in cities, I couldn't see the sky, couldn't tell what direction I was going, and there were too many people. People were just friendlier in small towns.

I never really talked about the war with anybody but I thought about it all the time. I didn't sleep a lot because I kept seeing faces of people I killed or reliving battles we were in. One incident I couldn't shake was an NVA soldier who I shot in the head with my .50 caliber. Most of his head was blown off and he still staggered another ten feet after he was hit. It was an awful nightmare. I thought a lot about Snake and all the adventures we shared. I was approaching Arkansas and it was like I was being guided to try and find Snake's family. I called my parents at least once a week to let them know I was ok and where I was. I was heading into Hot Springs, Arkansas, a place my uncle talked about a lot, and a place he traveled to when he was younger. He lived the life of a hobo for a while and hopped freight trains and traveled around the country that way. He always made it sound like a colorful life but I'm sure it wasn't a very pleasant way to live. I had to check out the area anyway. I skirted south of Little Rock to avoid the city traffic and wound up in Hot Springs on a Thursday. It was a pretty big town to me and I found a campground nearby to pitch my tent. It was a nice place and I spent two days there checking out some local attractions and restocking my food supplies. I found myself looking for things to do and excuses for not moving on. I had Snake's home address but no phone number and I knew his hometown was northwest of here. I had to do it; I had to find his family and apologize to them for being responsible for his death.

My stomach was churning as I approached Snake's hometown. I stopped at a gas station and asked if they knew where the Morgan family lived. They gave me directions and I headed for their home. I recognized the place from what Snake had described to me. I knocked on the door and a lady answered the door. I introduced myself and said "you may know me as Dirt Hog." She put her hands up to her face and said "oh my God, oh my God, yes I know who you are!" Tears poured out of her and she hugged me like we'd known each other for years. She said she was sorry, she did not know if I was alive or not. Jake spoke so highly of me she felt she already knew me well. I apologized for just dropping in and she said "nonsense boy, you come in here and sit down." I could see Jake's dry sense of humor in her. I started to say something but got this big lump in my throat and all I could say was "yes Ma'am."

She told me her husband would be home from work in an hour and Jake's little brother would be home from school shortly after. She also said I was staying for supper tonight and was not going to hear any excuses from me, so I should make myself comfortable.

When Mr. Morgan came home, Mary, she insisted I call her Mary, told him who I was. He shook my hand and hugged me and then we both cried uncontrollably. I was able to hold it in earlier with Mary, but not now. Months of feeling guilty for Snake's death finally came pouring out of me. Mr. Morgan said "it's so good to finally meet you, Jake spoke so highly of you and included you in most of his letters, and I know he loved you like a brother." I cried again and was finally able to say I loved him in the same way.

Mr. Morgan told me to call him Bill and asked me what I was doing here and how I found them. I told him I got out about six months ago and after getting out of rehab and then going home, it just wasn't the same for me. I wasn't the same and needed some time to figure out what I wanted to do with the rest of my life. I decided to do some traveling and ended up here. I kept Jake's address and when I got to Arkansas, I knew I had to find you folks. I knew I was looking for something but I didn't know what.

Bill grabbed my hand and said "son, the lord brought you here." I said "I'm sorry but I don't know what you mean." He said after they buried Jake, he and Mary both wondered if I was still alive and how nice it would be to meet me some day. He went on to say that they both prayed about it and they felt if I was still alive, the Lord would bring us together someday. I said "but you don't understand – Jake died dragging me to safety. If he wouldn't have come to save me, he might be alive today. It's my fault he's dead." Bill and Mary both hugged me as Mary said "that's nonsense, we know all that and we don't blame you." I asked how they knew. Mary said they got a letter from our Lt. explaining what happened and how in the face of heavy enemy fire Jake dragged his wounded partner to safety without regard for his own life. They knew that partner had to be me.

I did not know what to say. Mary brought out a framed commendation that was awarded to Jake posthumously for heroism in the face of battle. I felt a huge weight lift from my shoulders. It was the first time I admitted to anyone I blamed myself for Jake's death. I told them their forgiveness meant the world to me. Mary said "you poor boy, you've been carrying around that burden for too long." She said I must have forgotten how many times I saved Jake's life. She could remember at least three times that he wrote to them about. Then she wondered if there were any more. I said it was mutual; he covered my butt plenty of times.

About that time, Snake's little brother Ben came home from school. He was tall and thin like Snake and was a junior in high school. Bill introduced us and Ben said "so you're the Dirt Hog." I responded "yeah, that's me, nice to meet you Ben." Mary excused herself to go make dinner and I shared a few Snake stories with Ben and Bill that I thought she might not care for. Ben asked me if I really beat all them Marines arm wrestling and we took them for $100. I told him that was the truth. He said Jake told him I was one of the toughest men he ever met and I was his best friend. I told Ben, Jake never met very many tough men, but he was absolutely the best friend I ever had and I missed him deeply. Ben asked me where I was shot and could he see the scars and I showed him my leg and shoulder scars. Bill told Ben to go do his chores before dinner and to stop asking me so many questions.

Bill asked me if I would like to see some old pictures of Jake and I said of course. While looking through pictures of Jake growing up, I saw how much his life paralleled my own. Pictures of little league, high school sports, hunting, fishing, and family, I felt even closer to him.

Mary called us for dinner and it smelled good: country ham, browned potatoes, and corn. Before we ate, we all held hands and Bill prayed and included in his prayer a thank you to God for bringing me to meet with them. I thought to myself, he really believes that God brought me here. I loved my family and I know they loved me, but we never prayed together. Bill's prayer caused butterflies in my stomach and yet it seemed the right thing to do. The meal tasted as good as it smelled. We talked a while after dinner and Bill showed around their place and then he asked where I was going to stay that night. I said right out there in the back of my truck. He told me I was welcome to stay in Jake's old room. I told him thanks. But I don't sleep very well and sometimes I have nightmares and honestly I would be embarrassed if I woke everybody up during the night. Bill said fine, he understood, I could leave my truck parked right where it was. I told he and Mary thanks for their hospitality and I was going to turn in, it had been a long day. Mary said breakfast will be at 5:00am, see you then. I simply replied "yes Ma'am sounds good."

What a day. I was so nervous about meeting these people; I even screwed around in Hot Springs an extra day trying to get up enough nerve to meet them. They treated me so well I felt guilty. This God thing Bill talked about really had me thinking. It just seemed like a big coincidence to me but maybe it was true, maybe I was directed here God. Maybe the next day I would talk to him about it more. I was so glad to meet Snake's family, they were wonderful people. I slept like a baby all night, I couldn't remember the last time it was that I slept so well, and 5:00am came quickly.

Mary had a big breakfast of sausage, pancakes, eggs, and toast. I helped

Bill with some barn work after breakfast and he asked me if I would go with him later to meet some of the guys he worked with at the feed mill. I said I would be glad to and then I would have to leave because I wanted to be in Texas by nightfall. I said my goodbyes to Mary and Ben and they made me promise to keep in touch and I said I surely would. I said you folks have treated me like family and I will never forget it. We all prayed together before Bill and I left. I followed Bill to his job at the feed mill and he introduced me to several fellows that worked there. He then introduced me to the owner of the mill, who only had one arm. His name was Jim. Bill said we might have some war stories to share with each other. Jim told me he lost his arm in the South Pacific during WWII and lived through some pretty rough times. We shared a few stories and Jim told me he understood some of what I was going through and if I ever needed to talk or even needed a job to come and see him again. I thanked him for his time and thanked Bill as well and told him I couldn't say when, but he would be seeing me again.

In my heart I really did not want to leave but I was afraid if I stayed too long, I would not want to leave at all. That Bill sure seemed to know what to say and when to say it, but for now I was off for Texas. I had no idea where I was going other than to look for some place I could maybe be a cowboy for a while. I spent the night in a campground east of Dallas. As I approached the Dallas-Fort Worth area, I could see there were too many people for me. I decided to keep on moving and head for West Texas, which I heard was more wide open. I ended up in Amarillo in a couple of days and was pointed in the direction of a ranch that may be looking for help. Just outside of Amarillo I stopped at a diner for something to eat.

I sat in a booth in the corner and ordered my food. There were three young guys in the booth in front of me. I couldn't help but overhear their conversation, they were pretty loud. They were discussing guns, imagine that in Texas! The conversation wound around to which was the best all around deer rifle, anything from the Winchester model 70, Remington model 700, Ruger model 77, Weatherby Mark V and on and on, each guy had an opinion. One of the guys facing me must have noticed the smile on my face as I was listening to their conversation and asked "hey buddy, ya'll know anything about guns?" I said "ya' I know a little bit about them." He asked "what's your favorite?" I told him I'd tried just about every one of the different models they mentioned and in my opinion you can't beat the Winchester model 70. It's a clean, smooth action, dependable and durable.

I've fired probably 10,000 rounds through one and as long as I took care of it, it took care of me.

The guy asked "ya'll some kind of outdoor writer or something like that?" I said "no sir, I've spent some time in the military." He said he didn't know the military used Winchesters, he thought everybody used them semi-auto M-16's. I said yes sir, most everybody does. In my job, I used several rifles but my favorite was a Winchester model 70 with a match grade barrel, it was extremely accurate. He asked me if I was one of them snipers. I said "yes, sir." He invited me to come over and sit with them and I accepted; it had been a while since I got into a good bullshit session about guns and I always enjoyed it. Phil, the guy I'd been talking with, introduced me to Tom and Jay.

They were all full of questions about the war and what I thought about it. What was the longest shot I ever made, what calibers did I like, did I want another beer, where did I aim for mostly, give my buddy another beer, how many guys have you killed, give my buddy another beer, you ever been shot and you're money ain't no good here man, give my buddy another beer. The diner was ready to close for the night and the man behind the counter called me over and said he overheard some of our conversation and he wanted to shake my hand and say thanks for serving. He said he served in Italy in WWII and knew some of what I was saying to the boys. He also told me these were good boys and they just liked to raise a little hell when they got the chance. I said "thank you sir, that means a lot to me, not too many people now days are too quick to shake our hands for serving in the Nam."

My three new friends insisted I go with them to a local bar and have some fun. I thought, what the hell, I didn't have anything else to do. The bar was full of people, some of those people were some mighty fine looking young women, loud country music, and it seemed like everybody was having a good time. My buddies were kind of showing me off and I was enjoying it. I mentioned to Tom I'd sure like to have one of those cowboy hats most of the guys were wearing. He thought a little bit and grabbed me by the arm and led me up to the stage where the band was playing and whispered something to the guitar player. The guitar player winked and nodded his head at Tom. At the end of the song the guitar player said something to the lead singer. The singer motioned Tom up to the stage and Tom grabbed the microphone. He said "folks we have a special guest here tonight. We have us a genuine war hero just back from Vietnam and I want ya'll to make him feel right at home here tonight." Tom introduced me and then he said "my good buddy here says he'd sure like to have a nice ten gallon hat for himself and I was wondering if any ya'll had an extra one with you tonight." I was shocked, it rained cowboy hats up on the stage, there must have been 25 hats laying on the stage. Tom said "how's that boy, pick one!" I have a pretty big head and I tried five or six before finally finding one that fit. I grabbed the mike and said "thanks to all of you and if the fella that owned this hat meets me at the bar, I'd be glad to buy him a beer."

We drank beer, told hunting stories, danced, lied to each other and I met so many people I couldn't possibly remember their names, even if I was sober and I wasn't. We closed the bar at 2:00am and I think I crawled into the back of my truck on my own. About 10:00am the next morning Phil was banging on the back of my truck and saying hey man, you want a beer. I said hell no, get out of my way, I got to take a leak. The sun was so bright it hurt my eyes; I had one hell of a hangover!

Phil said he and the boys wanted to take me out to his dad's ranch and shoot some prairie dogs. I said I'd like to but I needed to get something to eat first. We went to the diner we ate at last night. The owner, Bob looked at me and said "it looks like the boys showed you a good time last night" and then he laughed. I ordered breakfast even though it was almost lunch time. After eating, Bob said "it's on the house, have a great day." I saluted him and said thank you, sir.

We were off to the ranch and met Tom and Jay there. They had several rifles in the back of a jeep and told me to pick one out. I found a Remington model 700 in a .22-250 caliber and said this will do. We drove out to a wide open flat prairie and watched a spot where there were a lot of holes maybe 200-300 yards away. I was sure these guys wanted to see if I could really shoot and not just blowing smoke to them last night. I asked what this gun was sighted in for and Jay said it was dead on at 200 yards. I said ok and we waited for one to pop out. I guess this was what they called a prairie dog town as there were holes all over in a cluster. One popped his head out of a hole at about 200 yards and I took his head off. Tom said "nice shot were you aiming for his head?" I said yes, sir. He said "ya know if ya wait a little bit they will come the whole way out of the hole and give ya more to shoot at." I said yes, sir. Another one popped his head out and I left him come the entire way out of the hole and then I shot his head off. I told them it was a good shooting gun but the trigger pull was a little heavy and the length of pull a little too long for me. I looked at them and said ok boys it's your turn to show me how well you can shoot. They each were fair shots and they all were shooting weapons that didn't fit them very well. A couple of the rifles had see through scope rings that were too high and I did not care for them. I talked to them about ballistic coefficients, trajectory, free floating barrels and seeing vapor trails on long range shots. I could see by the expressions on their faces I was talking over their heads. Phil was looking through his binoculars and said "I see one way out there, maybe 500 yards, think you can hit em'?" I said I could try. They were almost impossible to see at that distance and I had to wait for it to move before I could see it. I allowed for windage and bullet drop and squeezed the trigger; the animal flipped over backwards and was dead.

    I asked if there was a gun shop around and Phil said sure man, you're in Texas. I told them if they liked I could set up their weapons so they would fit and shoot better for them. They all said let's go! We got the parts we needed and went back to Phil's place. They had a nice reloading room and all the tools I needed. I fiber glassed the forearms, adjusted the trigger pulls, shortened the stocks on two of them and replaced scope mounts and rings and then torqued all the screws. One stock needed ½" of crown taken off and we were done. That night we would do some refinishing and the next day we would zero them in for each fellow. I talked to them about proper body posture and pressure points and breathing and then had each one of them practice all of those techniques. I think they were impressed; the next day they would be more impressed when they saw how much their shooting improved. I recommended some bullet and powder choices and we were back to the gun shop. The guys picked up what they needed and then we went back to ranch and they got busy reloading ammo. These guys had some nice equipment; it just needed some fine tuning.

    Phil's dad, Big Phil, came in and wondered what the hell was going on in here. Phil introduced me to his dad and said "Daddy, we are super tuning our rifles." I explained to Big Phil what we did and why and if he liked he could see the results tomorrow. The only thing he said was these damn rifles better look like they did when he left the house this morning or somebody was in deep shit and then he left the room. Phil said don't mind him, he always talks like that. We finished up the stocks on the guns later that evening and set them aside to dry. The boys and I did some partying that night and I met a couple of women I liked. The next morning we put the guns together and Big Phil went along with us to make sure we didn't screw up his guns. We got them zeroed in and everyone was impressed with how much better each gun shot, including Big Phil.

    Big Phil thanked me for helping the boys out and wondered if I was looking for some work. I said maybe, what did he have in mind. He took me into another room with a few pictures hanging on the walls and flipped a hidden switch and a four foot section of the wall slid open and behind it was a collection of twelve guns. Big Phil told me there were 150-160 guns in this room and some of them needed some work done on them, was I interested? I said I would be interested, if he could make me a list of what he wanted done I could probably get started the next day, unless his son got me too drunk that night. I really didn't plan on staying more than a day or two but I enjoyed being around these guys. Big Phil said I could stay in the old bunk house, it wasn't fancy but it would keep the rain off my head and the coyotes from chewing my toes. I said I was sure I'd slept in worse places.

Big Phil asked me if I had a rough time in Vietnam. I told him it wasn't pretty, but I thought we were doing the right thing by being there; the problem was the politicians wouldn't let us complete the job. Big Phil said "boy, you're in Texas now and we don't worry about them assholes here."

I started working on Big Phil's guns the next day. He had a very nice collection, a lot of Winchester model 70's, collector edition Winchester model 94's, a couple of nice Colt-Sauer's, Weatherby's, Remington model 700's and 760's and 30-40 older collector grade Winchesters. He also had nice collection of Colt revolvers along with some beautiful custom made rifles. While I was working on his guns, Big Phil brought one of his friends, Martin, in to meet me. Martin was a tough looking man of few words. Martin said he served in Korea and knew a little bit about guns himself. We talked about the military for a bit while he watched me work on the guns. He asked what I planned to do with my life and I said that's what brought me here, trying to figure out what I wanted to do. He said I should stop by his place that night; he would like to talk to me about a possible job I might be interested in. Martin told me Phil could give me directions and I should be there around 7:00pm. I said ok, I would be there.

Later that evening I stopped by Martin's house, he had a real nice looking log house in the woods. There was a black lab there to greet me and the dog named Buck and I became instant friends. I really missed having a dog around, most of my life I had a dog and really enjoyed Buck's company. Martin and his wife Carol welcomed me into their home. I guessed they were each in their mid-fifties. Martin asked me about my experience in Vietnam and about my knowledge of jungle warfare. He said Phil and the boys told him of my knowledge of guns and ability to shoot and that was good enough for him. I told him I was most skilled at stalking and moving in and out of situations undetected.

He told me he ran a private security business and provided security for various businesses around the world. He said his company also provided security for some foreign governments.

Martin told me he was looking for a few ex-military personnel to fill some vacancies he had and it sounded like I might fit the bill. He went on to say the job paid very well, I could expect to earn between $50,000 - $60,000 a year to start and all my travel expenses would be paid as well as medical and life insurance. I would be traveling a lot and may be away for a couple of months at a time. I would go through a training schedule with the group I would be working with, more to get to know them than to teach me skills.

It all sounded pretty good. I told him I was still recovering from a shoulder injury and I was not 100% yet. It may take another month or two until the shoulder was ready. I planned to spend that time seeing more of the west, especially Montana and Idaho and hopefully do some elk hunting later on. He said that was fine, he enjoyed elk hunting himself. I asked where I could expect to go and what I might do. He said given my experience, his company had clients in South and Central America, Africa, and Southeast Asia. As far as what I might do, it could be providing security for construction companies to observing government officials and militant groups in various regions.

My next question was "OK Martin, now I'm going to ask a question that maybe you don't want to answer, am I going to be a paid assassin?" He looked me in the eyes and asked "would you have a problem with that?" I told him "right now, today, yes I'm tired of killing. I don't want to kill children, I was forced to kill 12-16 year old boys in the Nam to protect myself and my men and I don't want to have to do that again." He told me his company was not in the business of killing children.

My next question was what happened to the men that I would be replacing? He simply said "some people quit and some people can't cuff it."

Martin gave me his card and said go enjoy yourself, you earned that right. In a few months or a year, if you want a job, give me a call and we will talk some more. I told him "fair enough, at some point I'm going to have to get a real job." We shook hands and I thanked him for his time, I said goodbye to Buck and was on my way back to the bunkhouse.

Driving down the road, I was thinking $50,000 – 60,000 a year; that was a lot of money to me. I'm sure Martin did not tell me about the danger involved but I had certainly been shot at for a lot less money. Other than sports, it was what I know best; however I'd have to get more details and think about it before I'd make any decisions. For now I was going to see the country. I went back to the bunkhouse and sacked out after calling my folks and the Morgan's.

I spent two more days working on Big Phil's guns and partying with the boys and then I decided it was time to move on. Big Phil paid me well and asked me if was considering Martin's job offer. I said I was but just not right now. He told me he and Martin worked together at times and that Martin was a square shooter and would not feed me a line. Big Phil shook my hand and told me I was welcomed back any time. The boys wished they could go with me but they all had jobs to keep them here. I told them I would be back through here sometime again, I just didn't know when.

CHAPTER 17

Back To the Woods

I was on my way to New Mexico. The eastern part of New Mexico was flat with a few rolling hills and not too appealing to me. I kept moving northwest and could see the Rocky Mountains ahead of me. It seemed like I would never get to the mountains, I could see them for such a long distance away. I made a decision to head north into Colorado and follow the mountains. This was what I wanted to see, beautiful country, mountains as far as I could see and not many people. It was so refreshing to breathe the fresh air; I saw elk and mule deer, even a mountain goat. I drove to a spot that said the elevation was 9000 feet and my truck was even gasping for air. I camped out almost every night and I felt like I could touch the stars at night, the sky was so clear. For me this was truly spiritual, I could feel my body and my soul healing, this was where I belonged. Maybe Bill Morgan was right, God had guided me to this place to give me time to think and to rest. I had not felt this relaxed in years. The people I did meet along the way were so friendly, when they asked you how you were doing, they waited for an answer, it wasn't just a cliché.

I kept moving north through Colorado and then cut over into western Wyoming and then on to Montana. I was taking my time, spending a few days here and there, just soaking in the mountains. I stopped in Missoula, Montana to get some gas and a bite to eat and asked at the gas station where a guy might find some part time work on a ranch around here. It was early July and the guy at the gas station told me of a few ranches that might be looking for some help and gave me directions. Like most everyone

I encountered on my travels he asked me where I was from and actually seemed to care. The first two ranches I stopped at were not hiring at the time but at the third ranch the owner said he would make a phone call to a friend of his and ask if he was looking for any help. He put me on the phone and his friend gave me directions to his ranch and told me to stop by and see him today. When I got there the owner introduced himself as Wes Nelson and said he was looking for someone to help set up camps for hunters coming in September and October. The job would only be for a few months, if I was interested he would give me a try. The pay wasn't great but they would feed me and put me up and would be glad to let me pretend to be a cowboy for a while. Wes introduced me to his wife Sally and son Clay and went on to tell me they owned 15,000 acres and leased another 20,000 acres which they ran cattle on. He said they had enough help for the fall roundup of the cattle but needed someone to help Clay with the outfitting business because the fellow who normally helped had broken his leg last week. Again I got to thinking: was this just a coincidence that I happened to bump into these folks at the right time or was it part of some master plan.

I was shown my room at the back of their house. I guessed at one time it was a summer kitchen, like a lot of older homes in the area I grew up had. I was about to make one of my childhood dreams come true - being a real cowboy - and if it would only be for a few months, that was ok with me. For the first time in a while I felt like I had some direction in my life. I could not imagine how big 35,000 acres really was; it seemed like a whole lot of land to me. My first job was fixing holes and sewing patches onto canvas tents and panniers used for carrying supplies on the pack horses, something I never knew a cowboy did. My hands were really sore after spending most of the day sewing. I didn't know much about horses but I was ready to learn. At the end of the day, Clay took time to show me how to saddle a horse and how to properly set the stirrup length so my testicles did not end up in my throat. Clay was twenty years old and seemed much older, he had obviously grown up on this ranch and he seemed to enjoy what he was doing.

We had six camps to set up for elk and mule deer hunters and we had to transport the equipment back into the mountains by horseback. After a few days of preparing equipment like portable wood stoves, cook stoves, old military cots, tents, food for the hunters and feed for the horses, we were ready to start packing everything up for the trip back into the mountains. We had a string of five pack horses and early in the morning, it was time to load them up. Loading up a pack saddle and strapping down panniers full of provisions on the back of a horse properly is an art form. Poor Clay showed me twenty times how to tie knots that would stay tight and easily loosen when unloading but I never got the hang of it. It is good I never went into the Navy because I never was very good at tying knots. When we went to unload, he had me untie the knots I made; I was glad because I was kind of embarrassed that I couldn't do them the proper way.

Our first trip was twelve miles one way on horseback. My butt was so sore; I led my horse the last two miles. I was really glad to see the little valley ahead of us with the remains of a camp from last year. We set up ridge poles for the tents and got them all stretched out, set up the cook stove, and installed small wood stoves in each tent for heat. We stashed the horse feed and some nonperishable food in a wooded cache up in the tree tops so the local critters wouldn't eat it all. We repaired the corral and hid some tools for horse shoeing if needed later. In the next two weeks we made five more trips of various distances and by the end of those trips I knew a whole lot more about horses than I did before starting this job. It was hard work and long days but I really enjoyed it; Clay was a good companion and we got along fine. The best times were sitting around a campfire at night listening to nothing but the crackling fire, coyotes howling, some whip-or-wills calling and an occasional owl hoot. The creeks were crystal clear, the smell of juniper and fir trees intoxicating, the air was fresh and clean, hell, even the smell of horse sweat soaked into leather smelled good to me. It was incredibly relaxing.

My shoulder was all but healed and my mind was healing as well. The nightmares and the night sweats were less than they used to be, maybe once a week. I know I woke Clay up a few times with my nightmares. I took some time to explain to him what I was dealing with but it always embarrassed me when I woke someone with my screams. I thought a lot about Snake and I wished he could be here to enjoy this with me; maybe he was. I had an ongoing contest with one of the pack horses whose name was Mother-In-Law. She seemed gentle enough when you were facing her but if you walked behind her in range of her left rear leg, she would nail you quicker than you could blink. You could see the whites of her eyes as she followed her victim, just waiting for the right moment. Everyday I would test her but she had not succeeded in kicking me, yet.

On our last trip out of the mountains, we crossed paths with a sheep herder in a big mountain meadow. He flagged us down and wanted to talk. It turned out he spent the entire summer moving his herd of 150 sheep from meadow to meadow, his only companions were a couple of dogs that helped to herd the sheep. He told us he had not talked to anyone in almost a month and was full of questions about what was going on in the world, who we were, and when we would be back. We talked with him for a while and he gave us some information about where he was seeing elk and where he was going next. Clay and I each gave him some food we had left over and he seemed happy for something different to eat. We wished him good luck and we moved on, both of us ready for one of Sally's good meals and a hot bath. Clay told me there were three or four sheep herders who used these meadows in the summer to fatten up their sheep. The land was BLM or Bureau of Land Management owned by the federal government.

We got back to the ranch a little before dark and got our horses unsaddled and turned out to pasture. They deserved a break; they worked hard the last couple of weeks, so did we. Sally had supper ready for us and told me I had received a phone call from my sister and I should call her right away. I left the number with my parents when I first got there and she must have gotten it from them. I called my sister Cheryl and she said she had some bad news. Mom and dad were both killed in a car accident the previous night. She was crying and it was hard to understand her when I asked what happened. I told her I would try to catch a flight home the next day and I would call her with the details in the morning. When I hung up, it was like somebody hit me in the chest with a sledge hammer. I sat down in a chair and cried. Sally came in and said "you poor thing, I'm so sorry." Cheryl had told her what happened and Wes was ready to come out and get me if we had not come back. All three of them wrapped their arms around me and tried their best to console me. We talked a bit and I told them I needed some time alone to sort through this. I went out to the corral and sat on the fence. I asked God why? I asked myself why. Why these two wonderful people? What did our family do to deserve this? I loved my parents deeply and now they were gone. Maybe if I wouldn't have gone away they would still be alive. I'd seen so much death and now more. I was starting to believe in all this God stuff and how he would take care of me, how could God condone something like this? The horse I'd been riding for the past few weeks, Walt, came over and nuzzled my hand as if he knew I was hurting. I rubbed his muzzle and he tried to open my shirt pocket where I kept pieces of carrots for him. Walt kind of brought me back to the reality of the moment. I gave him a carrot and went back to the house.

When I got back to the house, Wes had already purchased an airline ticket for me leaving Missoula the next day at 2:00pm. I would fly to Chicago, then Pittsburgh and on to Harrisburg. I asked if I could leave my truck at the ranch and pick it up when I got back. Wes said my truck would be here when I got back and he would take me to the airport. He told me if I could get back by the end of August, I could help with some of the elk hunters coming in the first week of September. I assured him I would be back by that time. Wes, Sally and Clay all prayed with me and I went back to my room to pack some clothes. At some point I fell asleep on the porch outside. I didn't sleep very well as some of the past year kept popping into my mind.

Wes dropped me off at the airport the next morning and after a long day of airports and airplanes I finally landed at Harrisburg late that evening. Cheryl arranged for one of our friends, Ken, to pick me up at the airport. Ken explained to me on the way home that a dump truck had crossed the center line of the road and hit my dad's car head on. My parents didn't have much of a chance. They were both pronounced dead at the scene. Ken dropped me off at my parent's home and told me if there was anything I needed to give him a call. It was eerie being in their house knowing they were not coming home. I spent most of the night looking at pictures and thinking about all the good times we had together. I loved my mother but my dad was my best friend; we did everything together while I was growing up. I was especially looking forward to hunting with him that fall and I was secretly planning to have them both come out to Wes's ranch and have dad hunt elk with me that fall. Now I didn't know what I was going to do.

The service was in two days. Throughout the next day, friends and family stopped by or called and it was exhausting dealing with everything. My two older sisters made most of the arrangements for the funeral as they lived close by. My sister Cheryl lived out of the area and she arrived around lunch time. She and I would be staying at our parent's house for the next few days to help out with things.

We all hugged and cried and shared memories of mom and dad. My other two sisters each had five children and they had their hands full dealing with them, so Cheryl and I kind of took over when we arrived. People were bringing food all day long and we were running out of places to put it all. Later that night, Cheryl and I finally had some time to catch with each others lives and it was really nice to see her again. She was eight years older than me but we were closer to each other than our older sisters. Cheryl was an accountant in the Pittsburgh area and seemed to be doing well, she was dating another accountant and he could not make it to the funeral because he was in California for the week. Cheryl was on the phone talking to him a lot and it seemed like she really liked him. She always worried about me being a little too much of an adventurer and wished I would settle down, sometimes she was like an extra mom. We talked well into the night and the next morning came really quickly.

Prior to the service we all said our personal goodbyes to Mom and Dad and got ready to greet folks at a viewing prior to the funeral. There were a lot of people attending and it was nice to know so many people thought well of my parents. After the service and after everyone else went home, Cheryl and I went to have a beer at a local bar and to wind down a bit. We met a few of our old friends and everybody was very nice about offering their respects to our family. We were both going to stick around for a few days to help tie up some legal affairs and it was nice to have Cheryl's experience to get through most of it. It was nice to spend time with her and I told her I didn't know where I was going to end up but wherever it was I promised to keep in touch. I told Cheryl I didn't want any of our parent's money right now and I didn't need it, I asked her to keep it for me. I also told her if she needed my share to go ahead and use it, I trusted her. We signed some papers with my folk's attorney and I signed my rights over to Cheryl at that time. I was getting restless and it was time to move on, it just didn't seem like my home anymore. Cheryl told me she hoped I found what I was looking for and no matter what I did or where I went, she would always love me. I told her I felt the same about her.

The next day Ken took me back to the airport and said he hoped to see me soon. I said I appreciated his help and I would look him up the next time I got back there; I knew in my mind I probably would not be coming back. I flew into Chicago and had a four hour layover until my flight to Missoula. I was wandering around in the airport terminal and bumped into a couple of G.I.s on their way home from the Nam. They were waiting for a flight out as well. We talked awhile and shared some stories and one of the guys said he spent some time at firebase Billy. I said no shit; I was there a little over a year ago, part of the sniper unit. They asked if I stayed in the snake pit. I said I wasn't familiar with a snake pit. They said "yeah, the snake pit was named in honor of a couple of crazy guys who ate snakes and rats, one of whom died defending it." They said the other guy was wounded and shipped back to the world. I laughed and said "well I'll be damned; I guess I'm the crazy guy who didn't die there." The soldier said "no shit, you two guys are kind of a legend there, we didn't know if you were real or not." About that time they called boarding for my flight and I had to go. I shook their hands and said "we were real!" I laughed to myself the whole way to Missoula about some of the dumb stuff Snake and I did and how probably those stunts have grown as they were passed on to new soldiers coming in. I really missed that old boy.

My flight got into Missoula late that night and I got a room at a local motel because I knew Wes and Sally went to bed early and I didn't want to wake them. I called the next morning and Sally came and picked me up and said howdy cowboy, you need a ride. I liked this family; they worked hard, they treated me well, and they allowed me to live one of my dreams: I was a cowboy. The next two weeks were spent actually being a cowboy, moving cattle out of some of the high country and loading them on trucks for shipment to the buyers.

By the beginning of September, the first archery hunters moved in. For the next two months we were busy: wrangling stock, packing in supplies and hunters, packing out hunters and their trophies, packing out meat, helping with guiding hunters, picking them up at the airport and delivering them back to the airport. I worked 12-15 hours a day, seven days a week and I loved it. I enjoyed spending time with most of the hunters; it was our job to make sure they had a good time whether they took an animal or not. Most of them were good sportsmen and enjoyed the outdoors as much as we did. We did have a few who we were as glad to see leave as we were to see arrive. One particular gentleman was filling in for a friend who got sick at the last minute and could not make the trip. This guy complained from the minute he got off the plane until we loaded him back onto it to leave. He didn't like the color of his horse, he didn't like the food, and he didn't like the bed he was sleeping in, and on and on. Clay and I had enough of this guy one day and decided this gentleman needed to be introduced to Mother-In-Law, the horse. We walked by the horse with the guy in just the right position and whack, she nailed him real good in the thigh - now he had something to bitch about!! He asked to be taken out of camp early the next day and we were glad to accommodate him. We found out later that Sally took him to town and he got a room at a motel to wait for the rest of his party to finish their hunt. Some of the hunters gave us tips for helping them and some did not. I helped a hunter from Texas get a nice bull elk and he gave me a $200 tip at the end of the hunt, which was the most I received from any one hunter. Most of the hunters tipped us from $20-50 for the week and we always appreciated it. We did not get a tip from the guy Mother-In-Law kicked.

The only problem I had with this job was it was going to soon be over. Wes allowed me to shoot an elk towards the end of the season as they needed some meat for the winter and elk meat is real tasty. By the end of November the hunters were all gone, the equipment was all brought back in to the ranch and stored away. My job was done. Wes said he would like to keep me on, but they just couldn't afford to do it. I understood and said maybe we could do it again next year. I told them I would keep in touch and Sally gave me a bunch of cookies and some jerky made out of elk meat to snack on while I was traveling. I also told all of them they helped me greatly to heal from the inside because of their kindness and willingness to give me a job, I would never forget them.

CHAPTER 18

Return to Hell

My sister Cheryl had sent me some money from our parents estate and I saved most everything I made working for Wes, plus I did receive some tips from some of the hunters so I had a pretty good bank roll saved up. I decided to head south as the snow was already flying in Montana. My shoulder was near 100% healed and I was in really good shape from all the hard work we had done the last few months. I was thinking I would work my way back down to Texas and check up on Phil and the boys.

I took my time traveling south, stopping in Wyoming and Colorado whenever the mood struck me. My last time through was early summer and I had been in a hurry for some reason. This time I wanted to soak in the beauty of the country. Every place I stopped people were getting ready for Christmas. I thought about heading back to PA for the holidays and spending time with some of my family but with my parents gone I thought it would just be too painful. It was a week before Christmas and I stopped at a fancy resort just outside of Colorado Springs to check the place out and look around. This place was beautiful, log interior with a 25 foot high cathedral ceiling in the main lobby and lounge area, a massive stone fireplace in the center, the look of the old west with all the frills. I was looking around the place and a young lady said to me "hey cowboy, can I help you with something?"

Then I realized I probably looked like I didn't belong here. I was dressed in old jeans and a flannel shirt with a crusty old cowboy hat and dirty boots. Most everyone else I saw was dressed nicely and some of them were staring at me. I apologized for my appearance and said I was thinking about staying here for a while. The young lady introduced herself as Lynn and said not to worry about my appearance, she was most comfortable dressed just the way I was. Lynn explained to me this facility had it all: spas, massages, great food, live entertainment nightly, a couple of bars, indoor swimming pool, and of course skiing. She did say there were a few rooms available on a limited basis and I would have to book a room for a minimum of three nights. I told her that would not be a problem; I would like to book a room for two weeks until January 2nd. She asked me how I would be paying for my room and I said cash in advance. I was showing off a little as Lynn was a nice looking young lady and I did not see a wedding band on her finger. I counted out the cash to pay for the room and I noticed her raise her eyebrows a bit when I did that. She told me where my room was and hoped I enjoyed my stay and then told me if I needed anything to just ask for her.

This place was great; it truly did have everything. I took a shower and drove into town and bought myself some new clothes and threw away some of my old clothes, except the hat and boots. When I came back into the lobby later Lynn looked at me and said "you clean up pretty good." I asked her what time she got off work and she said 6:00pm. I asked her if she would like to have dinner with me. She said she was not supposed to date guests of the resort. I said ok, how about if she would show me a nice restaurant that was not in this resort, after all she told me if I needed anything to ask for her. She told me to meet her in the parking lot at 6:15 and we would go out for dinner. We had a nice meal at a downtown restaurant and took a drive around the area and went back to the resort for a few drinks and to listen to a country band playing at one of the bars. We danced and talked and had a very nice evening. Lynn said she was also a part time ski instructor. I told I'd never been on skis in my life. I sat up some lessons for the next afternoon and we said goodnight.

I met Lynn at 1:00pm the next afternoon and she attempted to teach me how to ski. The skiing was kind of fun, being with Lynn was more fun. I'd spent the last five months with men and horses, smelling horse sweat and their farts and pretty much smelling the same from the men - the sweet smell of a woman was a very nice change. She had more lessons in the afternoon so I decided to hang out at the indoor pool. There were a lot of young people hanging out at the pool, mostly college kids I assumed were on holiday break. They were friendly enough until they found out I was just a cowboy and then they really didn't want anything to do with me. Damn snotty rich kids. After spending time at the pool I got changed and stopped at one the bars and had a few beers. An older gentleman came in and sat beside me and introduced himself as James. He told me he was a retired engineer and asked me what I did for a living. I hesitated but told him I'd spent the last five months working at a ranch up in Montana. He said he'd always wanted to do something like that but never did and now he was probably too old. I told him the pay wasn't great and the work was hard but the fresh air and the beauty of the mountains was terrific. He said he admired men who were willing to sacrifice big money for something they enjoyed doing. We talked about various things and he kind of renewed my faith in mankind.

Lynn and I spent a great deal of time together and I was afraid she might be getting a little too serious and frankly I was afraid I might be also. One evening she took my hand and said we need to talk. She said she really liked me and enjoyed my company but she was not ready to settle down just yet. She went on to say that she planned to go back to college after she earned some money working at the resort and she didn't want to be involved too deeply with anyone until she was finished with college. I laughed and I could see it made her angry. I said I'm sorry I'm not laughing at what you just said, I completely understand. I've been trying to come up with the right words to tell you the very same thing. That's why I'm laughing. We agreed to be friends and maybe at sometime in the future we would get together again. We spent the night together and the next morning we both agreed we would remember that night for a long time. I spent two more days at the resort then it was time to move on. I told Lynn I would see her again some day and we agreed to keep in touch. After two weeks of the "good life", it was time to get back to the real world and to get away from the spoiled rich kids at the resort.

I was off to Texas and two days later on a Sunday I pulled into Big Phil's driveway. He told me the boys were out wild pig hunting and they'd better be back shortly. He welcomed me back and said he wasn't sure if he'd ever see me again. We talked about where I'd been and what I had done and Phil said "boy, sounds like you been living your dream." Then he slapped me on the back with his big hand and said let's have a beer.

Big Phil said it was good timing on my part, because the next night they were having a bar-b-que. That was if the boys got their asses back here with a couple of pigs. He told me my old room was available but I might have to clean it up some. He had a few men here earlier to help with the fall roundup and they left things pretty messy and he hadn't gotten around to cleaning it up yet. Pretty messy was an understatement: beer cans, whiskey bottles, cigarette butts, tobacco juice in cups and God only knows what else. These guys were hogs; they should have been shot and bar-b-qued!! I decided to sleep in my truck and clean up the mess the next day. Sometime late that night I heard the boys come back and it wasn't long before one of them was pounding on my truck. It was Tom and he wondered if I had to take a piss. I thanked him for his concern and stuck the barrel of my shotgun out the door and told them to let me alone. But that didn't happen, I had to get up and have a beer with them. We had a good time talking and I had to hear about their pig hunt; they shot four of them so the bar-b-que was on. I went back to bed and I think at some point they did also.

The next morning I cleaned out the bunkhouse, which took half of the day, what a mess! Big Phil came out after I was done, (I think he was waiting until I was done) and said "boy, ya'll can stay here as long as ya'll want for cleaning up this pig pen." He told me the shindig was going to start around 4:00pm and I'd better put on my Sunday clothes 'cause there was going to be a lot of people here tonight. Lucky for me, I just bought some new duds up in Colorado Springs.

Big Phil had a big house and it was jammed full of people. It was a lively party: dancing, good food, plenty to drink, and my three sidekicks to keep things wound up. These guys were always up to something - spiking somebody's drink, trying to dance with every woman in the crowd, grab assing anybody, and they loved annoying Big Phil, who would threaten to kill them routinely. Later in the evening, I bumped into Phil's friend Martin. We talked a bit and he told me the job offer was still open. I said if he liked I could stop by the next day to talk about it further. He told me to stop by around 1:00pm. It seemed like there were a lot of wealthy people at this party and I got the impression there was a lot of business being conducted here as well, despite the boys' antics.

The next day I went to Martin's place and he told me he would like to see me shoot and see how I could handle myself. He had a shooting range set up behind his barn with targets out to 500 yards. He brought out a Weatherby 300 mag. and some beer cans and asked if I thought I could them at 500 yards. I said "yes sir, if the gun shoots, I can hit them." He rode his four wheeler out and sat up the cans then came back and handed me some ammo and told me the gun was sighted in for 200 yards. My first shot was a little low and kicked up some dirt on the cans. The second and third shoots each hit a can. Martin said that was ok. Next he took me to a horse barn that had an obstacle course set up inside. I had not done this for a while but wrestling horses, saddles, and packs and climbing mountains for months made this seem easy. I got through the course alright and asked Martin what was next. He took me into another room where two men were sparring on a mat. The room was lined with mats on the walls and the entire floor. I thought to myself this was no fly by night operation. Martin said "welcome to my rubber room." He introduced me to Gene and Howie, who were two of his employees. He said he would like to see me use some defensive moves against Gene first. Gene came at me hard and took me down, he wasn't screwing around. He let me up and turned aside and then came at me with a piece of 2 x 4. I disarmed him, took him down and pressed the 2 x 4 into his neck. Before I could react Howie grabbed me from behind and picked me off the mat and body slammed me back down. He was a big man so I went after his legs; he laid a forearm on the back of my neck that hurt like hell. I was able to flip him and put reverse pressure on his right elbow and wrist to immobilize him with my foot on the back of his neck. And he was done. We all shook hands and Martin said "ok boy, now we will talk some more." Martin told me he had me checked out and I was a good soldier. He went on to say he needed some help in Central America and that I would be gone from two weeks to a month.

If I wanted the job, I would spend a week training with the team that would be going down there. This job would pay $4500 a month and all my expenses would be paid while I was there. We would be providing security for important people down there. If I was interested he would need an answer in two days. I told him I would give him an answer by the next day. I thought about it hard - this was what I did best, the money was great, and I missed the excitement, why not? I called Martin that night and said let's do it. It was time to get a real job; playtime was over. I guess I was lost for a while but the last few months really helped to clear my head. I really liked working for Wes and Sally up in Montana but it wasn't enough to live on. I called my sister Cheryl and the Morgan's and told them of my plans and that I may not be in touch with them for a while. None of them seemed very happy with my decision but it was my decision. Nobody ever mentioned the word mercenary, but I knew enough about what was going on to know that's what we were. I bumped into a few mercs in the Nam and they were a hard nosed bunch.

I made arrangements with Big Phil to leave my truck and some of my things at his place. He told me he could not guarantee the boys would not strip it and sell it for parts while I was gone but he'd try to take care of it and he told me to be careful. The following day I was on an airplane with Martin to Houston to meet the rest of the team. Our headquarters were in an old airplane hanger, which looked like crap on the outside but was ultra modern inside. There I met the rest of my team: Mike Graham, Chris Taylor, Ken Murray and Ron Michaels. All were former military and looked to be in good shape. Mike and Chris were Marines and the others were Army. Martin told Mike to show me around as he talked with the other guys. These guys had top notch equipment: night scopes and binoculars, custom made sniper rifles, Colt revolvers, H&K semi-autos, grenade launchers, M16s - all top of the line weapons.

Mike said he heard I could shoot and told me to pick out a weapon. I looked them over and picked out a synthetic stocked .300 Win. Mag. on a Winchester Model 70 frame. He asked me why I picked that weapon when there were more modern weapons here. I told him it's mostly what I used in the Nam and I was comfortable with it. I fit it up to my shoulder and told him it was a little long in the stock. Mike said "no problem" and took me back into a room that was a dream come true for any gunsmith. There was any piece of equipment you might need. Mike introduced me to Bob the gunsmith and told me Bob would do what ever I wanted done to the gun. I told Bob what I would like and he said it would be ready the next afternoon. I also asked Bob if he could load up some 176 grain Sierra Boattail ammo for the gun and he said it was already done and handed me a case of 500 rounds. I asked him how the hell he knew what load I would like. He told me Martin called him two days ago and told him to make up my favorite load. I guess Martin really did have me checked out - I was impressed!

Mike and I talked a while and he asked me about my experience in combat. I told him where I'd been and what I'd done. He shared with me he had been at Khe Sahn when Charlie hammered the hell out of them. He said we probably wouldn't get involved in anything like that but we could get into some deep shit. He wondered if I had a problem with a Marine covering my ass. I said I didn't have a problem with that as long as he didn't give me a rash of shit about how much better the Marines were than the Army. I told him I was a hell of a good scout and could shoot the asshole out of a mosquito at 100 yards. He said he could live with that and he would have a mosquito for me to shoot at the next day.

Chris was a demolitions expert and kind of scary; he was always looking at something and trying to figure out how to blow it up. Ken was the electronics and communications guy and Ron was the team leader:

he was a deal maker, a hustler, and the kind of guy who made things happen. He was a supply Sergeant in the Army and had some combat experience, along with the scars to prove it. These guys were all hard core and experienced combat veterans. I was the new guy and would have to prove myself to them.

The next day at the shooting range, I saw a giant cardboard mosquito about four feet wide by four feet high with a bullseye in the center of it at the 1000 yard target. Mike said since I was in the Army he would not hold me to the high standards of the Marine Corps. The bet was on. I laid $20 on the table and Mike laid $40 down saying he wouldn't even get his gun out for $20, so I matched his $40. I told him to call the shot and he called closest to the bullseye. My shot cut the bottom of the bullseye at 6:00. His shot was ¼" to the right of the bullseye and I took his $40. Mike looked at me and laughed "ok kid, now let's shoot. Can you see that skeeter's eye?" I said "yeah, old man, I can see it." I guessed the eye was about 3" in diameter and there was a slight breeze blowing from the right. Mike told me to take the shot when I was ready and "oh, by the way, this shot is for $100." I made my adjustments and the shot hit low by ¾". Mike took his shot and it looked good but too close to call from this distance. When we got closer his shot was 1/8" closer than mine. I shook his hand and gave him the $100. I thought he would gloat but instead he said "kid, you can shoot." He asked me what they called me in the Nam and I told him they called me Dirt Hog and explained why. He said that was cool and he would call me Dirt. I asked him what I should call him and he said with a smile "Sir." He laughed and said I could call him Beans; the boys in his platoon gave him that name because of his love of baked beans.

We spent the rest of the week training, learning each other's body language, going over our mission and alternate plans. We boarded a jet and were on our way to Nicaragua. We landed at an out of the way airstrip and we were met by two locals who drove us to a beautiful home on the outskirts of a town. Our job was to provide security for some politician. Apparently there were some insurgents who wanted him dead. I'm sure there was a whole lot more to the story than we were told, but we didn't care as long as we got paid. Mike and I helped Chris set up some explosives around the property at various locations and we also put up some signal wires around the perimeter. All five of us were equipped with remote communications equipment and we could talk to each other 24-7. Mike and I took turns observing and resting for four days without incident. On the fifth day, the guy was going to move from the property, wherever he went – we went. We called him Butch because we didn't know his name.

We did this for three weeks with a minimal amount of incidents. We didn't have to fire a shot and only had to get physical a few times. It was pretty boring but at least we were not getting shot at. The last week of our tour went without incident as well. We were replaced by another team and we flew back home. The only significant thing I did while there was take down a couple of guys and pat them down for weapons.

We had a week off before our next mission and I hung around the Houston area. It was a nice place with lots of things to do and see. I spent some time fishing and hanging out with my team going over our next mission. We would be leaving for Cambodia and I thought about quitting, - I really didn't want to go back there - but I'm not a quitter. Mike wanted to go back and talked me into going. It seemed like he had some unfinished business but he never told me about it. Maybe I did also; the bastards did kill my best friend Snake. Our job was to go places the military could not or would not go. We were hired to protect private business interests in that country from Viet Cong takeover and we were told we would come home when the job was done.

Three days later, we were on a plane to Cambodia. I could smell that damn jungle before we got there. Our first assignment was to root out the enemy and secure the perimeter of an area that contained a few large buildings and what appeared to be a few housing units on the outskirts of a village. There were people moving in and out of the buildings and trucks moving in and out as well. There was some kind of manufacturing going on but we were not told what. Our first day we set up a wire and booby trapped a number of possible entry points. The compound was surrounded by a chain link fence but the fence was in poor condition. There were four security guards inside the compound and they were provided with specially marked jackets so we would not shoot them. The people inside the compound were instructed to wear a specially marked vest when they were outside for the same reason. Our orders were to shoot anyone not wearing the specially marked clothing. I hoped the people that worked there didn't forget their vests or it would be their last day of work.

Chris was in hog heaven setting up explosive charges all over the place. We cleared out the compound and inside the wire; it was secure for now. We blocked the entry points with barrels and pallets to try to funnel any intruders into a position that would give us a shot. I used one of my old tricks and put some rice at different places to attract the birds. If the birds flushed someone was coming. We were ready.

That evening everyone coming out of the buildings was wearing the proper clothing, good for them. The only intruders we had were a couple of stray dogs. The next two days were much the same and very boring. At the end of the fourth day a truck pulled up to the gate and it appeared to be broken down. It could be nothing or it could be a diversion. Mike and I were watching the back of the compound and we saw movement just outside the wire.

Chris had charges set up in that area and before we knew it, there was an explosion and we saw bodies flying through the air. We heard gunfire from the other end of the compound; the truck was loaded with enemy on the back. Game on!! Mike and I turned our attention to the gate where the gooks were trying to break through. It's all instinct from here; I was working my bolt, finding a target and moving to the next target. We kept them outside the gate and had them in a crossfire. Mike tossed a grenade at the truck and disabled it. A bullet struck the tree beside me and I turned to see two gooks running down hill at me. I shot one of them with my .45 and the other one was on top of me before I could fire at him. I shrugged him off my shoulders and he rolled off me and I was able to shoot him as he rolled away from me. I could hear Mike firing but I didn't know what he was firing at. Mike and I were standing back to back waiting for more, but it was over for now. We both thought we were ok and started to look around for any stragglers. We made sure the gooks were dead and I saw Mike take his knife out and remove something from each of the bodies. He came back to me with his hand all bloody and handed me two ears he cut off the men I killed. He said we would get $20 a piece for them in Saigon. I knew guys did this but I never did, I wasn't going to start now. I told Mike to keep mine if he wanted them, I didn't want them.

We worked our way down to the gate and met up with the other guys. Everybody was ok and we started looking around for any stragglers. We had five dead from our location; there were five more dead from the explosion at the rear and seven dead from the truck. Some of the locals helped to clean up the mess and took anything of value from the dead. I watched them picking around the bodies and knew they would do the same to me if they had the opportunity. The rest of our group went to repair the damage to the wire and fence from the explosions.

We spent the next six months in that area and had Charlie running scared. The Cambodian Army was gaining confidence in policing the area with our help and was able to take over. We were moved to another area and spent quite a bit of time training with the Hmong people and making hits on enemy leaders. Mike and I were doing a lot of hit and run ambushes and we found out we had a bounty on our heads. Ken showed us a couple of posters he found in a village and warned us to stay out of the villages. The bounty on us was equal to $500 US each, which was a lot of money to these people. He and I tried to lay low as much as we could and we pretty much lived in the jungle 24-7. Our other team members kept us supplied with food and other rations at different drop points. In a sick kind of way, I was actually enjoying living like this. The killing was an adventure and the adrenalin high always there. We lived like animals for almost three months, always on the move, looking for the next kill. How did that happen? I lost respect for the enemy, and was enjoying the killing. Mike had a whole damn bag full of ears he dragged around with him.

We were nearing a year since we had been in the states and it was starting to feel like this was home. I no longer minded the heat and humidity, the bugs and snakes and rats, I didn't sweat as much as I used to, my senses were at an all time high, I could smell people before I could see them, my hearing was much more acute, I had become the type of cold blooded killer that my former Army soldiers used to accuse me of being. Mike and I both felt nobody could catch us.

The day arrived when Ron came looking for us. We had not seen him for almost a month although we did communicate with him by radio. We found him. He looked at us and shook his head saying "you guys look like cave men." I suppose we did, we had not shaved in a while and our hair was long. He told us we moving down into the Mekong Delta where we had a new assignment. On the way out, he told us our first assignment was to get a bath, shave, and a haircut. We took a bath, but only trimmed our hair and beards.

In the Delta, we were protecting some private interests moving material up and down the river. It was more relaxed than in the jungle. We rotated time riding the boats and guarding warehouses, no running through the jungle like wild men, it was a piece of cake for Mike and me. Mostly we took down and blew up other boats that were trying to overtake the ones we were on. We carried rocket launchers and if they looked kinky, we took them out. The crews on the boats would put targets on the shore line and they would bet each other that we could hit the targets with our rifles while we were moving on the river. I enjoyed showing off for these guys and sometimes I would loan one of them my gun. One day one of the crew offered me a joint because I made him a pile of money that day. I took it and got stoned along with the beer I was drinking. Big mistake!! One joint led to another and another. I didn't know or care at the time but I was hooked. It seemed the pot gave me more courage; it certainly made me more stupid. I started doing some risky things, foolish things.

I still had a price on my head but thought nobody would recognize me because I kept the beard and long hair. I used to make fun of guys with their hair in a ponytail and now I was one! I went into a local village bar two nights in a row, which I had never done before. It was a rule I lived by for several years, never go to the same place twice. On the first night I was stoned and shooting my mouth off and everybody left me alone. On the second night when I walked in the locals were looking at me differently. I could see them pointing at me and in my arrogance I thought it was because they were afraid of me. Ron and Ken went with me because they could not talk me out of going. Chris followed us and came in alone, unknown to me. Mike stayed away because he had a bounty on him as well.

I drank one beer and a group of VC surrounded us at the bar. We all drew our side arms and faced the group of six men. They drew their weapons as well and we had a Mexican standoff. One of them said in broken English "we want this man", pointing to me, "we want no trouble with the two of you, you may go." I saw Chris sneaking up behind the man doing the talking and Chris pulled the pin on a grenade and put a choke hold on the guy. Chris was waving the grenade around with one hand and dragging the guy around with his other hand. In a few seconds there were only five of us left in the bar.

In one of the few sober moments I'd had for a while, I asked Ron "what do we do now?" Ron said we go to plan "B" and got on the radio to Mike and said "come and get us now!" The VC Chris had hold of passed out and he let him fall on the floor. Ron said Mike would be here shortly, be ready. Mike came flying in with the jeep, blowing the horn and flashing the lights. We ran out the door firing our handguns in the air and everybody outside scattered. We piled in the jeep and took off out of the village. Once we were in the clear Mike stopped the jeep and punched me in the mouth. He said "you stupid bastard, you could have gotten us all killed!" Then he handed me a beer and we all laughed like hell. Chris still had the grenade in his hand with the pin pulled and was laughing harder than any of us. He said "it's a dummy; you guys don't think I'd pop a live grenade do ya?" Yeah Chris, we think you would!

We were all a bit out of control and we were stoned most of the time. A lot of days we didn't even go on patrol. That was the main difference between military and mercenary, lack of discipline. Looking back we probably killed some people who didn't need killing because we just didn't care anymore.

We were in country for almost eighteen months and we needed to get out of there. We'd become sloppy and one or all of us was going to die. We were lucky so far; all of us had some close calls and a few cuts and scrapes here and there but no serious wounds. I once prided myself on being careful and moving quietly and unseen, now I didn't care who saw me. We talked tough but we all knew it was time to go home. I overheard Ron talking to Martin on the phone the next day and he told Martin to come get us out of here; we are done in and burned out. Some of it was the drugs, pot, heroin and the booze, some of it was we were starting to think we were indestructible. There was no honor in what we were doing anymore. We were simply paid to kill people and we didn't care who it was.

In two days, we were on a plane heading back to the States. Martin welcomed us back to Texas and said "you guys look like hell." I got a hotel room in Houston and for the first time in 18 months, I took a good look at myself in the mirror. It's not what I thought I would look like. I was 23 years old and saw a bearded, long haired, darkly tanned, rough and scared-looking man much older; I'd gone from 210 pounds down to 175 pounds, mostly from living on booze and drugs.

I sat in the shower for a long time and reflected back on what I had done. Overall we did a good job, we did what we were paid to do, and at times we were brutal and merciless. The shower hid my tears, and for the first time in a long time, I asked God to forgive me for the things I had done. I was asking myself questions like what the hell does God know about where we have been. How do I tell people I know where I have been and what I have done for the last 18 months? I decided the only people I would discuss it with would be those who had been there themselves.

The bed felt wonderful, the sheets smelled so fresh, I slept for 12 hours. I woke up with my hands shaking, my mind racing and unable to sit still, I needed a fix. I tore through my duffle bag and found a joint, the last one I had and burned it down. I was ok, I didn't think I was hooked, I supposed everybody who was hooked thought that. Mike came up to my room and said let's go, Martin wants to buy us some good old Texas steaks. That sounded good to me. I had not had a steak since we killed a water buffalo back in Cambodia six months ago. We met with Martin at a steakhouse and he picked up the tab for dinner and drinks. After dinner, he gave each of us $2000 cash and said "ya'll boys are going to Acapulco for two weeks on me for some R & R. You're rooms are booked and the jet will fly you down there tomorrow. When you get back we will talk about your next assignment."

I thought that was really generous of Martin and wondered out loud to Mike after we left the steakhouse "how he could afford to do all this?" Mike looked at me and asked "you really don't know do you Kid?" I asked "know what?" Mike said "the drugs man, what the hell you think we been guarding all this time?" I had my suspicions, but I really didn't know for sure that's what was so valuable to these people. I felt really stupid. I guess in my mind it was ok to be fighting for some idealistic cause or to try to free some oppressed people, but not for drugs. All the killing we did was to make a pile of money for some guys I didn't even know, it made me sick to my stomach. I threw up right there on the street. Mike looked at me and said "you stupid bastard, you think we'd go over there to help those worthless SOB's just out of the goodness of our hearts? Hell man, how do you think these guys can live like kings, and pay you and me more money than we've ever seen, simply by selling cows?" I guess I just didn't think. I went back to my room; I was embarrassed to realize I was so naive.

I got up the next morning and had breakfast with the boys but I didn't say much. Ron took me aside and said "look man, I overheard your conversation with Mike last night; I know how you are feeling. I was there myself, when I found out it was heroin we were babysitting. Right now you're thinking about quitting and feeling foolish. The bottom line is – where the hell are you going to make this kind of money with the skills you have? You're one of the best I've ever served with, this war ain't gonna' last for ever, why not make money while you can? You do not owe anybody anything, you got your ass shot up for your country and your country doesn't care." That bastard could talk anybody out of anything; he should have been a politician. I said "ok, let's go have some fun."

Acapulco was terrific, beautiful beaches, beautiful women, lots of food and booze; I didn't want to go home. While we were all on the beach one day with our shirts off, I noticed all of us had battle scars. As kids, my friends and I talked about battle scars, little cuts and scrapes that our mothers would patch up, mom would even call them battle scars. These were real battle scars; Ron had scars on both legs from shrapnel, Ken had burn scars on his arms and chest from a gas explosion, Chris had scars on his back and was missing half of his left ear from a miscalculation on a booby trap and Mike had scars on his chest, right arm and chin from being shot. I had my scars on my shoulder, leg and arm from being shot and stabbed. We all had little scars on our faces and arms from running through the jungle and getting tangled up with barbed wire. I was sure we looked like a motley crew to the fancy people who were also on the beaches.

One day on the beach, we joined with some college boys playing volleyball. We got a little rough with them and one of them told us we were a bunch of animals. We didn't care; we took it as a compliment. If they knew they played volleyball with five hit men, they might have been a little more respectful.

A few times we would be watching a newscast on TV in a bar and they would show shots of the war in Vietnam. Usually someone else in the bar would make comments about baby killers or something else stupid like that and we would want to rip their heads off but we never did. Once a particularly obnoxious gentleman commented how he was ashamed to be an American because of how out of control the soldiers were in Vietnam. My friends and I moved closer to his table and began conversing about where we were station in the Nam and the distaste we had for people who judged us without ever having been there. The gentleman and his wife left the bar.

None of us realized how arrogant and cocky we really were. We bullied people we didn't like and probably some we did like. It was a way of life for us - kill or be killed - it was difficult to turn it off when we did not have to be that way. We forgot how to act in a civilized society; we really did not fit in. I had begun to accept that this was who I was. After two weeks of fun in the sun, we wore out our welcome with the beautiful people. We'd been thrown out of a few bars and made asses out of ourselves most everyplace we went. It was time to get back to our world.

We flew back to Texas, all of us a bit restless with this docile lifestyle. Martin gave us a choice, we could go back to Cambodia and do some training for the government troops there or we could go to Africa. We talked it over and none of us wanted to go back to Cambodia. We were going to Africa, South Africa to be exact.

Our mission, we were told, was to again provide security, assist the government forces in putting down some civil unrest. Little did we know it would be over two years before we would set foot on U.S. soil again.

Africa was a different world: it was beautiful mountains with abundant game animals, vast grasslands like I'd never seen before, but they still had their share of those damn jungles as well. We trained troops in weapons handling, taught them about explosives, and tried our best to teach them all we could about staying alive. We moved from district to district and quickly learned not to trust anyone. These were very poor people and a lot of them would do anything for money. We had to watch each others' backs all the time. We often wondered if one of the troops we were training would end up killing us someday.

We were still smoking pot and using some heroin and the addiction was becoming a problem for all of us. We befriended an American doctor at a remote hospital who agreed to help us kick our addiction before it ended up kicking us in the ass. In return, we would provide the hospital and surrounding area with protection. For most of us it took two miserable weeks to get over the withdrawal symptoms and I know I was one mean SOB while going through it. Doc watched over us and made sure we didn't do something stupid. We each spent some down time when the withdrawal was at it worst and everybody steered clear of us when that was going on. Chris had the hardest time and we almost lost him a couple of times but he pulled through it and the entire experience made us closer as a unit. We owed Doc a lot and when we were all healthy again we raised hell with the local rebels. We led raids on the rebel strongholds for over a month and the area became known as off limits to them. The rebels called us the "White Lions." They didn't like us, but they respected us. We left a platoon in the area of the hospital to provide protection for Doc and his staff and never told anyone when we finally had to leave the area.

I thought I was pretty tough and I'd been hunting and killing for over four years but I never saw the level of mutilation I saw in the State of Rhodesia. Some of these rebels were brutal: they butchered people, and had very little respect for human life. It was one thing to kill an enemy who was trying to kill you, but this was a nasty place. There were times we wished we had not trained the troops we did. They were nearly as brutal as the rebels we were fighting. Many times we pulled our troops off bodies to keep them from cutting them up after they were dead. We moved from border to border, we really didn't know or care what country we were in as long as we got paid. I knew at this point we were at times protecting drug manufacturers and diamond smugglers, and the rest of the time taking out "enemies of the government."

Our team lost Ken the first year we were there. He was hit by enemy fire one evening while patrolling a work site. The rebels took his body and we heard from some of the local villagers that they cut off his head and put it on a pole and danced around it that night. They had a dance where each of us was killed by them and whoever killed us was a great warrior. The next evening we led a party of locals and hunted down the tribe of rebels responsible for Ken's death and killed them all, with great satisfaction. We found one individual with a carved wooden lion painted white hanging around his neck and assumed he was responsible for Ken's death. This time we did not stop the locals from mutilating the bodies. We did find Ken's head on a pole and most of the rest of his body and gave him a proper burial. It was a gruesome sight and one none of us would ever forget.

All three of us had some close calls and we all the scars to show for it - both physical and emotional. I'd never seen so many thorns. It seemed like every tree and bush had thorns on them. Snakes, lions, leopards, wild dogs, elephants, and hyenas along with the native people combined to keep us on edge most of the time.

It was not all bad though; this was a big game hunters' paradise. The abundance of wild game was incredible. We spent what little free time we had hunting and learning the native culture. We donated the meat from the game we killed to the local villagers and wherever we went we were welcomed. We all became hooked on learning from these people instead of drugs. Doc did us a great favor by helping us get sober and whenever we were near his hospital we helped out anyway we could. The terrain varied from open grassland to thick jungles. From steep, rugged mountains to flat grasslands where you could see for miles, Africa was as diverse as the US. I was particularly interested in the native culture and their tracking ability. These people were the most skilled trackers I had ever seen - without them we would never have been as successful as we were at our jobs. They taught me more in two years than I had learned in the previous twenty years. I came to love these people for their love of the land and the things in it. Compared to them, I was rich but I envied them. Despite the turmoil and unrest, I could make my home there.

I had one boy who accompanied me wherever I went, as did each of the other men in my unit. They were our interpreters, guides, and constant companions. Harold Motomba had become my friend. I did not like anyone calling Harold my "boy", which was the custom of most of the whites. I had no problem correcting folks who called him boy. They were told his name was Harold and I did not want him called boy. Harold was my gopher and my eyes and ears. He had incredible instincts, and I guess after a lifetime of being put down, it was difficult for him to look at himself as an equal to me, in my mind he was. Harold taught me things about tracking I never imagined I could learn. He once led us across a dry, parched desert ground that I thought had no sign at all, directly to a rebel compound. We would never have found it on our own.

We were nearing 24 months in this place and we were preparing to go home. The troops we trained were somewhat capable of maintaining some stability and it was now up to them to do it. I promised Harold that one day I would return and I would find him. We exchanged gifts - I gave Harold one of my rifles and he gave me a necklace he made. In the center of the necklace was a white lion he carved out of elephant ivory, it became one of my most prized possessions. Harold and I talked earlier about him coming with me to America but he felt his place was here with his people and maybe he would not fit in very well in our world. I thought to myself I didn't know if I could fit in my world anymore.

CHAPTER 19

Back to the World, Again

We flew out of Johannesburg, South Africa, and headed back to Texas, which I was starting to think of as home. This time we were one man short. It was weird being back home; I had trouble adjusting to the peace and quiet. I couldn't sleep for more than two hours at a time; I kept waking up thinking it was my turn to stand watch. Loud noises still made me jumpy and I was afraid I would have a repeat of my encounter at the cabinet factory years earlier. I felt naked not carrying around a weapon even though I had my handgun on me. The nightmares were back and I relived the past few years in my mind almost every night.

I'd been able to save a lot of money because I never got time to spend it. I told Martin I was going to take some time off and would call him when I was ready to go back to work. He said he would keep in touch and he had more work for me to do when ever I was ready. He took me back to Big Phil's to get my truck and on the drive back he indicated his business was expanding and he had plans for me but we would talk about it later; he told me to go and relax for a while. That old truck was like an old friend; it just felt good to sit in it, like my security blanket I guess.

I spent a few days loafing around in some bars and doing a lot of thinking. One day I tried to add up how many people I killed; I couldn't remember them all. As near as I could figure it must have been around 200. I was proud of the time I spent in the military but not so proud of the last 3 ½ years.

I called my sister Cheryl and told her I was back in the country and would like to see her. After she got finished chewing me out for not keeping in contact for the last few years, she agreed it was time for us to get together. I told her I would pay for an airline ticket for her and her husband to fly down to Houston and spend the weekend or what ever worked for her if she was interested. She informed me I would only need to buy one ticket as she and Jack had been divorced for over a year, something I would have known if I could remember to pick up the telephone and call her. She reminded me it had been almost two years since she had heard from me. I told her I would explain when she got here. She told me she was actually free this weekend and could use a few days away. I made airline arrangements for her and got a room for her at the hotel I was staying at.

Cheryl arrived Friday evening and it was great to see her. I could see from the expression on her face she was surprised by my appearance. She looked at me and said "Oh my God, you look so different." I didn't realize the last time I saw her I was Mr. Clean-cut. I now had a full beard and long hair and I'm sure I looked a lot older than I was. Cheryl was eight years older than me but didn't look it. We hugged and talked a bit and she said she was tired and ready to get some sleep. On the way from the airport to our hotel, she asked me where I'd been and what I was doing. I told her I was in Africa for the past two years and was unable to contact her at all. I did not give her a lot of details other than we provided security for different agencies. When we got to the hotel I told her to get some sleep and we would have all day tomorrow to get caught up with each others' lives and she agreed.

The next morning, we had a late breakfast and I gave her a tour of the Houston area. Like most women, I knew she liked to shop so I took her to a large shopping mall to do her thing. I normally don't like shopping but it was nice to be able to spend time together. I noticed she wasn't buying anything and figured she didn't have any money. I took her to a higher end clothing store and told her to pick out anything she liked and it would be my treat. She said that wasn't necessary. I told her it was because I left her with a lot of loose ends to tie up after our parents died and I always felt guilty about it. She looked at me and winked and said ok, she would be glad to help me get over some of that guilt. Besides, I told her I could afford it and it would make me happy to buy something for my big sister. She said I was her favorite little brother (and only little brother). Cheryl picked out some nice things and they looked great on her.

We went to a show that evening and had dinner at a nice restaurant.

Cheryl kept asking me about my life and after a few drinks I started telling her some things about the Nam and my job as a mercenary.

I told her I'd done some things that I was not proud of but I felt it was what I did best. She told me about her and Jack breaking up because of an affair she had with her boss and how it really screwed up her life. She got another job with a competitor and was making good money but she was not really happy with her life right now. Jack moved away and she had no contact with him since the divorce was final. Cheryl told me it was really important to her that she and I stay in touch with each other. Since her divorce, our two older sisters, who really liked Jack, had pretty much ignored her and she felt I was all the family she had left. That's why she was so pissed at me for not hearing from me for so long. I promised I would call or write as often as I could and told her I was getting tired of the life I was living. But I didn't know what else I could do to make a living. She grabbed my hand and said I could do anything I wanted with my life, after I got a shave and a haircut!!

I realized how much I missed my sister and having contact with family. My focus for so long was finding the next thrill or adventure that I really didn't take time to care about anybody but myself since Jake died. Cheryl told me she didn't care what I had done or what I did for a living, I was her brother and she loved me and nothing would ever change that. The next day as she was getting ready to board her plane I assured her she would be hearing from me on a more regular basis. We promised each other we would get together at least once a year and more frequently if possible. She left me with some words that really stuck – She said "I needed to focus on the people who were still alive and who cared about me and honor those who were gone by making something good out of my life." She always was the smart one in the family.

Cheryl was right - I did spend too much time thinking about those people I knew who were dead; there were a lot of them. I thought about Jake almost everyday. It hit me I needed to go visit Bill and Mary Morgan. The next day I took off for Arkansas. I got to the Morgan's on a Thursday and they welcomed me as if I were one of their own. I hadn't seen them for over three years, although I did speak to them on the phone a few times. Mary looked at me and said "boy, I need to fatten you up." She was also the second woman in a short time who told me I needed a haircut and shave. Bill said "Son, you look like you've been through hell." I didn't think he realized what he'd just said. He called me son and it hit me like a mortar round in my chest. I cried uncontrollably for a few minutes before I could talk. I thanked them for being so kind to me and told Bill no one had called me son since my parents had died and it really touched me. With my parents gone, these two were a wonderful adopted family.

We talked for a while and we shared what was going on in our lives. I told them I was sorry for not keeping in touch very often; it was difficult to find a phone where I was the last few years. Bill told me he quit his job over a year ago and was doing evangelistic work full time. Ben was in college and he and Mary were traveling the country preaching and teaching. They would actually be leaving on Saturday for some services in a town about 100 miles east of there. They suggested I go with them but I begged off and came up with a lame excuse of having a job interview back in Texas. I couldn't remember the last time I was in a church. Mary went into the kitchen to fix something to eat and Bill said to me "I see a lot of pain in your eyes." My reply was "I guess I'm just tired." He told me whenever I was ready, we would talk.

I felt really bad about lying to these folks about having a job interview and I apologized to Bill for doing it. I told him I'd done some things I wasn't proud of: I'd done drugs, I drank a lot, I'd killed a lot of people for money, slept with women all over the world and treated some of them badly. In my mind I was the last person God would want to see in a church. Bill laughed and said "you dumb ass, you're exactly the type of person God wants to see in church. Do you remember the first time we met, I told you God brought you and Jake together and later he brought you here to meet with Mary, Ben and me? Neither God nor I care what you've done with your past; we care what you do with the rest of your life. You loved our son like a brother and I don't know if you realize it or not from the first day we met you; we've loved you like a son as well." With tears running down my cheeks I asked Bill if that was his sermon for the day. He said that was no sermon, just honest feelings. This big, tough, mister macho was brought to his knees by mere words.

Bill forced me to look deep inside myself. I felt a lot of guilt for some of the things I had done. Bill prayed that I would release these things over to God - I tried to comply. He prayed for me for over an hour and I felt a huge weight leave my shoulders. When I looked up I was staring at a picture of Jake hanging on the wall. I told Bill if he didn't mind, maybe I would go with them on their trip and would really be glad to spend more time with them. Maybe I could learn more about this God stuff.

We arrived at a big church and enjoyed a meal prepared by the members of the church. I saw a poster hanging on the wall advertising

Morgan Ministries and apparently they were very good at what they did. I was a little embarrassed because I didn't have a suit or sports coat, just a pair of good jeans and a fancy western shirt. Most all of the men had suits on and the ladies were dressed well also. There must have been 200 – 300 people there. I was very uncomfortable being around this many people. I was used to hiding from them, not trusting anyone and I did not like anyone approaching me from the rear. I usually stood with my back against the wall. Bill preached a wonderful sermon on service to the church and Mary sang a few songs - she had a beautiful voice. Bill had an altar call to close the service and Mary sang very softly. It was very moving and I felt butterflies in my stomach each time Bill said come, come and let Jesus touch your heart. I felt drawn to go forward but did not. After the service they introduced me as a friend of the family and I was proud to be with them. Everyone was very polite and I thought to myself – if these church people knew who I really was they wouldn't be so happy to meet me.

The next day I went out and bought myself a couple of sport coats and ties and a new pair of cowboy boots. I stopped by a barber shop and got my hair and beard trimmed; I wasn't one of these people, but maybe I could look like them. When I got back to where we were staying, Bill and Mary were counting money from the previous night's collection. It had to be several hundred dollars. Bill must have seen the surprised look on my face and asked "You didn't think we did this just for fun did you?" I didn't know what to say, so I just said something stupid like "I didn't know." Bill said they didn't get into evangelism for the money, they felt they were called by God to do it. However they were doing quite well financially. I was glad for them.

I showed them my new duds and Mary gave me a big hug and a kiss. She rubbed my head and said I would turn some heads tonight. Bill said he would like me to come up front with him tonight and he would like to introduce me. I told him I didn't feel comfortable about that. He said that night's message was about sacrifice and forgiveness and he would be talking about Jake and the sacrifice he made for his country. He wouldn't ask me to say anything if I didn't want to, but he would be honored to have me on stage with him and Mary. How could I say no?

There were even more people attending the service that night. I was very nervous about being on the stage, sweat was pouring off me and it wasn't even hot in the sanctuary. That night Mary sang first, her singing was hypnotic to me - she had wonderful range. She could be a gravely alto and range up to a low soprano. I closed my eyes and my mind drifted to some of my boyhood memories. Mary's voice reminded me of Stevie Nix of the group Fleetwood Mac. Bill's sermon touched everyone and it was completely quiet in the church. He cried at times when mentioning Jake, as Mary sat beside me and held my hand. Bill shocked me when he said he no longer grieved for his son. He said he knew his son knew the Lord and he had made the ultimate sacrifice for his country. He said he missed his son everyday but knew that someday they would be together again forever. He then said God certainly does provide when we have a loss or are in need. Bill asked me to come forward and he introduced me. He said when the Lord took away his son; he sent him another one. A very special one, his son's best friend and partner in Vietnam, someone who spent almost two years with his son and experienced everything his son did. Someone who was willing to share those experiences with him and Mary and someone who was searching for something when he met Bill and his family.

I couldn't have spoken if I wanted to do so. Part of me wanted to say thank you to Bill for his words and part of me was choking back tears again. This God stuff sure seemed to make you cry a lot, and I was feeling very much out of control of my emotions. I was trained to not show emotion, and I was very uncomfortable.

Bill's message was clear and powerful and there were many people sobbing in the pews. I was struck by the command he had over the people, he was able to control their emotions with his words, sometimes humorous and like now reaching into their hearts and evoking compassion from them. Bill then made an altar call with Mary singing in the background. A lot of people came forward and Bill and the local Pastor prayed for them. They hung around the altar for a long time praying with each other, holding hands, some of them kneeling, others standing and swaying to the music, it was very moving. I was touched by the whole experience, but was also skeptical. Was this real or was it a show? Was Bill able to reach inside these people's emotions and make them feel good for the moment? Inside of me was still a hard ass that didn't trust anyone. I wasn't sure if I was ready to buy into this whole church thing. I loved Bill and Mary but I wasn't ready to accept this yet.

After the service, Bill winked at me and said "thanks man, you helped me hook them tonight." I asked Bill if all that emotion was real and all that "Jesus will make you feel good stuff was real?" He asked if I felt butterflies in my stomach and felt something pulling at me to go to the altar and if I did was that real. I answered yes and yes. He told me that was the Holy Spirit pushing me closer to the Lord. I had to think about that.

I accompanied them to several more services over the next few weeks and Bill included me at least one night in each of them. I even spoke a couple of times, briefly. At most of the stops, I would bump into a vet who served in Vietnam. We would share our experiences and it was easy for me to relate to them. Some of them would think I was an evangelist and I'd laugh and say "no way, I'm just a grunt trying to find his own way." I did like to sing and Mary and I were working on harmonizing together. While traveling one day, I overheard Mary discussing with Bill about buying a bus or a van and buying some new sound equipment. Bill didn't think they could afford it. I asked Mary how much she thought it would cost. She said they could buy a used bus in good shape for $12,000 - $15,000 and the equipment might be another $2,000 - $3,000. I asked if $20,000 would cover everything and she said yes, she was sure it would. I told them I had some money saved up and would not mind investing in their ministry. Bill stopped the car and asked "you serious?" I said "yes sir, I am." Bill got a big smile on his face and said "Son, Mary's been bugging me about a bus for the last year and I've been putting her off for that long." He winked at me and said he knew there was a reason he liked me!

We were on our way to Tennessee and Mary had a couple of dealers in mind we could check out near Nashville while we were there. We looked at buses and motor homes and more buses and motor homes - Mary was pretty fussy. She finally picked out a used bus that had been used by a band out of Nashville. It was very nice inside with all the comforts of home. The outside needed a paint job - it had bright flowery colors that were popular during the early seventies. Bill and I joked we could call ourselves the Flower Power Ministries. The dealer said they would repaint the bus and letter it to our liking, fill the fuel tanks and put new tires on it for $25,000. I said sold!! Morgan Ministries had its own bus and we would pick it up in two weeks. Bill and I worked out a deal where I would receive a percentage of the money they made to help pay for the bus.

I was suddenly an investor in a ministry team. A few months ago, I was in the African bush fighting rebels and trying to stay alive. Ain't life funny! I called my sister Cheryl and I told her she was never going to believe what I just did. When I told her I was going to be a part of a ministry team, she laughed and asked me if was smoking wacky weed again. I had to put Mary on the phone to talk to her and make her realize I was not stoned out of mind. Cheryl told Mary she didn't know what they had done to me, but whatever it was to keep it up. She told me that one of her prayers was just answered, that her little brother would get his head on straight. I told her

I would send her some pictures of the bus and all of us. Maybe someday we would be coming to her hometown.

On our way to pick up the bus a couple of weeks later, Bill stopped the car and we talked about me and my future. Bill said he would like me to take a more active role in speaking. He said he needed to know if I was ready to give my life over to serving God. I told him I was ready. I greatly admired the life that he and Mary had together and I felt I could be comfortable with this lifestyle. I liked to travel and was getting more comfortable about being around people. My problem was I didn't know how to turn it all over to God and I still didn't feel worthy. Bill asked "Son, you've heard me preach on those things before, haven't you been listening?" I said "yes sir, I have, that's why I'm still here." Bill prayed with me on that lonely country road and my life as an evangelist began that day. I was 25 years old and felt like I'd lived a lifetime already.

I watched and learned from Bill and Mary. Bill had a charismatic way about him, people liked him and trusted him, and I needed to try to emulate that style. I read and studied the Bible, read many different people's view points on religion and how it should be presented. I studied different Evangelists - not so much their teaching, but the person. Mary was a very gentle and caring person, but had strength inside her that even Bill did not have, and she helped me look inside myself many times. I could feel myself changing from the inside. My temper was not as bad; when people did air their concerns to me, it did touch me. When I was speaking to a group, many times I was unsure of what to say. Every time that happened the proper words came to my mind. Sometimes the prepared message I had was never used because another message would come to my mind totally unrelated to what I had prepared, but it fit the needs of someone there at that moment. It took me a while to realize it, but this was the Holy Spirit speaking to me. The words were not coming from my mind but my heart. I was learning to trust God. For years I never thought God talked to me but the fact of the matter was I was not listening. I was expecting a "lightning bolt" experience when God spoke. I was learning he spoke more subtly and often, if I just took the time to listen. I no longer believed in such a thing as a conscience, it was simply God speaking to me. I was learning, just as I had in the military, that I had a lot to learn. I was also hearing another voice. That voice was telling me I was a fool, I was not worthy of this position and I could not change who I was. Besides, why would I want to change who I was, I was getting rich as a hired gun.

We picked up the bus and it looked great. I could see Bill was pleased with the new paint job. When we got back home, Mary made the interior look like home. That bus took us all over the country for the next two years. Bill worked with me a lot to polish my speaking ability and to help me develop better people skills as well. Over time, my ministry was growing as well as Bill and Mary's. We were booked 18 months in advance. We purchased the latest in sound equipment, and the places we served were always full and the offerings were good. I spoke mostly about my life and would always relate better to younger people. There were times when the adventurous spirit stirred in me and I thought about my former life. I was surprised by the adrenalin rush I got from standing in front large crowd of people and I guess that helped to keep me settled down. I finally realized that was what I enjoyed about being a sniper: the rush that came from not knowing if I would live or die. I did take some time off, and most of the time I would go down to Phil's and hang out with the boys and do some hunting. I did spend some time with my sister and hung around the Houston area. I still enjoyed being alone in the woods and I still struggled with people getting too close to me in a crowded room but it was getting better. As Bill always said, everybody is weird in their own way.

We met a lot of people and made a lot of new friends along the way. The hardest part for me was trusting people. I would still have some flashbacks and got to the point of accepting that was the way it was going to be for the rest of my life. In the middle of a service one night outside of St. Louis, my mind just went blank, and for a good minute, I said nothing. In my mind I was seeing someone I killed, and it was like I was frozen in that moment. When I got my wits back, I explained to the crowd of people that I just had a message from God and I needed to take it. Bill trained me well, and the rest of the message went off without a hitch.

In a swing through Virginia, I took some time to visit a V.A. hospital. I met with a number of vets recovering from injuries both physical and emotional. I came to realize how lucky I was to have all my body parts and, I think, most of my sanity. I was brought up to believe there was no such thing as luck. "We make our own luck," my dad used to say. But now, after the things I've been through and seeing these men and the things they've gone through – I had to believe there was such a thing as luck. Or perhaps it was what Bill was trying to teach me – my life being spared was part of God's plan for me. My heart wanted to believe the latter, but my head was still taking credit for who I had become.

It was incredibly humbling to meet with these men. Some of them were missing arms or legs and trying very hard to put their lives back together. I felt very inadequate in ministering to these guys. In a lot of ways, they ministered to me. Their strength of will and determination was an inspiration to me. I prayed with those who wanted to pray and tried to provide encouragement for all of those I met.

One fellow I met was in a wheelchair - both of his legs were blown off by a land mine. He was determined to be, in his words, "the best damn wheelchair jockey in the hospital." He was constantly catching hell from the nurses for "popping wheelies" and racing around the hallways in his wheelchair. These men, who were true war heroes, were now heroes for each other. I was honored to be able to spend time with them.

Later in the day, I walked with some of the staff to a different ward. The guys in that ward had some type of psychological problems. Most of these men were very subdued and the spirit of overcoming their problems was nowhere to be found.

I saw a young man sitting at a table in a corner by himself, hell these were all young men. I approached him and held out my hand and introduced myself. He looked at me and asked "who the hell are you, another damn shrink come to tell me I'm nuts?" I said no I'm not a shrink; I'm just another grunt trying to figure out this crazy ass world. He asked me why I was there. I told him I was there to try to help in any way I could. He asked if I wasn't a shrink, how I expected to help a crazy bastard like him.

I told him I didn't know if I could help him, but what ever he was hurting from, I had probably been through myself. If he wanted to talk, I was willing to listen. He asked me if I ever killed anyone. I said yes, too many. He asked me if I ever killed any women or children. I said yes. He paused for a moment and I could see he was choking up, I was as well. I simply put my arm around his shoulder and told him it was ok, he wasn't alone.

We both cried, and for me and maybe him as well, it was the first time I shared my feelings and my fears with someone who truly understood. I'd shared some of these feelings with Bill and my sister and although they were sympathetic, they could not fully understand. This young man, John, understood. We shared our stories and the guilt we carried. He made me realize I still had a lot of guilt inside of me.

We talked for a few hours and it seemed like only minutes. This was turning out once again to be as therapeutic for me as it was for John. He was struggling with the visions of blowing up villagers and still seeing images of bodies and parts of bodies flying through the air. Little children caught in the craziness of war, their tiny bodies ripped apart, and knowing that he was responsible for some of it. Then to top it all off, coming back home and being called a baby killer; it pushed him over the edge. Up to this point in time, he had not been able to cope with it all on his own. John said the doctors were helping him, but he still had thoughts of suicide and at times he felt he deserved to die for what he had done. He said "damn it, I was just following orders, it wasn't my idea to kill those poor people."

I tried to tell him that was the point. He was a soldier following orders and although he may have pulled the trigger or thrown the hand grenade, that was his job at the time. I told him that I felt much of the same pain he did and there were still times when I saw visions of people I had killed. I'd come to accept that I would carry those visions the rest of my life. They would be a reminder to me of a time when human life had little value and it could end at any time. I told John of my walk with God and how Bill worked with me when my mindset was much like his. I left it up to John if he wanted me to help him in turning his problems over to God.

John said it sounded too simple. I assured him it was a process he would have to work at every day. His problems would not just magically disappear. The nightmares and the visions would creep in from time to time, as they still did for me. The difference was in knowing that no matter what, the Lord is standing right beside us, ready and willing to help us deal with anything that comes our way. I told John that God had already forgiven him of any sin he may have committed; now it was time that John forgave himself. I also told him if he would like, I would stay with him through the night and pray with him to help him release the pain within him and hand it over to God.

John looked at me and asked "what about these other guys?" I turned and looked behind me and there were two men standing there listening to our conversation. I didn't know how long they were standing there. I asked them if they were interested in what I was saying and if they would like to join us. They both said yes. I spoke to a nurse and asked if we could have a private space somewhere where the four of us could talk. She directed us to a small meeting room and then brought us some sandwiches and drinks. The other two men, Dave and Mike, shared their stories and they were much the same as John's. Feelings of overwhelming guilt and problems with drug abuse, as well as feeling nobody really cared.

We talked and prayed throughout the night. I led the men through a process some people know as the "seven steps." It is a process of acknowledging sins, fears, doubts, and guilt, and releasing them to God to be cast out of their lives so that they can be released from the bondage placed on them by outside forces or their own minds. What is important to God and should be important to them is what they do with the rest of their lives. They must realize they cannot change the past, but more importantly that God has already forgotten their past deeds. They needed to take their past experiences and use them as a learning experience to help them help others - not make the same mistakes they may have made in their lives. Even in the case of war, where we as soldiers didn't have a voice in the decision making process, we needed to accept that what we did was done to save the lives of others. Unfortunately, in war times innocent people will die but we, as soldiers, need not carry that guilt with us. Throughout the night, there were many tears, many screams of anger and relief, and the power of God's love encompassed the entire room. By morning we were all exhausted, but when I looked at each man, I saw a spark in their eyes that was not there the day before. They were hugging each other and there was definitely some healing taking place in the room. A doctor came in and said he didn't know what went on in here last night, but it looked to him that it was something good. He thanked me for whatever I did and I said don't thank me, thank God. These men were not completely healed, but they were at least given some tools to use along the way. The process for me was very rewarding; I learned a lot about myself and had some hints into the power God had given me to do his work. Once again I saw the truth in what Bill taught me.

The entire process of healing fascinated me. The first time for me was when I witnessed the healing power of a shaman in Africa and tried to learn as much as he would teach me. It was an eerie power, and I felt uncomfortable with it. It was a power that he used to have control over his people. Even with my limited knowledge, I felt it was an evil power, used for his benefit mostly, but nonetheless, it was real.

The power I felt the previous night was real as well. It was a calming, confident, feel good power. It was not the dominating, intimidating power that I learned earlier in order to survive in the jungle. I could feel the power of God's love and grace pass through my hands when I touched each one of these men. It was so strong that it would turn them from quivering in shame and guilt to calmness and thankfulness addressed to God. I found myself awestruck by what was happening. It was actually kind of scary for me; I turned my hands to my face several times, to look at them and try to figure out what was happening. I had no idea that I had this power and, looking back, I don't believe I had it before that day. The only logical explanation was God placed me in that hospital and used me as an instrument of healing.

I gave the men at the hospital my phone number and told them to call me anytime and promised I would keep in touch. We had established a special bond and I assured them they had helped me as much as I may have helped them. I left that hospital feeling incredibly good about myself and the prospect of creating a healing ministry bouncing around in my head.

In the next few weeks, I spent a great deal of time reading and studying about healing, mostly in a spiritual sense but also physical healing as well. I spoke with other evangelists about the subject and they encouraged me to pursue it.

I related my experience at the hospital to Bill and Mary, and they were both excited to hear of my gifting from God, as they called it. I was feeling like a kid with a new toy, and wanted to go around touching everyone with a problem and heal them. Bill warned me to go slow and always remember this was a gift from God, I was simply the vehicle he chose to channel his power. It was not something I should use to show people how cool I was. Also there was no guarantee it would work again; that was up to God and God would let me know when the time was right. It was up to me to be listening.

The next day, Bill and Mary sat me down and said we needed to talk. They had been talking it over and decided it was time for them to slow down. At the end of that year, they were only going to travel six months out of the year and the rest of the time they would be developing a radio ministry. They wanted me to carry on their traveling ministry and they would help me find someone to take their place. We started interviewing prospects to join our team in each place we served. While in Oklahoma one week, we met a couple – Bob and Terry Howell, who sang at one of our services. Bob was 31 years old and Terry was 29 and they sang and played music very well together. Bob played the guitar and Terry played the keyboard. We talked with them about our plans for the future and asked them to consider an offer to join our team. They seemed flattered and shocked at the same time and said they would discuss it and pray about it.

The next day, Bob asked if he and Terry could possibly travel with us for a week or two to see if they would like it. We thought that was a great idea. None of us would make any commitment until they gave it a try. The bus was a bit crowded with five people in it, but we managed. I slept on a padded bench that went with the kitchen table. With two women on board, I ended up peeing outside a lot because the bathroom was usually occupied. Bob and Terry fit in well; they had a down home, country style that the crowds liked.

While we traveled, Bill was teaching me how to read the crowds and give them what they wanted. We kept notes on what type of preaching and music each particular group liked. Most of the time, we would book a return visit for the following year or perhaps every other year. We also kept notes on who had money at each of the stops. Often times, these would be little old ladies who were widows with lots of money to donate to our ministry. Since I was a reasonably good looking young man, it was part of my job to suck up to these ladies. I would go to their homes for dinner, which was a treat for me, because I got tired of eating on the road. When they came to the service we would make a fuss over them and tell the crowd what good cooks they were and the ladies loved the extra attention. It would usually earn us an extra $500 - $1000 per week in donations to our ministry. A few times I did get propositioned by women twice my age, but declined as politely as I could, saying God would not approve.

We were a nondenominational ministry, not affiliated with any church. One of the things that annoyed me was all these people referring to themselves as Christians or other people they knew as Christians. Their inference seemed to be that all good people were Christians or that only Christians knew God. To me, the term Christian was no different than Republican or Democrat; it meant nothing as far as one's spirituality. This was one thing I could not talk about for fear of offending people. I was also testing the healing part of the ministry and trying to work in a healing service whenever I felt God was leading us in that direction. There were some positive results in some of the services, where people proclaimed to be healed and it was always a very emotional time when that occurred. There were also times when someone asked for a healing and nothing happened. Most of these occurred when I did not feel like I was getting a sign from God to proceed with the healing. For me it was a learning process, and many times I felt totally out of control, but God would lead me in the right direction and it would all work out.

After a two week trial run, Bob and Terry said they liked it and they would like to join us. They signed a contract with Bill to be with us for the next year. We worked out a schedule for everyone with the idea that Bill and Mary would taper off the traveling even more in the future.

CHAPTER 20

The Ministry Grows

So began another chapter for Morgan Ministries and for me as well. In the next year, Bill and Mary's radio ministry took off. Mary was making recordings, Bob and Terry were making recordings, and we were selling them on the road. Bill and Mary were traveling less and less as they were busy with radio and recordings and looking at maybe doing some TV shows. We set up a schedule of being on the road for three months and then off for a month. Bob and Terry agreed to sign on for another year and things were going well. One of my months off, I drove down to Houston and spent some time fishing. In my travels, I decided to swing by Big Phil's and say hi to everybody. When I pulled in, there seemed to be quite a commotion going on around the place. Little Phil came out to greet me and said one of his Dad's business partners had just been shot to death the day before. I saw Martin and Big Phil and a few other men I didn't know sitting on the front porch talking. I always thought Big Phil was tied into Martin's business but until that day, I never knew for sure. Big Phil and Martin came over and shook my hand and Big Phil asked me if I ever met Red Jacobs. He told me Red was shot to death the previous night at his home a few miles away. I said no, I never met him and told him I was sorry for his loss. Big Phil said the police were saying it looked like a robbery gone bad. I was not sure what his connection was to the police, but Phil always seemed to know what the police were up to. I went into the house with little Phil and of course we drank a few a beers. He looked at me and said he didn't know if I would drink anymore since I was a preacher, I told him a few beers never hurt anyone. Apparently Red had no family left, so Big Phil was on the phone making arrangements for Red's funeral. Big Phil came into the room and pointed his finger at me and asked "Ya'll are a preacher now, aren't you?" I said "yes sir, I am." He said "good, you're going to do Red's funeral." I told him I'd never done a funeral. "Well, then it's about damn time you did one" he snapped back at me. I told Phil I didn't know anything about Red and his response was he didn't think Red would mind.

I called Bill to find out what I should say for the funeral and he gave me some passages of scripture to read and words to say. So I did Red's funeral. I guess it really didn't matter what I said. Everybody seemed anxious to get the funeral over with, so they could go back to Red's favorite bar and celebrate his life or death, I wasn't sure. Before I left the funeral, Martin wished me good luck at my new job and he told me to stay in touch. I said goodbye to the boys and left for Arkansas the next day.

Our team was going to move into some areas we had not been in before in southern Ohio, West Virginia, Virginia and western Pennsylvania. They were all large rallies in stadiums. We would be sharing duties with other evangelistic teams and that was the first time I'd ever done that. The money was good; we were guaranteed $1000 per night plus a percentage of the gate receipts. We would spend three nights at each place.

I was very nervous for the first time in a while. It was difficult for me to be center stage in a large gathering of people. In churches I could always keep my back covered by a wall or some kind of barrier, now I was in the middle of a field with people all around me. For five years I stayed in the shadows and prided myself on my ability to hide or disappear - my life depended on it. I still didn't like somebody coming up behind me unannounced. Now there were hundreds of people behind me; I found myself always checking my back trail and looking over my shoulder. There were only a few people I trusted and they were not there. Those old demons would just not go away. I was afraid I might do something stupid, so I asked Bob and Terry if they would stand behind me while I was speaking and explained why to them. They agreed and said they would pray for me.

There were 10,000 people in the stadium that first night. Bob and Terry sang before I spoke and they did a great job. Their music was more upbeat and the crowd couldn't help but sway to the music and tap their feet. They made my job easier by putting the crowd in a good frame of mind and their music helped me to relax as well. My message that week had to do with God changing people. I normally used myself as an example: if God could change me, he could change anyone.

Although we believed in what we were doing, it did get to be a drag after a while, like any job. Sometimes I would get a motel room to give Bob and Terry some privacy and at times they would get a room and I would have the bus to myself. For me there were women at the various stops but nothing serious. Mostly dinner and sometimes dancing, sometimes sex in the bus. I still drank a beer occasionally but I had to be careful to project the proper image everyone expected from me.

At times I missed being wild and roaming the bush. I did not miss sleeping on the ground, ducking bullets, the bugs, snakes and only taking a bath once a week. The thing I missed the most was the thrill, the rush you can only get from cheating death. Sometimes I would bump into some young, cocky kids who didn't have any respect for anyone or anything and wished I could kick their butts in public but I never did. At times I felt like two different people, the old me and the new me. The old me would keep sneaking out every now and then, wanting to go out and raise some hell. Bill would keep telling me I needed to turn it all over to God. I wasn't sure I knew how to do that. It was something I preached about but really didn't know what I was talking about. In talking with other evangelists, we all had skeletons in our closets. We were human but the public expected us to be prefect.

Our next swing was into Virginia, where we had three more bookings. We were to spend a week in Richmond at a revival in a big church there. I did not really care for city life, but that's where the money was. We could no longer afford to do the small country churches on a regular basis, although we did do a few each year just because we liked them. Two days after we were in Richmond a member of the church we were serving was murdered. He was a banker and apparently a very influential member of the community. It put a damper on the services we were doing and after three days the board of directors of the church decided to cancel the rest of the services.

CHAPTER 21

My True Mission

We had seven days free until our next engagement and I went to the airport and bought Bob and Terry airline tickets to Florida. They needed a vacation and so did I. I drove the bus to our next engagement, rented a car and drove to Nashville for a few days R & R. I was also going to try to line up some new bookings for the area. While in Nashville, I stopped by a veterans outreach program that helped vets struggling with addiction and adjusting to civilian life. I talked with a number of guys and tried to offer encouragement to them. I was told there were some vets who were living on the streets and could use some help. I went to find these guys and to try to understand how they got to that point. I found four guys huddled in an alley, living in cardboard boxes and eating out of dumpsters. I told them I wasn't there to preach to them, only to help them if I could. I asked them what I could do to help them. They all said nobody could help them, nobody cared. I told them I cared.

I told them if it were not for the help I received from a few friends, I might be right there with them now. These guys were broke financially, emotionally, and spiritually. It hurt me deeply to see these once proud soldiers reduced to this lifestyle. I helped them gather up their things and said we were all going to a restaurant around the corner and dinner was on me. One of the guys, Tommy, said they wouldn't serve them in there. I said "The hell they won't!"

When we walked in, everyone in the place stared at us. I said to the waitress "my friends and I would like a table for five, please." She said she didn't know if one was available. I looked around and saw plenty of empty tables and whispered in her ear that the one in the corner in the back would be just fine. She guessed that would be alright. We seated ourselves at the table and a man came out of the kitchen and asked to speak to me alone. He asked me what the hell I thought I was doing bringing these bums into his restaurant. He was a man older than me, I guessed around fifty. I introduced myself and the four men with me. I told him my friends and I came in to have a nice dinner and talk over our tours in Vietnam. He looked at us for a minute and didn't say a word. Then he asked "you guys all served in Vietnam?" Everyone replied "Yes, sir." He hung his head and said "I'm sorry guys, I'm really sorry, I've seen you guys around here before but I just kissed you off as a bunch of worthless bums too lazy to work." He stood tall and saluted, tears ran down his cheeks, and he was obviously embarrassed as he said "I served in the Army in Europe and I saw a lot of action and lost a lot of good men. You guys order anything you want and it won't cost you a penny." He turned away and said I'll be back in a few minutes; I have to do something in the kitchen. I turned and saluted my four new friends seated at the table. I walked back to the kitchen to thank Max for his generosity and he was weeping like a baby. I told him thanks and the Lord would bless him deeply for what he had just done. He just motioned for me to go and I respected that.

The guys ate a good meal and Max provided dessert as we shared our war stories and what happened after we came home. The four of them had problems with booze or drugs, had bad experiences with the trauma of war, and felt their country abandoned them. They all had problems and for whatever reason, they fell through the cracks in the system.

Max came out with a bag of food for the guys to take with them and he looked at me and said "Who the hell are you; I've never seen you around here before." I explained to him who I was and told him to think of me as just one of them. Max said to me "you stop by here tomorrow morning for breakfast at 8:00am, we need to talk some more, and bring these gentlemen with you." I took the guys with me and got them two rooms at the motel I was staying at. I then called Bill to see how much money we might have to spare to help these guys. I called some organizations I knew to see if we could raise some funds to help vets like these. I left a message for a fellow I knew with the Veterans Administration to get the ball rolling on some type of rehab program to enroll them in.

Bill called me back later that night and said we had $5000 we could spare right now. He told me that perhaps I'd just found my calling - helping these vets. He also told me he and Mary would start thinking of some ways to raise more money for a program like this. Maybe Bill was right – God had a plan for me and if I was patient, it would all come together.

The next morning, we met with Max and another gentleman named Carl Peters. Max had called Carl the previous night and they had a proposal for us to consider. Carl owned a number of rental properties and he had a few that needed some work done on them. If these four men were interested and thought they could do it, they could do the work on the properties and live in one of them rent free until they finished the jobs. The guys looked at each other and felt between them they could do the work. Carl said his son would supervise the projects and his company had all the tools the men would need. If they were interested, they could go look at the house they would be living in right now and we went to take a look. Carl said this house was the worst of the three houses. It was pretty bad, but compared to sleeping in a cardboard box, it was definitely a step up. It was amazing to me how all these things fell into place in one day's time. I believed that it was all part of God's plan.

This whole project started to snowball and over the course of the next year, it grew to include similar programs in five other cities. Max hired one of the guys to work in his restaurant, two of them got remodeling jobs with Carl, and the fourth got a job as a mechanic in a nearby garage. They were all enrolled in counseling programs and doing well. We continued to raise money for the programs where ever we went and donations came in from a number of other organizations as well. We were able to purchase five other houses in different communities and called them Jake's Houses. I was really pleased with how this mission turned out; it was vets helping other vets. A wonderful example of how a simple idea can turn into a big deal when people allow their passion to be funneled in the right direction. Obviously I was not the only one who had compassion for these vets. I was humbled by the generosity of the communities involved. I realized that all the crap I went through in the past had prepared me to be able to relate to these guys and to help them out of the hole they'd fallen into. This group of soldiers of war would hopefully become spiritual soldiers in their lives. I was seeing more and more that God did have a plan for each of us, it was up to us to follow that plan. The whole project was a part of the healing ministry that I had not even considered previously.

Morgan Ministries had branched out into radio, TV, and now a veteran's outreach along with doing the road trips. We were all very busy and enjoying what we were doing.

CHAPTER 20

A Love Renewed

Bob, Terry, and I continued to travel while Bill and Mary joined us occasionally. Ben was out of college and was managing everything we were doing. I was getting weary of the travel and thought about settling down but didn't know if I'd be comfortable in one place. Besides, I knew I would miss the adrenalin rush I still got from speaking in front of big crowds.

I was still an adventure junkie and I did a lot of hunting when I was not working. I still loved the woods and the solitude that I could find there. I was able to go to Alaska, Canada, and my first love, Montana, and stay with Wes and Sally at their ranch. I tried skydiving, racing cars, snake hunting with my bare hands, and any other thrill I could find. I had some close encounters with bears and moose, almost fell off the side of a mountain hunting mountain goats, and after bow hunting for bull elk numerous times, I still got chills up and down my spine from hearing the bugle of a bull in rut. For me, there was something deeply spiritual and refreshing about being alone in the mountains. I came away from those experiences feeling energized and renewed. There was a part of me that wanted to experience everything I could while I was able. The money was good and I could afford to do anything I wanted.

There were a few ladies I'd been seeing on a steady basis in different locations. Sometimes they would each travel with us for a while. We would introduce them to our crowds as assistants or interns to the program. Terry would shake her head and ask me if I was ever going to settle down. There was still a battle within me, I missed the soldiering but I felt a commitment to Bill and Mary and all they had done for me.

It was now four years doing the ministry and many of our engagements were repeats and in many cases we were renewing old friendships. On a swing through Pennsylvania one evening, we were in a church about fifty miles from my old hometown. At the end of the service, a lady approached me and shook my hand. It was Trudy, my old flame from high school. She said she saw in a newspaper ad that I was going to be there and she wanted to come see the new me. She looked great and my heart skipped a few beats as we talked. I felt like a clumsy school boy as I searched for the right words to say. I asked if she lived in the area and she said did. She said she and her seven year old son lived in an apartment complex about two miles from the church. Trudy told me she and her husband got divorced a little over a year ago and she was picking up the pieces after the divorce. I said I was sorry to hear that (but I really wasn't). Trudy asked if I was married and how in the world I ever got into this line of work. I suggested we grab a bite to eat or coffee somewhere so we talk more. She said she had to get home that night for her son but asked if I could make it for lunch the next day. You bet I could!!

How about that; I hadn't felt this way in a long time. Terry asked me who I was talking to for so long after the service. I asked her why. She said because I was gushing like a little kid with a crush on his teacher. I said she was just an old friend and Terry rolled her eyes and said "yeah, right."

The next day, Trudy and I met for lunch and spent most of the afternoon together. We shared what we'd done with our lives since we last met and talked about family and what some of our old friends were doing. She worked as a legal aide and she and her son Jeff did a lot of things together since Jeff's father left. Her husband had a drinking problem and took off with another woman and paid virtually nothing in support of Jeff. Trudy said Jeff would soon be home from school and if I wanted to meet him it would be fine with her. We went to Trudy's apartment and she introduced me to Jeff, as well mannered as a seven year old could be, and her neighbor Beth, who was watching Jeff until Trudy got home. Beth and Jeff were watching the local news about the murder of some high profile drug dealer that had been shot the previous night. Trudy told Beth they should not be watching stuff like that on TV. Jeff said "but Mom, you said already that we should shoot all these bad drug people." I tried to hide it, so I had to turn my head and laugh.

We had one more day in the area and I spent most of it with Trudy and Jeff. Jeff wanted to see the bus I lived in and he thought it was really cool. Trudy and I decided to stay in touch and there was certainly a spark between us. Terry was on my case big time about being in love and she enjoyed seeing me act out of character. She would walk by me singing "love, love me do" or puckering up to mimic a kiss. She was right, I was in love. I'd come to realize I had been in love with Trudy since high school. None of the ladies I dated in the past few years made me feel so out of control the way she did.

We finished our tour in Pennsylvania and moved on to Virginia. I kept in touch with Trudy by phone almost daily and we were making plans to get together when the tour was over in a few weeks. After the Virginia tour, we would be headed to Florida and do some stops at some retirement communities which were always a part of our swing through the south. They were always very lucrative for us, as there seemed to be a lot of wealthy people living in those communities. I made plans with Trudy for her and Jeff to meet me in Florida after our services were finished. I sent her the plane tickets and we met in Orlando. I had a week until our next engagement and we would be able to spend it together. Jeff was really excited about the plane ride down and all the things to see and do around the Orlando area. I was excited to just be around him and his mother. The week went very fast and on the next to the last day of our time together, I asked Trudy to marry me. She seemed shocked and said she would have to think about it. The next day she called me and said I should come over to her room, we needed to talk. When I got to her room, she told me she wanted both of us to explain to Jeff that I asked for her hand in marriage. If he approved, she approved. When we explained to Jeff we were thinking of getting married – his first question was "does that mean I get to sleep on the bus?" We both laughed and said we would talk about that later. I asked Jeff if he would be ok with his Mom and I getting married and he said he thought it would be cool. We all hugged and Trudy finally said yes. We made tentative plans to get married when our tour took us close to home, which would be in about six weeks.

It took some convincing and planning but I finally got Trudy to agree to quit her job and travel with us. It would obviously be a big change for her and Jeff, and me as well. She was afraid I didn't make enough money to support all of us. After showing her the numbers she agreed it would be ok. We got Jeff enrolled in a home schooling program and everything was falling together. We asked Bill to marry us during one of our services near to home. I invited my sister Cheryl, Big Phil, Martin and his wife, and of course the boys to my wedding and to my surprise, they all showed up. Big Phil and Martin handed me an envelope and told me it was just a little something to get us off on the right foot. Later when I opened the envelope, there was $5000 cash in it. Trudy almost choked on her drink when she saw what was in the envelope. The boys were pretty well behaved except for hogging most of the dances with Trudy. Cheryl had a smug look on her face most of the time and I suspected she had a part in Trudy and me getting together again. Later I thanked her for her part in putting Trudy back in my life, she just winked and gave me a big smile and said "nothing's too good for my baby brother." I'd known for a long time there was something missing in my life; Trudy was it. I felt I had come full circle; she and Jeff brought a lot of joy to my life. So our life together began.

    I had to remember to introduce Trudy and Jeff at each of our services, mostly because I was happy to do so, but also because I didn't want an embarrassing moment with one of the ladies I had dated in the past. The lifestyle change was very different for me and it was a big adjustment, but I was really glad to share my life with both of them.

    Trudy gradually worked her way into singing harmony with Bob and Terry and fit in very well. We did have to buy a larger bus with three bedrooms and two baths. Jeff seemed to be adjusting to his new lifestyle well although he said his Mom was a harder teacher than the teachers he had in school. Bob was teaching Jeff how to play the guitar and what all the electrical stuff was about. Bob gave him the title of Jr. Engineer. I was truly happy for the first time in years. I had to learn to share my thoughts and goals with Trudy, something I had never done before. In the past, if I wanted to do something, I just did it, as long as it fit into our schedule. We prayed and asked God to guide our lives and as long as we took the time to do that, He would always show us a way to get through our problems. It took a few months for all of us to get comfortable with our new lifestyle. Bob and Terry were both very understanding and they had become family as well. They were a part of most of the decision making process when it came to business and they were a valuable part of the team. Trudy developed a children's ministry and she and Jeff would usually run a program for those churches that wanted one while we were ministering to the adults. She was very good at working with children and once again, I could see how God's plan would fall together if we would just allow it to unfurl.

    Our life together was great; Trudy brought out a side of me that I thought had died with Jake. Aside from the Morgan's, I'd never let anyone else into my life; I guess I was afraid of losing them. It was just easier to put up walls and not allow people to get too close. Martin had taught me years ago to never trust anyone, because everyone had their price and sooner or later your closest friend could turn on you. I was trying hard to break away from the hard assed attitudes I had adopted to survive earlier in life and to also break the bondage of guilt I still carried with me from my past life. Trudy and Jeff were a vital part in helping me do that. They gave me something else to focus on, more importantly someone else to focus on, instead of myself. I'd come to realize I had led a very selfish life, feeding my ego in war and in the ministry. It was very easy to allow people to put me up on a pedestal as an evangelist and if I wasn't careful, I could get to believing I belonged there. I had to constantly remind myself my job was to serve the people, not have them serve me.

After one and a half years of traveling, we decided to buy a house near Bill and Mary's place. Trudy liked the house and for me it was a new experience - I never owned a house before. I had been talking with Bill about doing less traveling and he was planning to retire soon so it seemed like the right time for me to take over his job. I would continue to travel maybe three months out of year, and spend the rest of my time in the studio taking over the radio and TV shows that Bill and Mary had done for years. We bought the house and settled in, and for the first time in my adult life, I had roots. We had some remodeling to do to the house and we decided we would work at it on our own when we had time and eventually we would have things the way we wanted them. I was a bit nervous about the whole roots thing, I didn't know if I could adjust to living in one place all the time. I'd spent so much time on the road; it just was my way of life. I was 32 years old and I guess it was time to settle down and act like most people expected me to. I'd have to find something to feed my thrill seeking habit or try to break it. It did seem like we were more of a family, living in our own house. It was nice not to have to worry about making too much noise or interrupting a conversation, something that we always had to worry about while traveling in the bus.

When I no longer had to travel as much, I would be able to devote more time to the house. We both felt when Jeff got to be high school age; it would be good for him to go to a public school. Trudy and I also planned to have another child sometime in the future and it would be a good place to raise a family.

I liked this whole family thing and I guess the people around me could see a difference in me. A number of people commented about my demeanor being much more relaxed and I was smiling more. I didn't realize I was so uptight before.

I spent as much time as I could with Jeff, trying to teach him the things my father taught me. He was like a sponge soaking up whatever I could show him. We spent time camping and fishing, and my plan was to try to adopt him as soon as I could.

On one of our camping trips, apparently I had a bad dream that woke him up. The next morning, he asked me if I was dreaming about snakes. He said I kept hollering snake, snake. I had to explain to him that Snake was a nickname for my friend in the Army, who died saving my life. Of course Jeff wanted to know all the details and I shared with him some of what happened. He asked me if that was how I got the scar on my shoulder. I said yes, that I was shot in the shoulder. I asked him when he saw the scar on my shoulder. He said he saw it the night before when I was getting undressed. Jeff hugged me and said he was sorry my friend the Snake was killed, but he was really glad that I wasn't because he wanted me to be his new dad. Wow, powerful words from such a little guy! I told him I would be proud to be his new dad.

Both Trudy and Jeff asked questions about the war, what I did, and about my life as a mercenary. Although I didn't really want to lie to them about it, I never really told them everything. I was always afraid if they knew everything, they would think less of me and our relationship would fall apart. One evening I got out some old pictures and shared them with both of them. Jeff couldn't believe that it was me in some of the pictures. He said I looked pretty scary with the long hair and beard and the guns hanging on me. I told them that I was living proof that God can change anyone. It was a statement I used a lot in my ministry and one I believed in. Little did I know that they would both embarrass me by making up a photo board of some of my old pictures to be displayed at some of our stops for all to see. It was certainly visual proof that I had changed! In my heart I felt that by having them in my life, they made me more of a whole person and they were my inspiration to continue in ministry.

There were a lot of days I regretted living the life I had previously, and a lot of days I felt totally unworthy of the blessings God had given me. I know there were times when Trudy could sense that in me and would ask what was troubling me. I told her that some days I felt like a yo-yo, being pulled in two different directions: one by God and the other by Satan. I was feeling more of a responsibility to the people I was preaching to and also to her and Jeff. I shared with her that there were some things I had done before we were married that I was totally ashamed of and at times it became a real burden for me. Trudy told me she didn't care what I had done in the past, she loved me and Jeff loved me and we were going to spend the rest of our lives together. She also told me maybe I needed to listen to some of my own sermons now and then. We agreed to continue to work through these issues and when I was ready to talk some more, she would be ready to listen. She was right: sometimes the preacher needs to be preached to. Bill had always been there for me, willing to listen and mentor me when I got off on the wrong track. Now I had another mentor - my wife, who was willing to listen and it meant the world to me.

As a pastor, there can be a lot of pressure put on one by other people expecting them to be perfect. At times it can be overpowering if one lets it get to them. One of my pastor friends suggested to me that if I didn't have anything to hide or be ashamed of it should not be a problem; he snickered as he walked away. He was right in principle, but my life was not that simple or maybe I was not willing to let it be that simple.

I was finding out there was a whole lot more to running the business than just preaching and putting on a good show for the people we served. Bill was slowly breaking me in to learn his job and once again, I had a lot to learn. Ben was great at managing everything and kept us all on schedule. He was the driving force behind the success of our operation. He was a good businessman and made sure we all towed the line when it was necessary.

Bill and I were in the process of interviewing candidates to take my place in the traveling ministry and we were having trouble finding someone who we felt would fit. I talked with a man from Los Angeles, California, on the phone that had been recommended to us by a fellow evangelist. After a phone conversation with the man, I agreed to fly out to visit him in person and to sit in on some of his services.

Trudy and I flew to L.A. and met with the gentleman, Tom Wilkins, and found him to be a very forthright person and we were pleased with his demeanor. His teaching that evening was non-denominational and straight forward. We met with him after the service and talked with some of the people he served and we both felt this was our guy. We agreed to meet with Tom again in the morning and discuss the job further. Trudy and I had a nice dinner later and took a little tour of the city which she enjoyed. I was just along for the ride; I still didn't like cities. We went back to our hotel room to relax; it was nice to be alone, between working and spending time with Jeff we didn't get a lot of time to be alone. It was valuable time for the two of us and we vowed to do this more often. The next morning Tom wanted to show us a mission project he started and we went to take a look. Tom created a bit of an oasis in a very depressed area. They provided shelter and food for women and children who were victims of abuse. Tom was rightfully proud of what he and his volunteers had accomplished there.

We were looking around at the houses and talking to some of the people who lived there when two men with handguns came around the corner of one of the houses. They were hollering for a woman named Lucy to come out of the house. Tom stepped in to try to settle them down and told them to put the guns away. Tom reached for one of the guns and it went off. I instinctively jumped the second man and took the gun away from him. I could see the other fellow pointing his gun at Tom. I told him to drop the weapon or I would shoot. He turned to face me with the gun pointing at me and I fired and hit him in the chest knocking him backwards. This all happened within a few seconds and when I turned to check on Trudy she was lying on the sidewalk with a pool of blood around her head. Oh no, not Trudy, she must have been hit by the first shot that was fired. I kneeled down to help her but it was too late, I knew she was dead, Trudy was dead. The love of my life was dead. This was not a nightmare, this was real, I'd seen a lot of dead bodies but this was my wife, that S.O.B. killed my wife. How could this happen? We were here to do God's work. The man that shot Trudy was dead, the other one was not, and I was going to change that. My mind snapped and I hit the guy with everything I had. I kept on hitting him until the police pulled me off him.

The police pinned me to the sidewalk and put me in handcuffs until Tom told them what happened. I just kept thinking Trudy would get up, that it was only a flesh wound, but deep down I knew it wasn't. The paramedics arrived and after checking Trudy they said they were sorry, there was nothing they could do for her. My whole body went limp, the last few minutes flashed through my mind: why Trudy, she never hurt anyone, why not me, Lord, why not me instead of her. All the shit I'd done in my life, I should have been shot, not her. The police told Tom and me we had to come down the police station to give our statements. Trudy's body would be taken to the county morgue to be examined. When we got to the police station, I was in shock - people were talking to me but their voices were muffled. They escorted me into a room where they asked me a bunch of questions and I signed a piece of paper. They told me I could go but not to leave town.

Tom took me back to his place after he gave his statement and we just kind of hung onto each other for a while, neither one of us knowing what to say. I had to call Jeff, but how do you tell an 11 year old boy his mother was dead. He was staying with Bill and Mary and I called and talked to Mary. She said they would take care of Jeff until I got back and she would explain it to him as best as she could. I told her I would call and talk to Jeff the next morning.

The police came to Tom's house later in the day and said I needed to go with them to the station again. They said they would explain why when we got there. Once there, a detective told me that the man I had beaten died. They were considering charging me with his death. They asked me how a preacher learned to beat a man like that. I told them I wasn't always a preacher. They knew that, I could see they had my military records in front of them. They asked me what I did while I was employed by MPC, Corp. I told them I was a mechanic. The detective said according to my financial records I was a very well paid mechanic. I told them I was a very good mechanic. I was getting annoyed with their questions and said "look, I was defending my wife and friend from two armed men, if that's not reason enough to use deadly force, what is? Yes, I have extensive training in hand to hand combat but haven't used it in years." I was angry with myself for losing control and I honestly didn't realize I beat that man so badly. The police had a job to do and I would have to deal with it later.

I was told they would be handing my case over to the District Attorney's office to decide if I was going to be charged with any criminal action. I was free to go but needed to let them know if I was going to leave the city. I told them I would be leaving to take my wife's body back to Arkansas to bury her. I went back to my room and called Jeff and it broke my heart to hear him cry. He asked me why his mom was shot and I couldn't answer that question. All I could say was it was just some freak thing that happened. I told him I loved him and missed him and we would be home in a few days. To his credit he asked me if I was ok and told me to be careful. I promised him I would.

The next day I was informed that Trudy's body was ready to be picked up at the morgue and I went to see her there. It was such a shock to see her lifeless body. I had flashbacks of Jake and my parents lying dead and there wasn't a thing I could do about it. One day we were laughing and enjoying each other and making plans for the rest of our lives, and two days later she was a pale lifeless form of what she used to be. I made arrangements with a local funeral director to prepare Trudy's body and we would fly back home in two days. Bill arranged to have the funeral the day after we got back. The police granted me permission to go home but told me they would contact the Arkansas State Police to keep track of me while I was there.

Trudy and I arrived back home and Bill, Mary and Jeff met us at the airport along with a hearse to transport Trudy's body. Jeff wanted to see his mom so we opened the casket inside the hearse for him to see her. It was heart wrenching to watch him react to seeing his mother's body. He clung to her body and did not want to let go. Jeff and I spent most of the evening talking about death, how much his mother loved him and how sometimes bad things happened to good people. He needed to know God was taking care of his mom now and even though she could not be with him physically her spirit would always be with him. She would be watching over him and guiding him through his life. He could always talk to her in prayer and she would always respond. Jeff fell asleep in my arms and I wondered if my words made any sense to him. I prayed that God would heal his broken heart and mine as well. I carried him to bed and slept on the floor beside him until morning.

The funeral the next day was well attended and it was nice to know so many people cared. Bill conducted the service and did a great job. Jeff was a trooper until they lowered the casket into the ground; he buried his head in my chest and cried, for both of us it was so final. Trudy was the love of my life and I'd wasted so much time ignoring that fact. We shared 18 months together and it was great. Then in an instant it was over. I had no desire to go on with the ministry at this time. I felt so lost without Trudy; other than the Morgan's, she was the best thing to happen in my life since my parents died. We planned to have a child of our own but now that wasn't going to happen. I still had Jeff and I loved him like my own and he was a part of her. It seemed my life was surrounded by death. I understood that death was part of life but why had I cheated death so many times, why was God keeping me around? Was it God at all or was it the Devil keeping me around to do his dirty work? Jeff was not my biological son, and now that Trudy was gone, was his real father going to want him back? Was I going to lose Jeff as well? Once again it felt like I was starting over again.

The next day I met with my attorney and told him I wanted to set up a trust fund for Jeff. I'd accumulated several hundred thousand dollars that I wanted Jeff to have for his future. I needed this done quickly as I might end up in jail for what I had done in LA. I also wanted Bill to be the administrator of the trust. My attorney assured me he would get on it shortly.

A week later the LA Police called and said they needed me to come back and talk with them some more. I agreed I would fly back to LA the next day. I arrived at the police station and met with a detective and an Assistant DA. They said they viewed the shooting of the armed man as self defense. The beating death of the other man was questionable but given the circumstances, they felt they would not be able to find a jury that would convict me. Therefore, I would not be charged in either death. I was warned the family of the beating victim could sue me in civil court. I understood that and thanked them for their consideration. They told me I was free to go, and that was good news.

I went back home and tried to pick up the pieces. Jeff and I spent a lot of time together and I remembered how much it meant to me when Bill called me son for the first time. One day while we were out wandering around in the woods I called to Jeff and said come here, Son. It felt good to call him son and he came up to me and said "what do you want, Dad?" From that day on we were Father and Son. My attorney came through and called one day to say the trust fund for Jeff was completed. Bill and I got all the papers signed; it was a good feeling to know that Jeff's future was secure financially, no matter what happened to me.

We hired Tom to take my place on the road and he was doing a good job of filling in for me. I was learning Bill's job and still going out on the road when Tom needed a break. Jeff got enrolled in a regular school and for him it was a good thing.

About six months after Trudy's death, a car pulled up and two men in suits got out and knocked on the door. The two men came in the house and introduced themselves as FBI agents. They said they were investigating a series of murders that had occurred over the last several years. They told me the FBI had established a pattern that some of the murders were occurring while my ministry team was in the area. They also said they knew that I worked for MPC Corp. and had personal ties to Big Phil and Martin. The FBI knew they were major players in the MPC Corp., which was a front for drugs being sold in this country.

They asked me if I had any thoughts on that. I asked if they were accusing me. They said maybe me or a member of my team. I asked what evidence they had. They told me all the murders they were investigating were very clean and efficient, and performed by someone with my skills. They also said they were watching the two men who jumped us in LA. They knew that the men were after me, not some woman named Lucy. They knew there was a contract out on me by my former boss Martin because he was afraid I would roll over on them after I quit working for him when I got married.

I asked if I could have a few minutes to myself and they agreed. I thought about my life: I'd done a lot of ugly things. I thought about Trudy and how I was going to live without her, and of course Jeff and how I was going to take care of him. I asked God for forgiveness for what I had done and the people I hurt. Throughout my entire ministry I felt like a yo-yo. There were days when I felt very close to God, when I knew I was doing the right thing. There were also days when the other side of me, the trained killer, came out. The adrenalin rush, the excitement, the thrill of getting away with something. The truth was I never quit killing, I was a contract killer up until the time I married Trudy. I told Martin I wanted out after that, and I thought things were ok between us after that. I was a gun for hire and I was paid a lot of money to eliminate people who became a threat to the business. The ministry was a perfect cover, who would suspect a preacher? Red Jacobs was my first contract kill because he was skimming money from his partners; the banker in VA who was laundering money for the business was killed for the same reason. In all, I killed eight different people while in the ministry. I didn't know how much the FBI knew, but I had a feeling I was going to find out.

For almost seven years, I got away with it. In my heart I knew this day would come. I was ready to end it. I asked the agents what they wanted. They said the men I killed were all involved in the drug trade and maybe they should thank me, but they were not going to do that. One of the agents said I must be one cold S.O.B. to kill Red Jacobs and then preside over his funeral. They suspected I was the cleaner for the company and they wanted all the information I could provide them about MPC Corp. I told them that would be a death sentence for me. The agents said they could protect me, but I doubted that. The clincher for me was they knew I asked my boss to let me retire after I got married. They also knew the two men responsible for Trudy's death were actually sent to kill me by Martin. I had no idea Martin hired those two men to kill me. They thought Martin felt I got the message not to talk after my wife was killed. What Martin didn't realize was I never would have talked to anyone if he hadn't had Trudy killed. I was really pissed to know Martin was responsible for Trudy's death. It made sense; he was not going to let me walk away from the business. Loyalty and honor meant nothing to these people. I refused to do the last job he gave me and at that point I became a liability. They were afraid I would turn on them. The bastards killed my wife.

The FBI wanted names, locations, shipping details, and contacts. I asked what was in it for me. They told me if they got what they wanted from me, they would provide me with a new identity and they would relocate me to another country. The agents told me the choice was mine: go to prison for the rest of my life or cooperate with them and start a new life somewhere else. I thought about it for a little while, and came up with some things I wanted in return. I told them there were three things I wanted: I wanted to go to South Africa, I wanted to take Jeff with me, and I did not want Morgan Ministries to be destroyed by what I had done. I needed them to track down Jeff's real father and have him waive all custody for Jeff and have full custody granted to me. If they did that for me, I could give them all the information they needed to bring down the entire operation. I told them I would not give them any information until I had court documents stating I had full custody of Jeff. The agents agreed. The agents also told me any money I had that they could prove was paid to me by the company for the hits that I did, the FBI would confiscate. They would leave us enough money to get a fresh start and that would be it. I didn't care much about the money; I just wanted Jeff to have a good life and hopefully be able to spend it with me.

In four days, the agents came back with a court order granting me full custody of Jeff. I didn't know what the agents told Jeff's father and I didn't care. Jeff and I were taken to a safe house where I provided the FBI with everything they needed to know about the company. I gave them enough information to take down operations in Texas, Pennsylvania, and Virginia, along with operations in Cambodia, South America, and Mexico. It took a couple of months and things came down as promised. The FBI got what they wanted: Martin, Big Phil, and their partners were in jail, and there were indictments issued for 40 different operators including some of my old partners in crime.

CHAPTER 22

A New Life

The story we gave to Bill and Mary was Jeff and I wanted a new start in life and we going to go to South Africa to look into starting a new ministry over there. It was our hope that they would come and join us whenever they could and certainly we would keep in touch. I never really told Bill what was going on with the FBI investigation and knew that after things settled down and I knew they were safe, we would have that discussion. The fact was we were given one way tickets and I was told by the FBI if I ever came back to the US, I would be arrested for murder and sent to prison for life. We landed in Johannesburg, South Africa, to seek out a new life together. My first task after we got settled in a hotel was to try to find my old friend Harold Motomba. It took two weeks but we finally tracked Harold down. He was working for a rancher in the northern part of the country. It was so good to see him again. Harold was using his tracking skills to assist hunters in retrieving game and helping out on the ranch when they didn't have any hunters. Harold asked me how I found him and I said he was the one who taught me how to track people down! He laughed and said "I teach you good." Harold introduced me to his boss, Roy Spaulding. Roy was 75 years old and looked 55, except for a slight limp in his right leg. Roy invited Jeff and me to spend the night, and we accepted. We had a wonderful meal of impala that evening and sat by a big campfire and listened to stories of Roy's adventures in the bush over the last 40 some years. I could see Jeff was soaking it all in as he was all ears to Roy's stories. He fell asleep while we were around the campfire and I wondered if he was dreaming about being in the bush himself.

I was a little apprehensive about going back there because I wasn't sure if there was still any bad blood between the rebels and the folks I used to work for there. Harold assured me that most all of the rebels that were there when I left were gone. He said our team was very highly regarded among the villagers that remained. He thought many of them would be glad to see me when they found out that I was back.

Harold asked me if we were just on a holiday and how long we might stay in Africa. I explained things to him and said we were looking for a place to call home and we were thinking we might make our home in South Africa. I said it would be up to my partner to see if he liked it here. Harold asked me if I needed access to the funds he and I stowed away when I was here before. I told him I did. When I was working as a mercenary with Harold, we confiscated a considerable amount of money and uncut diamonds from some of the gentlemen we eliminated. I left most of the loot with Harold, as I trusted him completely and did not want to get caught smuggling diamonds into the USA. Harold told me he sold the diamonds two years ago and spent some of the money on his family. I told him that was fine, the money was as much his as mine, I planned splitting it 50-50 with him all along. Harold looked at me with his eyes wide open and said "you mean that?" I said sure, you risked your life as much as I did. Harold said "but my friend, I don't think you realize how much those diamonds were worth." I acknowledged I did not. I thought maybe $100,000 - $150,000. He told me he got $600,000 for the diamonds and we had another $200,000 in cash. He said he spent $20,000 on his family and himself but the rest was all secure in a safe deposit box in a bank in Johannesburg. I was shocked, more shocked than Harold when I told him half of it was his. I had no idea we accumulated over $800,000. Jeff and I were a lot better off than I thought.

We stayed at Mr. Roy's a few more days and we enjoyed his company. Roy asked me what I planned to do. I said I wasn't sure, I thought we would look around for some property and maybe do a little ranching. He said he was getting too old to keep up with everything and was considering taking on a partner. He asked if I might be interested. He told me Harold spoke very highly of me and that was good enough for him. I said I'd talk it over with Jeff and let him know. I knew Jeff liked it here; he got to do some hunting and Harold was teaching him about the bush and he made friends with some of the other kids whose parents lived and worked on the ranch. It was an easy sell - Jeff looked at me and said let's do it.

The next day, I signed an agreement with Roy to buy 50% of his operation for $250,000. The ranch itself consisted of 7000 acres, mostly open plains with about 1500 acres of mountain land. The main house, which we would share with Roy, was huge: 4000 square feet, and it already had two separate living areas. There were four smaller houses or cabins for guests to stay in, and another four mud and thatched roof houses for the staff to live in. There were 500 head of cattle and a herd of goats that numbered around 100. There was a string of eight horses and three Land Rovers for transporting clients, as well as a stake body truck for hauling game. There was currently a fence being constructed around a 2000 acre tract. In addition the ranch leased another 10,000 acres adjoining the property for hunting purposes.

I was one lucky S.O.B.; a few months ago, I was very close to spending the rest of my life in prison. Now I had a friend in Harold whom I could trust with my life, a new business to sink my teeth into, and a young man whom I thought of as my son and I had a chance to make a difference in his life. I was given yet another opportunity to do the right thing and I didn't want to screw it up this time.

I got Jeff enrolled in a school; he had to travel 30 miles one way everyday but never complained about it. He and I moved into the main house and it was more than enough for us. We had three bedrooms, two baths, a large kitchen and dining area and a large living room with an 18' cathedral ceiling. Roy, whose wife had passed away two years before, lived alone in the other half of the house. Roy had two children, a son and a daughter, who had no interest in the ranch and lived away from the area. We had housekeepers who took care of our laundry and cleaning and prepared the meals for us each day, as well as for our hunting clients.

After we got settled in, I wrote a letter to Bill and Mary and my sister Cheryl. I sent along some pictures of the property and of Jeff and his friends. We invited them all to come and visit and encouraged Bill and Mary to come and spend some time developing their ministry there. Jeff and I loved it and the only thing missing was Trudy. We both talked about how much she would have liked it here. Sometimes when we were outside, each of us would get the feeling someone was looking at us and we came to accept that it was Trudy watching out for us.

After being there for a year, Bill and Mary did come to visit and we had a great time with them. One evening while they were with us, I asked

Bill to take a walk with me and I told him about the killing I had done while I was still working for him and the real reason we relocated to South Africa. He looked at me and said "I knew you were in some trouble and I figured when you were ready you would tell me about it. I don't care what you did in the past. Like I've told you all along, what is important is what you do with the rest of your life. Yes, I am disappointed in what you've done but I can not change that. Mary and I will always love you and Jeff and nothing you do can change that."

Over time Bill and Mary came back several times and did create a ministry of their own in Africa. Roy passed away at the age of 79, and I bought his share of the ranch from his children. Harold, who got married the year before and his wife Molly moved into the main house with their son Jacob. I made Harold foreman of the ranch and eventually, he would become a full partner. Jeff grew into a fine young man and I was very proud to call him Son. After college, he came back to the ranch and became a well respected professional hunter. The locals called him "little white lion." Jeff married a young lady from Johannesburg, Alicia, and a year later they had a son who they named Billy.

Jeff took over the outfitting business and I concentrated on developing a fine strain of cattle for the ranch. I totally lost my desire to kill anything, and I could only give God the credit for that. I occasionally guided some hunters, especially some repeat clients who had hunted with me in the past. Many of our clients were Americans, so we were kept abreast of what was going on there. Sometimes one of the ranch hands would call me White Lion in front of one of our clients and they would be curious as to where that came from. I would try to explain that it was a part of my past that I would prefer not to talk about it. If they persisted, I would simply tell them it was from a time when I was young and crazy.

We shared many adventures together from antelope hunting to zebra hunting. I never remarried as I'd come to realize I could never give someone else the love I had for Trudy. I did spend much of my free time ministering to the local villagers and providing funding for them to build schools, improve water and sanitation, and help them to improve the quality of their lives.

The scars in my heart were healing. I learned that preaching was a small part of ministering. True ministry was how we lived our lives every day and the respect and true concern we showed to our fellow man. The locals still called me White Lion, as my reputation from years ago was passed on to their children, but that part of me is gone. God truly guided me through many twist and turns in my life, most of which I created. Bill was right all along; I needed to allow God to guide my life. I also realized that it was a process that I would deal with throughout my life. There were still days when I looked over my shoulder to see if someone was following me, times when a gunshot would cause me to dive for cover. The difference now was: I was allowing God to guide me through those days.

Sometimes people are not what they might seem to be. Some people are very good at deception and there is evil and goodness in all of us. It is a choice we each must make, as to which road we will follow. For me, the road was very crooked, sometimes evil, and sometimes good. Unfortunately, it took the death of my wife to convince me which road was right for me. It is a consequence I will have to live with for the rest of my life.